Murder in the Family

Ramona Richards

"If you can't get rid of the skeleton in your closet,
you'd best teach it to dance."
—George Bernard Shaw

MURDER IN THE FAMILY BY RAMONA RICHARDS
Published by Firefly Southern Fiction
an imprint of Lighthouse Publishing of the Carolinas
2333 Barton Oaks Dr., Raleigh, NC 27614

ISBN: 978-1-946016-76-8

Cover design by Elaina Lee
Interior design by AtriTex Technologies P Ltd

Available in print from your local bookstore, online, or from the publisher at: ShopLPC.com

For more information on this book and the author, visit: www.ramonarichards.com

Brought to you by the creative team at Lighthouse Publishing of the Carolinas (LPCBooks.com):
Eva Marie Everson, Jessica R. Everson, Shonda Savage

Library of Congress Cataloging-in-Publication Data
Richards, Ramona
Murder in the Family / Ramona Richards 1st ed.

Printed in the United States of America

Praise for *Murder in the Family*

"Ramona Richards' newest, *Murder in the Family*, kept me flipping the pages to learn more about Molly and her Aunt Liz and Carterton . . . oh, so many little twists and turns to delight readers of romantic suspense. A perfect blend of intrigue mixed with emotional depth, this book is highly recommended."

~Robin Caroll
Best-selling author of the Darkwater Inn series

"I love, love this story of family, and greed, and murder. Ramona Richards creates the best characters, and Molly McClelland is no exception in Murder in the Family. Strong, witty, and fearless . . . I want to be Molly, and I want to live in Carterton, Alabama."

~Patricia Bradley
Award-winning author of the Logan Point and Memphis Cold Case series

"Murder in the Family is a delightful mystery with vivid and interesting characters who capture your heart and you wish the story would never end."

~Susan Sleeman
Bestselling and award-winning author of the Truth Seekers series

"Murder in the Family is filled with quirk, charm ... and murder! Ramona Richards has penned characters so well written you feel like you know them. The suspense, humor and romance in this story makes reading a delight. A must read for mystery lovers!"

~Kellie Coates Gilbert
Author of the popular Sun Valley Series

"Ramona Richards' Murder in the Family is Southern-fried suspense at its best. You won't want to miss it!"

~Barbara Cameron
Best-selling author

"Great fun! Ramona Richards's latest is a Southern-fried treat: a clever murder mystery with a sprawling cast of entertaining characters and a setting that comes alive."

~Rick Acker
Bestselling author

"Read in one sitting, Murder in the Family is possibly the best fast-moving page-turner I've ever read. From page one, it held me captive until the very last page ... and then I wanted more. Masterfully written and never predictable, I was completely invested in the characters. Ramona Richards has a new fan—me!"

~Ane Mulligan
Bestselling author of Chapel Springs Revival

"A large family shares one emotion—hate for the relative brought in to divide the belongings of the woman who died . . . or was she murdered? Prepare to pick your favorites, and to be surprised at the outcome."

~Richard L. Mabry, MD
Best-selling, award-winning author
of medical suspense with heart

"A tightly woven plot in an atmospheric setting, Ramona Richards's evocative Southern crime novel and its memorable characters will linger long with readers. Well-crafted with touches of humor and romance, a story of obsession, family legacy, and forgiveness. A must-read."

~Lisa Carter
Bestselling author of His Secret Daughter,
A Vast and Gracious Tide, and The Stronghold

"Ramona Richards does a fantastic job of showing the loveable, quirky, strange, and sometimes vile sides of a typical small town in the South. At one point, I thought she might have researched my relatives before writing this book. I thoroughly enjoyed seeing how Molly's strong resolve to help others and honor her beloved aunt's wishes ultimately provided the stability, family, and love Molly had always longed for. Great job, Ramona!"

~Shellie Arnold
Author of *The Spindle Chair*

"Ramona Richards is a master of spinning intricate story webs, and Murder in the Family is her best yet. Just like the home Molly McClelland inherits from her hoarder aunt, this thrilling novel is filled with dark secrets, treasures, and more than one surprising twist. The realization that the enemy could be a family member makes the story even more consuming. I couldn't put it down!"

~Karen Barnett
Award-winning author of the Vintage National Park series
and the Golden Gate Chronicles

Acknowledgments

The list of people who had a hand in this book coming to be are endless, but here are a few of them, to whom I owe enormous thanks and probably a steak dinner or two.

Sandra Bishop, who encouraged me to indulge in my fascination about why people hoard, to look deeper into the reasons.

Eva Marie Everson, who loved the book from the beginning and wanted to buy it.

Jessica R. Everson, who has some unparalleled editorial skills.

Jamie, Marcheta, and Sunny, who kept repeating, "Don't stop," and who are the first to recognize how crazy I get when I'm not writing.

The conference attendees who listen to my endless rabbit trails and ask me why I don't put them in a book.

And . . . finally . . . thanks to John, Bradley, Reagan, Tina, Meredith, Marty, and Randy. My rocks who keep me grounded and going in this stage of my life.

Dedication

This one is for Teri, who has been my publishing partner, beta reader, and unfailing encourager since galleys were paper, type was hot, and stripping involved X-ACTO knives and tape. We survived and thrived through it all. That, and a bucket of chicken.

1

"Aunt Liz, you can't keep doing this. It's going to get you killed."

And it had.

Molly McClelland's own words to her aunt now haunted her. Elizabeth Morrow was gone.

Accident?

Murder?

Whatever it had been, Aunt Liz's death had turned Molly's carefully crafted world upside down. Now Molly found herself in the one place she never wanted to be: sole heir to a disaster.

Molly sat in her ancient blue Explorer, staring at the building that housed her aunt's attorney, unwilling to go in. Exhausted from a two-day drive, part of her wished all of this would just go away, that she'd wake up from a dream to find she had never left her friends, never trekked back to the one place she swore she'd never see again. Molly squeezed the steering wheel, her knuckles white, as family duty warred with the urge to flee back to her real life, her real family in Missouri.

What there is of it.

"Stop it!" Her words hissed through clenched teeth. She refused to let this place—these people—worm their way back into her soul. She'd spent too many years divesting herself of the past. "I love my life now." All of it.

No, she didn't live in Missouri. Molly didn't really *live* anywhere. But she'd come to Alabama from a series of supercell thunderstorms near St. Louis and photos that would pay a lot of bills. The month had just started, and April had always been one of their busiest months for storm chasing. But after only one phone call, Molly had been forced to bolt for Alabama while her business partners and best friends, Jimmy and Sarah, had remained behind. And at a moment when Sarah needed her most.

Molly closed her eyes, the image of a gray and comatose Sarah swimming behind the lids. *No, this is no time for tears. Focus. Get through this quickly so you can get back to them.* She brushed her eyes and sniffed, glancing up at the third-floor windows again.

Dear God, what a phone call that had been. Aunt Liz had died, leaving Molly her entire estate. "I still can't believe you did this to me, Aunt Liz." Molly squared her shoulders, peeled her fingers from the steering wheel, and ran her hands through her dark, windblown curls. "But I'm here now. No second thoughts. Jimmy will take care of Sarah till I get back. Just get this over with." She paused. "And stop talking to yourself."

This was the meeting with Russell Williams, Liz's attorney, to find out *why*—despite all Molly's requests otherwise—Liz had left the estate to Molly. Williams seemed to be a nice man, at least over the phone, but he apparently had little idea what kind of chaos her aunt's will was about to unleash.

It's just stuff. I don't want any of it. Molly knew without a doubt that Liz had died because of a houseful of stuff. Williams had explained that a stack of storage containers had toppled, crushing Liz's chest, smothering her. Why? Why had she lived like that, to the point that her own hoarding had killed her? Why hadn't someone helped her?

Or maybe ... just maybe ... someone in her family had killed Liz because of something in the estate. It did sound like a most convenient accident.

Molly hated the thought. But Molly knew her family, even if she hadn't laid eyes on most of them for nearly twenty years. She despised them, and she wouldn't put it past any of them to murder for greed. She'd left and never looked back. Even when she'd returned to Alabama to photograph tornadoes, Molly had avoided Carterton and her entire family.

She grinned wryly. *Must be quite telling that you'd rather face an F5 than your family. There is something desperately wrong with you.*

Molly looked up at the sky. "So what in the world am I doing here now?"

No answer. No need. Molly knew why. Face it. The estate was now hers. Although what she was going to do with it, she had no idea. "Maybe I can refuse it. I could be back in Missouri by Monday." She checked her watch one more time. It was time.

The law office occupied the top floor of the three-story Georgian redbrick, with a small parking lot ringed by an overabundance of shrubbery, primarily azaleas and knockout roses in bright reds, pinks, and whites. Irises and tulips filled in the bare spaces along with lines of monkey grass. Molly had parked in a corner space, away from the building and close to the shrubs. She took a deep breath and released it slowly, steeling herself for the next few hours, watching the blossoms shift and wave in a light breeze. She grabbed her purse, a narrow crossbody bag she draped over her shoulder, and swung her legs out.

The springs of the rickety Explorer squeaked as Molly slid into the warm morning, sneakered feet thumping on the pavement. The scent of the rich blooms wafted over her, and she hesitated, looking up at the sky, this time at the bright blue contrasting with puffy cumulus clouds. Amidst the floral swirls, her stormchaser's nose picked up a hint of ozone.

A front's moving in. Rain by late tonight, early morning. Not a surprise. Alabama in the spring and summer almost always held the promise of some strong, juicy storms. Molly used her key to lock the door, tucked the ring into her jeans pocket, and turned, drawing up short so she didn't trip over the two women who seemed to have materialized in the empty space next to the Explorer.

"Molly? Molly McClelland?"

They were a matched set, although at least twenty years separated them. Stout women in denim skirts, they also wore too-tight t-shirts and sneakers. Wild shocks of brownish hair that longed for a brush wafted in a dozen directions.

Molly, at five-nine, towered over both of them, and she took a step back, trying to get a better look, and bumped into her SUV. "Do I know you?"

"You're Molly McClelland, aren't you?" The older one stepped closer, while the younger stared mostly at the ground, glancing up occasionally at Molly. The older one wore glasses, and her hair had unruly shoots of gray throughout. Her t-shirt was a plain yellow that added a sallow tone to her pale skin. The younger one's dark brown t-shirt declared her allegiance to a country music star who would probably be amused by the shape his face took when stretched across her substantial bosom.

Molly moved to go around them, grazing her shoulder against the Explorer's mirror. She winced. "I am, but you'll have to excuse me, I have an appointment—"

They blocked her path, planting their feet in a wide stance, like twin sumo wrestlers. "Oh, we know all about that appointment. We have to talk before you see that interfering lawyer."

Greed brightened their eyes, and Molly bit her lower lip. She wanted to laugh and cry at the same time. They had to be family, probably cousins, although she didn't recognize them. Typical. This is why she left Alabama in the first place. She tried to go around them again. "I'm sorry, but—"

The older one put up an arm to stop her, and Molly got a whiff of rotten food and stale tobacco. She grimaced as the woman leaned toward her. "What gives you the right to inherit? We're the ones who took care of Elizabeth, right up to the end, especially Lyric here."

Lyric grunted an affirmative, and Molly shot a glance at her. *Lyric? Who names their kid Lyric?* "I'm sure, but—"

"No buts, Miss Molly. That estate is properly ours. You need to sign it over. Liz had no right to give it all to you." A hand shot out, two fingers poking Molly in the chest.

Molly froze, her eyes narrow, annoyance building in her gut. Her voice dropped, a harsh growl sounding in her tone. "Don't touch me. Ever." The woman stiffened, but Molly continued. "You want more stuff. So you must be kin to me."

"We are. You don't recognize us? We're cousins! I was Kitty Peevey. Filbyhouse now. Lyric's my daughter. You don't remember me?"

The angry words were out of Molly's mouth before she could stop them. "Certainly not like this. The Kitty Peevey I remember dreamed of being a ballet dancer and getting out of Alabama. She would never assault a perfect stranger in a parking lot and demand that she give her more stuff! Especially if you were involved in her death. Were you? If you were taking care of her, why did you let her die like that?" Molly lunged at them, and both women took an astonished step backward. Molly dodged left, then right, scooting around the two. Kitty and Lyric couldn't move fast enough as Molly sprinted toward the front door, but they squawked after her.

"How dare you! We didn't have anything to do with it! That old woman died 'cause she was a fool!"

Their shouts faded as Molly fled into the coolness of the lobby, desperately bounding for the elevator. A glance to her right revealed Kitty and Lyric lumbering through the doors, voices still raised at her, along with at least one fist. Molly bolted for a door marked "Stairs," and headed up, hoping she could reach the third floor before the elevator. She did, pushing into Russell Williams' office through glass-paned double doors, shaking and confused.

The receptionist's head snapped up in alarm. A tidy, richly dressed woman in her fifties, her eyes widened at Molly's abrupt appearance. Then, without missing a beat, she said, "Lock the door, Miss McClelland. We've been expecting you." She then pressed a button on her desk phone and spoke into her headset. "Miss McClelland is here. And, from the look of things, Kitty and Lyric are still lurking in the parking lot." The receptionist paused, listening, although she kept her eyes on Molly, who fumbled for the deadbolt and turned it.

After a moment, the receptionist spoke again into the headset. "Yes, sir." She pushed two more buttons, paused, then said, "Security? Third floor. Stat," before severing the connection. She unplugged the headset from the phone and stepped from behind the desk.

Molly ran her hands through her hair again, trying to fan away some of the heat in her face as the older woman approached. Molly stood almost a foot taller, but the receptionist clearly had command of the office. Her pixie-cut, steel-gray hair framed a petite face sculpted by smooth and natural-toned makeup. Her tailored navy suit gave off the air of a commander awaiting battle orders.

"I'm Shirley. Have a seat, hon." She touched Molly's arm with reassurance. "Would you like a beverage? We have Cokes of all kinds, plus filtered, spring, and sparkling water."

Molly barely mumbled, "Filtered water would be fine—"

"I'll be right back. Mr. Williams will be out in a moment." Shirley motioned at the door. "Ignore what you might hear out there." She disappeared down a hall behind her desk.

Molly couldn't sit. Too much energy from the encounter still surged in her veins. She paced, breathing deeply, brushing her curls out of her face. Who *were* those women? And why were they *here*? In her mind, she paged through her aunt's most recent letters, searching for a mention of either Lyric or Kitty Filbyhouse.

The outer office of Russell Williams & Associates allowed for a long pace. Soft dark-green carpet padded her steps around the cherrywood receptionist center. The desk matched the walls, with their beveled panels and subtle, impressionistic artwork. The Queen Anne chairs for waiting clients looked comfortable in their sophistication. A faint scent hung in the air, masculine but clean, like linen dried outdoors.

Molly stopped, remembering. Several months ago, her aunt had mentioned someone moving in with her, to take care of daily tasks. Was that Lyric? But why would they think …?

Shirley returned, and Molly accepted the offered goblet of ice water gratefully. "What was that?" She motioned toward the door.

"We've had a few … visitors this week."

"My relatives?"

"Kitty and Lyric have been the most persistent."

"They said they'd been with Aunt Liz at the end."

Shirley paused. "Did they? Well … Mr. Williams will have to explain all that. But if I were you, I wouldn't believe anything any of your relatives say in regards to your aunt."

Molly smiled down at her. "Friendly advice?"

"Survival skill."

Molly laughed, but her nerves made the sound quiver, and she ran one hand through her hair yet again, her fingers tangling in the dark curls.

A look of concern crossed Shirley's face. "Would you like a brush, dear?"

Molly jerked her hand free. "It wouldn't do any good."

"It might help calm you down."

A roar sounded outside the door. "Molly McClelland! You're a thief! You belong in jail!"

"Dear heavens," Shirley muttered.

Molly scowled at the door. "It never stops. The greed. It hasn't stopped in three generations. Destroyed my family, everything I cared about."

The ruckus changed as two deeper, muted voices joined the fray. Molly took another step back away from the doors. Shirley touched her back. "Security guards, dear. No worries. They're familiar with the situation."

"Molly?" The bass voice behind her sounded smooth, dark, and soft, and it overpowered the commotion outside the door.

She turned … and tried to hide her surprise. Her imagined picture of a Southern lawyer ran between Ben Matlock and Atticus Finch, but the tall man in front of her was nothing like either. *More like a retired NBA point guard,* was her first thought.

Close-cropped white hair emphasized the deep brown of his skin and eyes. He stood a straight and lean six-foot-five at least, and his three-piece, pinstriped suit looked as if it cost more than a new car, seeming to flow over and caress him instead of just "fitting well." The elegance of his image extended to his cuff links, tiepin, and the silk handkerchief tucked in the pocket. Even the fine lines in his broad face seemed to have been placed there by an artist instead of age.

His face twitched a bit as an odd thump hit one of the doors, but a smile lit his eyes as he extended an arm toward Molly. "Russell Williams."

She shook his hand. "Molly McClelland." But she couldn't ignore the sounds from the hallway. Molly pointed a trembling hand at the door. "They killed her, didn't they? Tweedledum and Tweedledee out there. My whole family would gladly kill for more stuff. One of them killed her."

2

Russell froze for a moment, then glanced at Shirley, whose lips pursed with concern. He cleared his throat and pushed his shoulders back. "There's no evidence that Elizabeth Morrow's death was anything but an accident. I know you don't want to be here, and Liz explained to me that you were estranged from your family."

Molly stared at him, eyes wide with disbelief. "'Estranged'? Is that what she called it?"

Another thud hit the door, and Molly jumped, stepping away from it.

Russell continued. "But I am an officer of the court. You might want to be cautious with such accusations."

"You've had to hire guards."

"Yours is not the first family who didn't like the way a will turned out."

"Bet it's the first to turn hoarding into an art form."

A short bark of a laugh escaped from Shirley, and she coughed to cover it up.

Russell's mouth jerked in amusement, and his arms opened in welcome. "Please. Come this way."

Russell escorted her down the hall behind Shirley's desk, past two comfortable offices where younger people appeared hard at work. At the end of the hall, he held open a door for her, and Molly entered, feeling drastically underdressed in her jeans and cotton shirt. Everything in the room seemed to be made of cherry wood—the paneled walls, the expansive desk and matching credenza, the conference table for six sitting to the right of the desk, and the coffee table to the left, which stood between a leather couch and two chairs. Large Impressionist landscapes hung at each end of the office. A wall of bookcases behind his desk held a plethora of the expected law books, but also artifacts from Africa, photos of Russell with various state and national leaders from the 1960s and 70s, and two framed diplomas—a bachelor's degree from Fisk University and a law degree from Howard.

Molly didn't hide her awe. "This is bigger than my first apartment." She touched the edge of his desk with caution, as if it might cut her. "And infinitely better furnished."

Russell chuckled. "Business is good." He motioned for her to sit in one of the wingback chairs in front of his desk as he returned to the chair behind it.

"I'm glad." Molly swallowed hard, still trying to regain her composure. Her resolve to walk away from the inheritance had been reinforced by the encounter in the parking lot. She just wanted it over and done with. "At least we can be comfortable while we deal with this nasty business." Her words sounded harsh, even to her. "I'm sorry. I don't mean to be rude." She paused, then gripped the arms of her chair as she settled. "It's just that … I don't want any of this. I told Aunt Liz that. I can't understand why she did this."

"Don't apologize. You're in a tough position." He nodded toward the front of the office suite. "And, as you can see, I'm well aware of the predilections of your family. They have visited often since her death."

"Was it really an accident? Or did someone in my family make it happen?"

Russell sat stone-still a moment. Finally he leaned back in his chair. "As I said, there's no indication that it was anything but accidental."

"She suffocated under a pile of crap."

"She was a hoarder. Her house was—"

"I know what her house must have been like. She also—apparently—had a live-in caregiver. Lyric, if what those two women said is true."

He gave a bare nod. "Lyric lived there, yes, but she wasn't around twenty-four seven. Liz … Ms. Morrow …" His voice trailed off, and he cleared his throat. "The coroner ruled it an accident."

Molly hesitated, recognizing the roadblock, then relented. Now was not the time. As she calmed down from the confrontation, the exhaustion from the last few days threatened to overwhelm her. Her shoulders slumped, and her voice sounded more weary and bitter than she meant it to, but she was too exhausted to be polite. "Is there anything I can do to make this go away? I don't want the estate. She knew that. We even talked about it. I told her not to leave me anything. Not a morsel. Not a shred. Not. A. *Button.*"

"But she did. You can't make it 'go away,' but we can try to get through it as quickly as we can. There are a number of things you'll need to—"

Molly shifted in the chair. "Why can't Mickey inherit? I'd be glad to sign it all over to him."

Russell hesitated. "Mickey?"

"My brother. My mother's other child. Aunt Liz's nephew. If Aunt Liz didn't want to leave it to one of the other many little nephews and nieces, she could have left it to Mickey. I'm sure he's around somewhere. At least Liz never mentioned that he'd died. He'd be wiser about getting rid of everything than I would be."

"Your brother. Molly, how long has it been since you've talked to Mi—your brother?"

"Twenty years. Same as most of the family. I left when I was eighteen and never looked back. Aunt Liz was the only one I had any contact with."

Russell's voice remained steady, quite lawyer-like. "Your brother is not in a position to inherit."

Molly hesitated. She'd never quarreled with her brother. They had both just left Carterton, never looking back. Not even for each other. But she hadn't considered that he might be … "So. He's dead."

"No. Just take my word for it."

"Okay. For now. If not Mickey, then why not Kitty and Lyric? If they want it so badly, why didn't Aunt Liz just give it to them?"

Russell reached for a thick accordion-style folder on one corner of his desk. "We can go over all that in a few moments." He pulled a white business envelope from the folder. "Before we start, Liz—Ms. Morrow—requested I give you this." He slid it toward her. Molly picked it up and fingered the sealed envelope with only her name on the front.

"I have no idea what's in it," Russell continued. "And she requested that you be allowed to read it in private. So I'm going to step out. I'll be right outside when you finish." He rose and left the office, pulling the door shut behind him.

Molly stared at the letter, feeling sure that it would be a plea to follow her wishes in the will. *I can't, Aunt Liz. I just can't deal with these people again. You knew that!* She stared at the envelope a few more minutes, then pushed her thumb under the flap and broke the seal. As she unfolded the sheets, she noticed the quivery handwriting. It was dated only a few days before her aunt's death.

*March 10*th

My dear Mollybelle—

Molly closed her eyes, an unexpected ache of grief washing over her. Only Liz called her that anymore, a nickname of affection, sincerity, and comfort. She sniffed, straightened, and opened her eyes to continue reading.

Please forgive me. I know you do not want this. And, to be honest, I never intended for you to have it. Until a few months ago, my will was completely different. But some things have happened here that make this necessary. So I hope you will spare me a few minutes to explain.

I fully suspect that even if you drove straight to Russell's office, you will have by now met Kitty and Lyric. Recently I overhead them making plans about where in their home my big-screen television would look best. And the antique secretary from the hall. And the living room sofa. And the ... perhaps you get my drift here. The list sounded quite endless, and it sounded as if they planned to act soon. At least to this old woman's ears.

They are determined women. Avoid them if you can. Do not believe them. I overheard Kitty refer to Lyric as my caregiver. As if. Sitting around watching TV and occasionally scooting out to McDonald's does not a caregiver make. Lyric takes me to the doctor, but only so that her mother can have access to the house. Obviously, there was a method to their madness. Inheritance. I've noticed some things missing, but nothing major. They won't find what they're really looking for, not until I'm dead, maybe not even then.

And I'm quite concerned about what they may be adding to the piles that fill these rooms. Don't be surprised by anything you discover when you inventory the house. I'm frightened. I only trust Russell at this point, and I can't leave it to him.

This is why I'm turning to you.

It will be the same with Bird and his scions, as you well know. He'll be into it with Kitty before my body is cold. He is a grandfather now, and you will not be surprised to know that none of those apples fell far from that rotting tree. RuthAnn and Tommie Jane are here in town, and their children have studied at the feet of the master, Bird the Avaricious.

In fact, none of the greedy grappling will surprise you. But what I'm about to say may.

The very reason that I've decided to leave it to you is precisely because you don't want it. You have no desire to clutch it to your chest like a starving chipmunk and scamper away into hiding with it. While I know, in fact, that you will have a desire just to burn it and walk away, I beg you to consider this:

Not all of your relatives are clutchers and plotters. Some are, in fact, quite deserving. Some could use help from the estate. Kitty's niece has a special-needs child, and they are struggling. Although Kitty's brother inherited the family's propensity for greed, his daughter did not. Probably because of her mother, who divorced that evil creature as soon as she could and whisked her children out of his sphere. The niece, darling girl, is as far from being like Lyric as you are. She even has trouble asking for what she needs, much less what she wants. Another cousin is a reservist who lost his job when he was deployed. Others would respect the stories behind some of the pieces and cherish them for their history, not just their monetary value. Some of the items in the house hold great memories for a lot of people. Some of the items ... well, you'll see when you go through them. Remember: family takes care of its own. That's what we do.

And despite all your anger at what happened in the past, you have something Bird, et. al, will never have: compassion. You protest voraciously, but I know you as I always did. You care. It's the very reason you've been so angry for so long, so shut off from your own family. You care deeply.

So why didn't I make those arrangements myself? Two reasons. One is that I simply don't have time. There is a lot of stuff and a lot of family. I'm not strong, and if God doesn't take me quickly, one of the family probably will see to it I get to Him sooner than later.

The other is that Bird and Kitty will get in the way, and I simply do not have the strength to fight them. But I know you do. You have a good heart but a constitution of steel. And the temper to meet them head on.

So I don't expect you to keep anything. But I beg of you to consider getting rid of it in a way that will be fair and equitable—and quite possibly heal some old wounds that have haunted this family for far too long. You aren't the only one who was damaged by what happened in the past. There are more wounds out there than you can imagine.

You'll find in the house (hidden well, but I know you'll find it) a journal containing a list of names, and some of the possessions I'd like them to have. You will find notes on each piece that will explain why. There's other information in the journal as well. There are boxes of journals under my bed, which you might also find intriguing.

You'll also find in the paperwork with this letter and the will a quitclaim deed, giving you the house immediately. You're my executrix, so you should be able to act on my behalf. Check with Russell on this. The legal paperwork will take some time, and I wanted to give you the power to handle things without waiting. It's ammunition to use against Bird, Kitty, and the others if you want to … or permission to sell it right away if you don't.

If you agree to do this, Russell will help you and help keep you safe. He's done what he can for me. Also the local sheriff. Good man. He's watched out for me as much as he can. You'll like him.

This is important. You mentioned to me that because of your work, you have a gun. Keep it close. You may need it. Kitty and Lyric will be nuisances to you, but Bird is dangerous. Do not turn your back on any of them.

I love you, Mollybelle. And I love our family, despite the problems. There are still good people in it. More than you realize. You are the only one who can help them. I hope you find it in your heart to carry out my wishes. And forgive me.

Love,

Aunt Liz

Molly dropped the letter on the desk and stood, gripping her curls as she paced. A bizarre mix of emotions swirled in her: frustration, anger, and sadness the most prominent. She did not want this. She hated it. Her entire body tightened, and she dropped her arms to her sides, stopping in her tracks as it all closed in on her. She felt as if bands of steel had wrapped around her, smothering her. As if all of Aunt Liz's possessions had fallen on and around her.

But she also could not rid herself of a haunting memory: the sight of her mother and Aunt Liz upon discovering that their own mother's house had been stripped bare by Bird and his sons while the sisters had gone to arrange their mother's funeral. It had broken both of them. Her mother had collapsed on the spot.

Molly clenched her eyes shut, trying to push it away. The words burst from her in a hoarse whisper. "Bird took everything from me! My family. My home. *Everything!* You can't ask me to do this! How could you do this?"

Because you can stop it. This time you *could stop it. This gives you the power to stop it.*

The realization rocked her and Molly stilled. If she didn't stop it, what happened twenty years ago would be repeated, all over again. Bird and his children—and now grandchildren—would pick the house clean like buzzards on the bones of a carcass. The rest of the family would be left with nothing. Could she really let it happen again if she had the power to prevent it? Who would be hurt this time if she let all Aunt Liz cared about be stripped away again by narcissistic relatives who cared only for themselves?

Molly had stopped next to the window overlooking the parking lot. Three floors below, Kitty and Lyric circled her Explorer, peering into the windows and testing the locks. Kitty banged on one of the door handles, as if trying to make the lock pop. A security guard came out of the building and shooed them away. But Molly knew they would never quit. It would never end.

*Unless **you** stop it.*

"They killed Liz," she whispered, her breath fogging on the window. "One way or another, they're responsible. If I do this, they'll come after me too. It won't be easy." And Molly knew all too well how vicious her uncle and his kin could be. That she'd seen up close and personal.

Molly's gaze shifted to the sky. Those puffy clouds were thicker, building more in the west, and a slight gray color spoke of the gathering moisture. And they reminded her that she usually charged toward danger when others sought shelter. "They think they know me. They don't."

Molly straightened her shoulders and swallowed hard, pushing away the claustrophobia that threatened to strangle her. She crossed the room and opened the office door. Russell stood on the other side, waiting. Molly nodded for him to come in.

He settled in his chair. "Well?"

She sat as well and pushed the letter toward him. "Please read this."

Russell hesitated a few moments, but reached for the sheets across the desk. He pulled a slim pair of gold-rimmed reading glasses from his pocket and slipped them on. As he read through the letter, Molly watched his eyebrows go through a series of arches and descents. When he finished, he paused, pressing the letter flat on his desk. Finally, he raised his gaze to meet hers.

"Why didn't you tell me she'd signed a quitclaim deed?" The calm in her voice surprised her.

Russell cleared his throat as he pushed the letter back toward her. "For the same reason she didn't mail this letter."

"You wanted me here before I had all the information."

He nodded. "Will you honor her request? Have you made a decision? Do you want to go through the will and the estate paperwork?"

She shook her head. "Neither. Before I do, I'd like to see the house."

"I understand." He opened a drawer and pulled out a set of keys. Then he pressed a button on his phone. "Shirley?"

"Yes, sir?"

Russell's next words left Molly staring at him in another round of astonishment.

"Please call Sheriff Olson and tell him to warn the deputies. We're on our way. We'll need protection, at least two men."

3

The journey to Elizabeth Morrow's home felt like a chaotic three-car funeral procession. Russell led the way in his charcoal-gray, late-model Mercedes, a big car as polished and immaculate as he was. Molly followed at a safe distance since Kitty and Lyric tailgated her in an ancient Impala that seemed to be constructed primarily of Bondo and dust. At times, the Impala lunged so close to the Explorer, Molly couldn't see its headlights. She found ignoring them next to impossible, since they kept swerving and blowing the horn at her. Each jerk of the Impala toward her made her heart tighten and jump a little. Her Explorer had seen some rough territory, but she didn't think it would survive a battle with the Chevy tank following her.

Suddenly, the fact that Russell had sheriff's deputies guarding her aunt's home sounded like a great idea. It had startled her, but he'd explained during the elevator ride down that Aunt Liz had arranged it with the sheriff before her death.

So she'd suspected they wouldn't give up until she was dead. Even after.

The deputies had taken up guard, along with some private security folks, after the 911 call, which had, fortunately, come from a friend, not Lyric or any of the family. Russell also had the locks changed immediately, since Lyric had made duplicates for every key used in the house, even the ones for the upstairs bathrooms and the attic.

In retaliation, Kitty and Lyric—and occasionally Bird and some of his family—had started haunting the law office, undeterred by the security guards Russell had hired. The guards looked like former linebackers to Molly, making her relieved to see them when she'd returned to her Explorer. They'd held Kitty and Lyric at bay while Molly and Russell left, but the Impala had caught up quickly, despite the fact that it belched white smoke out the back and appeared ready to blow the head gasket at any moment.

Molly glanced one more time in her rearview mirror at the weaving car, trying to ignore the twinge of fear their behavior created. *Aunt Liz, what have you done? What have* I *done?*

Molly pursed her lips and focused again on the broad rear of the Mercedes. Despite the fact she'd told Russell she had not made a decision, Molly knew she had. Unlike the rest of her family, Aunt Liz had stayed in touch after Molly left Alabama. Her persistence had annoyed Molly at first, but eventually she accepted her aunt's contact. She'd never really stopped loving her—no fault for the past rifts lay at Aunt Liz's feet—and Molly knew her decision to leave the state and family behind had hurt Aunt Liz.

She could do this. She could honor her aunt this much. After all, it shouldn't take that long, maybe a week or two, then she could turn the house over to Russell to sell and be done with it. A couple of weeks. Mama always said you could walk a mile with a rock in your shoe if it was the only way to get home.

So her decision *was* made. Of course, the fact that Kitty and Lyric had irritated her beyond reason didn't exactly discourage her. By now, she wanted to make sure they'd never lay a hand on a single molecule of Aunt Liz's property.

With a sly smile, Molly began to play with the Impala. Slowing down and speeding up for no reason. Hitting her brakes unexpectedly. After a while, they backed off a bit, even if they did continue swerving and leaning on the horn. Molly grinned. "Don't mess with me, girls. You will *not* get what you want."

When Russell abruptly slowed the Mercedes, Molly realized they approached the last long curve before entering Carterton. She winced as she heard screeching brakes behind her, and the headlights of the Impala disappeared from her rearview mirror, too close to her bumper to be visible. *Now will you back off?*

And they did, a little, as Molly frowned, looking around. She hadn't even noticed they had left the Gadsden city limits. Twenty years ago, long stretches of pinewoods had lain between the two communities. This curve had been lined on both sides with tall Southern pines so thick that deer were a nuisance to nighttime drivers year round. But the pines had been cleared; now parallel brick walls bordered the road, broken only by gated entrances to upscale subdivisions. Behind her lay stretches of strip malls and similar house clusters. Had all the little towns surrounding Gadsden really run together?

Apparently so. They passed the gas station Molly remembered as the beginning of Carterton. Beyond that, the road suddenly divided into a boulevard, headed by a rose-filled island with an elegant sign that proclaimed, "Welcome to Carterton! Southern Hospitality at Its Best!" Precisely spaced Bradford pear trees stood in the boulevard greenway, and the speed limit dropped to twenty-five miles per hour.

Molly gaped at the other changes. The city hall had sprouted a second story. The Baptist church had acquired a fellowship hall, a Sunday school wing, and an enlarged parking lot. On the opposite side of the boulevard, new constructions completely blocked the Methodist church and the old general store from view. The old depot had been refurbished as a restaurant, and a shiny new strip of stores next to it boasted a hair-and-nail salon, a tattoo parlor, a chiropractor's office, and a Dollar General.

"A Dollar General," murmured Molly. "You've hit the big time, Carterton." But even her inner cynic felt slapped at the growth her hometown had experienced. "I guess nothing stands still for long." Behind her, Kitty pounded the horn. "Except my family."

The Mercedes turned up a narrow side street, and Molly followed slowly, bracing herself again as her mental movie of childhood continued playing. In it, Maple Street had been a narrow lane leading to the public swimming pool a mile from the main road. A half mile in, one of the town's wealthier families had built matching Victorians on either side of the street. Built in the early 1920s and intended for their twin daughters, the tree-filled lots had remained unchanged for more than fifty years. When both women died within days of each other in 1970, the houses were sold at auction. Aunt Liz, already accepting her role as maiden aunt in the family, bought one, then renovated and furnished it top to bottom with comfortable but elegant décor. The house became a second home to her many nieces and nephews, who often stayed over.

Molly, who had come along ten years later, winced as delicious memories of days in that house returned, along with some less pleasant. “A mostly normal childhood,” she whispered. For years, those two Victorians had stood alone on the street, painted queens that represented the town’s elite. As Carterton had grown, that had changed as developers bought the land around them.

Today a dozen or so houses lined both sides of the street, surrounding the Victorians like serf cottages around a castle. All looked relatively new—and somewhat identical—with their half-brick half-vinyl siding constructions. Some of the trees remained, and Maple Street was still lined with maples. But many had been cleared to make way for narrow yards littered with bikes, balls, and play sets. Neat bushes remained netted with last year’s Christmas lights, and random forsythia and azalea bushes dotted unexpected spots. On the right, behind the lots and the houses, an expansive pine grove between this neighborhood and the next ensured privacy and a place for kids to run and play yet be safe.

In this constellation of new, lower-middle-class residences, the two Victorians shone like suns with their gables, scrollwork, and blue, green, and pink paint jobs. The one on the left looked polished and welcoming, with fresh paint, a neatly trimmed lawn, paved drive, and a matching storage building to one side. The one on the right, Aunt Liz’s home … not so much.

Russell turned into the rutted gravel drive of the house, and the last of Molly’s pleasant memories dissipated as she looked at the tattered and unkempt front yard. Three white wooden steps led up to the house’s wide, wraparound porch. Faded white latticework ran from the rail to the roof along the front and sides, almost invisible behind overgrown morning glory and moonflower vines. The house was bad enough, but Molly grimaced at the sight of a mud-covered black pickup backed up to the house. Next to it, a red-faced, paunchy, and almost bald man stood nose-to-nose with a lean, calm deputy, one of at least four officers that she could spot. The overall-clad man’s scratchy voice reached Molly even through the closed windows of the Explorer as he demanded his right to access the house and its contents. Next to him, a woman waited, hands on hips, a scowl on her narrow face. Her jeans and t-shirt had seen hard times and hung loosely on a thin frame. Her wispy, whisky-shade hair was more squirrel's nest than hairdo.

"Bird," Molly whispered, anger building to slice through her again. "And his lovely wife Nina. Vultures at the site of the roadkill."

She parked behind the Mercedes and slid out of the SUV, resisting the urge to dig her gun case from beneath the seat. Instead, she glanced at Russell, who stood beside his car, watching her closely. As she approached him, he whispered, "Are you all right?"

She nodded. "Keep me from killing him, will you?"

"Just try not to do it in front of the sheriff."

She glanced at the four officers. "Which one is he?"

He nodded at an older, uniformed man still on the porch, and Molly headed that way, even as Kitty and Lyric's car crunched to a halt behind them. Their screeching joined Bird's. The shouted words blended together in one accusatory shout. *This is our stuff. You have no right to keep it away from us.* Same song, different pitch, a talent-show reject stuck on repeat.

Molly hesitated as an unmistakable odor hit her, a combination of rotting food and molded cardboard. And something even more pungent. The scent of a landfill. But … no, this was not just the stench of garbage … this was the scent of a tornado-crushed town, three weeks into the aftermath. Somewhere in that house were dead animals. Her eyes narrowed. Blossom—

She had no time to think about it. Bird had spotted her. He shoved a finger in her direction, then dodged around the young deputy, closing in on Molly. "You! You're the cause of all this!"

Nina, following a foot behind Bird, joined the fray. "Tell her, Bird! She has no right!"

Molly detoured behind the Mercedes, putting the big car between her and Bird, whose bellows echoed off the steel of the cars. He followed, but her duck around the car gave her time to reach the porch where Russell and the sheriff waited near the top of the steps. A few of the deputies clustered near the base of the steps, moving a few feet backward as Molly approached. She stopped on the second step, glancing from Russell to the sheriff, who nodded a welcome.

Molly returned it, remembering that Liz had thought highly of this man.

"You have no right to this!" Bird marched to the steps, halting only when the young deputy caught up with him and blocked his path again. Nina thudded into Bird's back, and the sheriff moved closer to Molly. Bird was not deterred. "You're not family anymore! I'm her next of kin! This house is mine!"

Kitty punched him in the arm. "Ours! Lyric took care of her! Liz promised."

"Yeah!" screeched Lyric, a few steps behind her mother. "It's mine!"

Bird glared, stepping away from her, almost tripping over his wife.

The overwhelming reek strengthened, and Molly's eyes began to water. She'd had enough. Molly threw up her hands and called on her best over-the-roar-of-the-storm voice as the anger finally pitched out of her. "ALL OF YOU! SHUT UP!"

They stared at her, stunned. Behind her, Russell made an odd choking noise.

Molly pointed at the blue Explorer. "*That* is all I want to own! But Aunt Liz had other ideas!" Bird opened his mouth, but Molly screamed. "Shut it!"

"Now wait a minute—" Kitty started.

"You, too! All of you, be *silent* for *one* minute!" Surprisingly, they waited. "Aunt Liz signed this house over to me before she died. Legally, it's now mine. She did it for her own reasons. You don't like it. I don't like it. But I *will* honor her, and as long as I breathe, *you* will, too, or I'll sic every single one of these fine officers on you.

"And I will be distributing her property according to *her* wishes. Not mine, and certainly not yours. She's charged me with this because she couldn't trust any of you to do it without getting greedy. Guess what? She was right. Obviously. That's our family history, which you are amply demonstrating today."

Molly paused, trying to calm herself, but the anger boiling within would not be quieted. Her voice dropped, taking on a harsh, bitter tone. "Now understand this. I will stand between you and every piece of trash in this house until her wishes are granted, and I can promise you I'm just as mean and ornery as any of you. Probably more so. Get used to it."

Lyric whimpered. "But she promised me that—"

"Then it'll be in her will," Molly snapped. "And if anyone tries to take anything behind my back, I'll hunt you down with every legal recourse I have available." She snapped an arm out, pointing at each of them. Her voice rose in volume, echoing over the lawn. "Do *not* tempt me. I am *not* Liz. I've spent a lifetime hating everyone in this family *except* Aunt Liz, and I make my living chasing down tornadoes, so don't think I won't take you on."

Bird glowered at her, the sparse wisps of white hair left on his head flipping about in a light breeze. "So what's next, Your Majesty?"

The breeze also stirred up the odor of the landfill again, annoying Molly. "I will work with Mr. Williams on Aunt Liz's desires, then make inventory for the will probate. We'll have to see what happens after that." She stared at Lyric. "Where's Blossom?"

Kitty gasped, indignant. "You're asking about *the cat*?"

Molly ignored her, keeping her stare on Lyric. The younger woman looked at the dirt. "She ran away after Aunt Liz died."

"Great. So y'all run off everyone, including the cat."

"Don't think we're just going to slink away," Kitty said. "I don't care what the will says."

"I would expect no less," Molly said. She turned and stepped onto the porch, a little surprised by how dark and cool the miasma of covering vines made it. She looked up at Russell. "You have the keys?"

He nodded but hesitated. "This may not be pleasant."

She held out her hand. "It'll be fine. My memories of this house aren't all great anyway."

His eyes softened in concern as he pulled a ring of keys out of his pocket. "Are you sure?" He separated one key from the cluster and held it out.

She took it. "I'm sure." With the deputies behind her, Molly unlocked the door and pushed it open.

And gagged.

4

The stench rolled over Molly like a dump truck, pushing her backward on the porch. Her relatives, clustered at the bottom step, hooted as she gagged again, bending over to fight the nausea that roiled through her stomach. Russell placed a comforting hand on her back. "I'm sorry," he whispered. "The house has been closed up since her death."

Molly straightened, pressing her hand over her mouth a few moments, glaring at him. Finally, she sputtered, "So who else is dead in there!?"

More guffaws emanated from Bird, but both Kitty and Lyric glowered at her. "See what Lyric had to put up with?" demanded Kitty.

Russell turned his back on the group and leaned close to Molly. "No one. Liz was—" He stopped abruptly, searching for the right word. "A collector of family memorabilia."

"So that included dead animals and rotten fruit?" She stared at him. "You said 'hoarder,' but this is unbelievable. No 'memorabilia' smells like that! I know that smell. Something's dead in there." She pushed the door back, but it stopped halfway, blocked by something. She stared, stunned at what she saw in the opening.

A narrow path of hardwood floor weaved its way among mounds of trash bags, clothes, boxes, books, and newspapers. To the left, Molly could see the edge of a staircase leading up, also piled high with unrecognizable lumps. On the right side of the path, the top of what might be an antique secretary peered over a mound of storage containers. In front of the door sat two boxes so heavily laden they had collapsed into each other. Something greasy oozed from the corner of one of them. She turned again to Russell. "How long has it been like this?"

"See!" Kitty called out. "See what Lyric put up with?"

Molly whirled. "Shut up! Lyric should have gotten off her fat butt and helped Aunt Liz deal with all that … stuff!"

Kitty started toward her, but was stopped by one of the deputies. "You have no idea what you're talking about!"

Molly looked up at Russell again. "Why didn't you tell me it was this bad?"

His shoulders dropped. "Because I knew you wouldn't come. And this really needs to be handled."

"Yeah, with a match and a few oil-soaked rags."

That comment caused even more outrage at the bottom of the steps. "You can't do that!"

Molly glared at them. "Yes, I can! It's my house now! Don't *tempt* me!"

Bird shouted. "You don't know what's in there!"

"Guess what? *I* don't *care* what's in there!"

"But Liz did," Russell murmured. "And she trusted you with that."

Molly stilled. Russell was right. She'd accepted Liz's task. She'd declared it in front of the rest of her family, such as they were. She looked again through the half-open door. The odor still made her nauseated, but she'd smelled worse after a tornado strike on a town. She could handle it.

A movement to the left caught her eye, and she found herself staring at a pair of beady, reflective eyes about halfway up the stairs. Rat. Of course there would be rats. Maybe that's the smell. Dead rats. With a sudden flickering movement, it vanished. Molly pulled her shirt collar up over her nose and started to enter, but the sheriff cleared his throat. She glanced at him, and he pointed at her feet.

"You might want to put your jeans inside your socks, ma'am. Y'know. Fleas." It sounded like the voice of experience speaking.

"This is getting worse by the minute," she muttered. She looked from him to Russell, then turned and slammed the front door. She marched off the porch and headed for the Explorer. Russell followed, a frantic note entering his voice for the first time. "Molly, you can't leave. Where are you going?"

"I'm not leaving," she said over her shoulder. "I'm getting my cell phone." She yanked open the door of the SUV and pulled her smartphone from her purse. As she punched it awake, she saw that Jimmy had still not sent her word about Sarah's condition. Maybe nothing to tell. Or maybe it's something he doesn't want to tell.

She shook off the thoughts and opened her browser. Less than two searches and three phone calls later, Molly found a pest control company willing to tent and fumigate the house on a Saturday—tomorrow. Another two calls, and a dumpster would be delivered Monday morning. Russell listened silently, his eyes slowly widening with surprise, as the deputies kept Bird & Company from moving within eavesdropping distance. As she ended the last call, Russell nodded approvingly.

"I wouldn't have thought of that. Are you good with the cost? I can make you an advance on what you're going to inherit, if you need it to get this done."

Molly smiled wryly. "I'll keep that in mind. Storm chasing doesn't pay all that well. I actually make more selling photographs of winterscapes and sunsets to regional magazines. But one advantage of owning nothing but a car is that you don't have many expenses. I'm fine for now."

"Let me know if you need help. Liz said you'd take charge and get things done. I honestly didn't expect it would be this quickly."

An image of her quiet, intelligent, and reserved Aunt Liz flashed through Molly's mind. She'd been a schoolteacher, beloved by most of the kids in town, including Molly. She looked up at Russell. "In the fifth grade, she tried to teach me to share leadership. I was always the captain on the playground, head of the group at reading time. It didn't really take." He chuckled as she nodded back toward the house. "But I will have to get in there to make some preparations for the exterminators."

Walking back toward the house, she nodded again at the man Russell had pointed out as the sheriff. Russell picked up on her cue and introduced them. Sheriff Gregory Olson, with his neat gray mustache, steel-gray hair, and sun-wrinkled face, reminded Molly of an Old West hero. Wiry and lean, he stood only a couple of inches taller than Molly, but when he shook her hand, his grip felt like iron.

His blue eyes, however, twinkled with kindness. “Miss Molly, I can’t say I envy you.”

“I appreciate that, Sheriff. You wouldn’t by any chance know where I could lay hands on a set of Tyvek coveralls, would you?”

His brows lifted. “Like we use at crime scenes?”

“Yes, sir. With booties, gloves, and a mask.”

He nodded. “I think I can get you one or two by morning. What time do you need them?”

“Around nine. Maybe a little before.”

“Do you want one of my boys to hang around tonight?”

“If you can spare one, I think it would be a good deterrent.”

“Not a problem. They’ve gotten used to watching out for Miss Liz, but I didn’t want to assume anything with you here.”

“I appreciate it.” Molly paused and lowered her voice. “By the way, exactly how notorious are my … relatives here in Carterton?”

The twinkle vanished. “I wouldn’t turn my back on any of the ones here, if that’s what you mean.”

“It is. Thanks. Can you … um …?” She made a “go away” gesture at Bird.

“Get them to leave?”

She nodded. “I held them off but it won’t last long. They aren’t really afraid of me. Yet.”

He tipped his hat at her, and she and Russell watched as the deputies escorted Bird, Nina, Kitty, and Lyric off the property. They grumbled and shot her foul looks, but they left. As Bird’s truck drove out of the yard, she nodded at their departure. “Nina didn’t say much.”

Russell watched as the truck disappeared down Maple Street. “She never does. Some folks think she’s not quite right in the head. Others think she’s an abused wife, which wouldn’t surprise me. She does seem devoted to the kids and the grandkids.”

“Stockholm syndrome?”

“Maybe. She never attempts to leave. Who knows? Maybe she really loves him. Stranger things have happened between heaven and earth.”

Molly leaned against the front of the Explorer, half sitting, bracing her rear on the bumper. She turned her attention to the house, observing it closely for the first time. The walls remained the dark blue of her childhood, but sometime over the past twenty years, someone had painted the shutters, trim, and scrollwork an odd combination of pink and neon green, though not recently. Split strips, curled slivers, and broken blisters of paint covered the house. The vines on the latticework curled over the roof, trailing along the gutters and pushing their way beneath shingles. Torn window screens and leaves that clustered in gutters like spiked fans added to the ambiance of neglect.

"How long had she been a hoarder?"

Russell shifted uncomfortably and crossed his arms. "I'm not sure. It seemed to come on slowly. I didn't notice at first. Some family member or other would drop off a piece they no longer had room for, but didn't want to get rid of."

"So she became their storage bin."

"Yes. Then about six, no, seven years ago, one of the cousins took sick, and his children brought almost the entire contents of his house over here when they moved him to a nursing home. She didn't want to say no to anyone, and everyone said it would be temporary, that he'd get well. But he didn't. Liz had such a tender heart. But that triggered something in her. After that, it got out of hand in a hurry. About three years ago, she stopped letting me come over."

Molly glanced sideways at him. Something in that last statement held more tenderness and regret than she'd expected from someone who was only a lawyer to a client. Her curiosity spiked, along with a rising suspicion. "How long have you known Aunt Liz?"

He shifted from one foot to the other. "Since we were kids. My dad worked in the fields with her dad." He paused. "Your grandfather. When we were barely old enough, we worked with them." He looked out at the low light of the horizon and into the past. "As a teenager, Liz could really pull her weight. Better worker than Bird ever thought about being, even though he was older and a boy. Regina—your mama—was already out of the house, working in Gadsden. Liz handled the field work as well as helping your grandmother in the house."

Molly peered at him a bit more closely. The muscles in his face had relaxed, and a light sheen glistened in his brown eyes. "Russell?" she asked softly.

He answered without looking at her. "Yes?"

"Are you the reason Aunt Liz never married?"

His whole being seemed to sharpen at the question. He uncrossed his arms and looked down at her. "Why would you ask that? You've never married."

She stood up straight and faced him. "Yes, but I'm aggressive, difficult, and mouthy to boot. I have a rough look, and I'm a nomad. Men seem to find that intimidating. And I won't even get into what I do for a living. But you're right. Aunt Liz had the most tender heart of anyone I've ever known. And in her teens and twenties, she was a beauty, like Cher with curly hair. Mama used to say her sister could have had any man she wanted. But she never wanted any of the ones who came around. Maybe because she was already in love?"

Russell stood stock still for a few moments, studying her. His eyes narrowed, and the skin around them seemed darker than before. Molly waited. Finally, Russell nodded, as if he'd made up his mind about something.

"I got a scholarship to Fisk University in Nashville. It was the late '60s. The Loving case had been decided, but there was no way we could be together, not here, not there. So we thought it best for me to go. Stay away. I tried. Fisk, then Howard for law school. I came back when my mother got sick, expecting to hear that Liz was married with a bunch of babies. She was still single. So was I. In her words, 'nothing else ever felt right.'"

"Why didn't you elope, go up North somewhere?"

He shrugged one shoulder. "Too entrenched, I guess. We were both involved in churches here, and she had a good place teaching fifth graders at the elementary school. My mother was sick. Then her dad, and later her mom. By that time I'd joined a firm in Gadsden. It's not as easy as you might think to pick up a law career and go somewhere else. I guess we got comfortable with the way it was."

"Kinda like Tracy and Hepburn."

Russell snorted a laugh, the most undignified action he'd taken since she'd walked into his office. "Only not as romantic. Or as high profile."

"How did you keep it a secret?"

He paused, then looked down at his hands, which were broad with long slender fingers, his palms as pale as the tops were dark. He stared at the deep lines in them, almost as if he could see the past as well as the future. "I'm not sure we did. By the time I came back, it was well into the '70s, but still a dangerous time for such a thing. Seriously risky for her as a teacher. But we were never blatant, never declared anything in public. No one asked, we didn't offer. She took enough heat for being my client that we didn't risk anything else. Over the years, we just became set in our ways. Most folks no longer cared—" He paused and shrugged one shoulder. "—except for Bird. He continued to hassle her about it, use it to threaten her, until the day she politely reminded him that I was a lawyer with a high success rate in court."

They both grinned at the implication, but Molly narrowed her eyes. "You said you were both in church. Did it ever make you doubt? At all? That God would put you through something like this?"

He shook his head. "Why should I doubt God?"

"You've met my family. They'd make Jesus doubt faith was worth it."

He scowled. "No. God may allow evil to exist, but He doesn't condone it. He helps you get through it, deal with it."

"I'm not so sure."

He hesitated, looking at the house with a deep sadness in his eyes. "I do sometimes wonder why He doesn't always give us enough strength."

Molly put a hand on his arm, her voice softening. "It's not about strength. You couldn't have stopped it."

His eyes narrowed in puzzlement as he studied her again.

"You couldn't have stopped her from being a hoarder."

His voice dropped almost an octave. "I'm not so sure."

"You know my family. You knew Liz. She spent most of her life trying to be the peacemaker. Taking in everyone's stuff is a logical outcome."

He shrugged, as though unconvinced. Molly squeezed his arm, then released it. "Will you be here in the morning?"

He nodded. "As soon as I can. Wouldn't miss it. What are you going to do tonight?"

"Get a motel room. Get some sleep. Check on my partners."

Russell frowned. "Your partners?"

She crossed her arms. "I work with two partners, Jimmy and Sarah. The day you called, Sarah had gotten hurt while we were shooting a supercell that produced two funnel clouds. She's in the hospital."

"Wow. I'm sorry."

Molly shrugged. "Lousy timing. But Jimmy convinced me I'd be of more use here. Get this out of the way. When Sarah's well, we can get back to work right away."

"Reasonable. But are you sure you'll be safe to stay alone?"

Molly hesitated. "Probably for now. Bird's mean and definitely capable of coming after me physically. But my guess is they'll try to get around me another way first. Twenty years ago, it got ugly only after they ran out of options."

"That's when Mickey got hurt."

"You knew?"

"Liz told me. Just remember that I have a condo with a guest room, if you need it." He gestured at the Explorer, curiosity on his face. "Is that really *all* you own?"

"Pretty much. I own the equipment for chasing. Why?"

"When Liz told me you were a storm chaser, I had this image of you traveling around with all this high-tech gizmo gear and a slick team of experts to help you, talking in a jargon no one else could understand."

She grinned. "If you won't believe everything you saw in *Twister*, I won't think all Southern lawyers are Matlock."

He laughed. "Deal."

"Yeah, there are teams like that, but most of us are cowboys. We travel light. Jimmy, Sarah, and I each have our own cameras, but we share some items for work, like a laptop and a high-end video recorder. I left both of those with Jimmy so he could work on our latest pictures and videos while I'm here and Sarah is healing. Gear is expensive, and we're in too many situations where it can be damaged or stolen. And it's more about the photographer than the gear, like most professions. Everything I need fits in one good-sized padded case."

"Another way not to get tied down."

Molly smiled. "You got it."

"Ya know, having a home base is not a crime."

She licked her lips, pausing before answering. "No, it's not. But it *is* a slippery slope. I'd rather chew glass than ever end up like Bird or Kitty."

His voice dropped. "Or Liz?"

It hurt every fiber of her being to say it. But she had to admit it. "Or Liz. I just can't."

"Excuse me."

They spun to face the man standing near the back of the Explorer. His denim shirt and jeans hung on a lanky frame. He snatched a University of Alabama ball cap off his head, crushing the cap in his twisting hands. A thick shock of dark-red hair stood out in all directions above and about a ruddy face. He nodded at the lawyer. "Mr. Russell, good to see ya again. Are y'all here about Miss Liz?"

Russell nodded. "Finn."

"I'm her niece, Molly McClelland. And you?"

He shuffled forward, heavy work boots stirring dust out of the gravel. He stuck out his right hand, a wide smile crossing his face. "I'm Finbar Eccles. Finn. I used to do a lot of work for your aunt, back when she'd still let me."

Molly shook his hand, but her eyes narrowed. "When she *let* you?"

Finn shook Russell's hand, then moved back a respectful distance, and Molly realized Finn stood almost as tall as Russell. "Yeah, the last year or so, she stopped hiring anything out. I tried—" he gestured at the house with the ball cap. "—ya can see it needs work—but she wasn't having it."

Molly glanced at Russell, who nodded slightly. "She was trying to get Lyric to leave."

Smothering a grin, Molly looked back at Finn. "So you know the house pretty well."

Finn nodded vigorously, causing several clumps of hair to flop back and forth. "Like the back of my hand."

Molly nodded. "So what was it like the last time you were in it?"

Finn frowned, his gaze shifting to the house. "They had already dumped all that stuff on her, so it was starting to get pretty bad. She told me repeatedly she didn't know what she'd do with all of it. I volunteered to help her take some stuff to the Goodwill, maybe get it auctioned, but she started getting sick, and that plonker Kitty sold her on the idea that she should keep it all." His mouth twisted. "For 'prosperity,' as Kitty kept calling it. No sense of irony, that one.

Then turned around and moved her skitter daughter in on her. That's when Liz stopped hiring me."

Molly tilted her head sideways as the word "plonker" confirmed the Irish lilt she thought she heard mixed in with the light Southern accent. "How long have you been in the South, Mr. Eccles?"

He straightened, smiling, and shoved the cap down over the crown of hair. "Long enough to be a good, solid fan of Alabama, Ms. McClelland."

Russell coughed. "Anyone with a sense of self-preservation does that."

Finn bowed slightly. "True dat. And, please, call me Finn."

"And I'm just Molly. You live around here, Finn?"

He pointed right. "Two houses over. And I can tell you the whole neighborhood is waiting to see what you'll do with all this."

"Well, tomorrow we start with fumigation." Molly crossed her arms. "The tents will arrive midmorning. Then we start removing the trash. After that, inventory. Beyond that …" She spread her arms wide. "I have no idea."

"I suppose Mr. Russell here has told you to keep an eye over your shoulder?"

Russell's bass voice rumbled. "I have."

Molly looked Finn over. "What have you seen?"

Finn looked toward the house, his face somber. "Bird. Nina. One of them shiftless grandkids. LJ. He's Leland's boy. And Eddie. Scrawny young'un. I think he belongs to one of the sisters. RuthAnn? Tommie Jane?"

"RuthAnn," Russell confirmed.

Finn nodded. "Just poking around where they don't belong. Some other folks, too, I ain't never seen before. Looking in the windows, nosing around. This was all before she passed. I checked on her every day, that's why."

"I thought Lyric was here all the time."

Finn made a noise that was halfway between a snort and a cough. "Ain't hardly."

Realization flowed over Molly and she straightened. "You found her? You're the one who called 911."

Finn's chin shot out. "I was. I did. Dug her out, too, from all that pile o' garbage. But it were too late." His eyes grew moist. "I should have—"

Molly put a hand on his arm. "Don't. Don't do that to yourself."

He looked grateful, then shook his head. "But she told me. The night before when me and the missus took over some dinner. After Lyric left. Miss Liz told me she'd heard 'em talking, talking that they were gonna kill her."

5

As Molly expected, rain dowsed Carterton just before dawn. By the time she arrived at the house, a faint steam hovered over the grass as the sun burned off the damp. She sat in the Explorer, letting the air conditioner run, relishing the last few moments of cool. Everything glistened, but Molly knew the beauty would be overwhelmed by mugginess. She had to smile. "It would not be Alabama without humidity."

Sheriff Greg Olson pulled into the drive just after eight thirty. Molly watched in her rearview mirror as he got out, put on his hat, and dug a package out of his trunk. He didn't have the rolling stroll she'd seen in so many officers in the past. Instead, he strode, as if every step had intention. He slammed the cruiser's trunk and headed toward her SUV.

Molly felt more than a little puzzled at how relieved she felt to see him. "One day," she muttered. "You've known the man a gigantic twenty-four hours. Probably just because he's on your side." She shook her head as she got out. "Later. Think about it later."

Greg greeted her with a nod. "Good morning."

"Thank you for this. I wasn't sure where I'd get one otherwise."

"Amazon. They can overnight them."

She laughed. "I'm sure they can."

As he handed her the crinkly package holding the crime scene coveralls, he examined her closely, his focus never leaving her face. "Are you sure you want to tackle this alone? I, or one of my officers, could help."

Molly hugged the package, surprised at how much noise it made. "Thanks, but I'm good. It's just a few prep stages for the fumigation—

opening cabinets and such, and it'll help me refamiliarize myself with the house. I haven't been in it for more than twenty years. I know the house itself hasn't changed much, but the contents ..." She glanced away toward the house, then rolled her shoulders and looked back at the sheriff, whose gaze remained on her. Molly resisted the urge to squirm. Instead she cleared her throat. "Have you ever been in a town a few days after a tornado has moved through? Smelled the garbage ... but something else as well?"

He nodded once. "Fortunately for me, it was only animals."

"There's something else going on here, isn't there, besides the hoarding?"

Greg remained silent for a few moments, still observing her. Then he pulled a small vial of Vicks VapoRub from his pocket. Her eyes widened as he handed it to her. "Smear it under your nose. Even with the mask, the smell can overwhelm you. That suit is going to be hot. Don't let yourself get overheated. It's easier to do than you might imagine. Do you have water on site?"

"I have a case in the back of the Explorer and a cooler full of ice."

"Good. And if you need anything at all, call out. I'm leaving two guys here all day, and I'll be stopping by occasionally."

"I will." She paused then asked, "Is this in your regular duties as sheriff?"

He smiled. "There is nothing about this situation that's part of my regular duties, Miss Molly. But Liz was special. What happened to her has my town in a tizzy. This needs to be resolved, and I want to see that her wishes are followed, if at all possible. It's good for you to be here for her. No matter what happened in the past."

He touched her shoulder briefly and headed for his car. Molly watched him drive away, wishing for just a moment that he'd stay. She'd been in Carterton less than twenty-four hours and had already met three people she hoped to know better. A record.

"Then again," she muttered, "how often do you stay in one place more than twenty-four hours? That's a record in itself."

Molly shook her head and headed for the house, wishing that others here in Carterton, however, would definitely stay away. She hoped Bird and Kitty took her last warning to heart.

Both had tracked her down at the motel last night to berate her about the house, with Bird giving ominous warnings about the damage the fumigation would cause. She'd listened, silent, as they ranted for a few moments, then told them that the fumigation would start at two in the afternoon, and if they tried to stop her, she'd have them arrested for trespassing on her property. Then she shut the door in their faces. Earplugs did the rest until the motel manager threatened to call the police. They gave up and slunk back into the night.

Far more disturbing to her was the silence from Missouri. No call or text from Jimmy. She and her storm-chasing partner had not parted on the best of terms, but still, she thought he'd realize she'd want news about Sarah, about how serious the brain injury had been. An injury caused by storm-flung debris the same day Molly had received the call from Russell.

She shrugged. No matter. If she wanted to get back to them as soon as possible, Molly had to focus on other things. She tore into the package and shook out the Tyvek coveralls, slick and impervious, and slid them on over her cargo shorts and tank top. She spread a finger's-width of the pungent salve under her nose and tucked the bottle away in a pocket of her shorts. She slipped on the booties, making sure they were impervious to fleas. She zipped up the suit, and, with the hood up, a mask over her mouth and nose, gloves on her hands, and the booties over her sneakers, she looked like a ghost. "Appropriate," she mumbled as she placed the key in the lock one more time.

The ointment helped, but a strong odor of decay still reached through the mask. This time, however, she knew what lay behind the door, including the rats that scurried from one box to another, slipping between the cracks. Molly reached for the switch just inside the door, and the foyer blazed into light. She stared for a few minutes, listening to the skittering of tiny claws and trying hard to get her mind around everything.

How does someone get this way? This extreme?

She stiffened, preparing to be slightly off balance, then picked her way through the rows of boxes and bags, the stacks of magazines and newspapers, trying to touch as little as possible. The tall furniture she had spotted yesterday was, in fact, an antique secretary hidden behind the containers in the foyer. The desk of it lay open, stuffed with mail and flyers, some for community events dating back two years. Behind the glass doors of the hutch, however, stood neat rows of Hummel angel figurines, which her aunt had collected since college, twenty-five or thirty of them. Hundreds of dollars in collectibles.

"Wonder how much of this isn't really treasure, just trash." Molly ran a finger down the joint where the two doors on the hutch section met. The quality of the wood and the craftsmanship were obvious, even to her untrained eye. "And how much treasure is beneath the trash."

Just beyond the secretary, an archway to her right revealed a room, but no path allowed even the tiniest access. Turning on the light, Molly spotted the corner of what looked like a Tudor cup dining table, its legs bearing the sturdy double-cup acorn design. The chairs for it were turned upside down on the table, their legs rising like masts on a grounded sailboat from the mounds of junk around them. A box near the door had ruptured, spilling out a tumble of phone books. The black letter dates of 1975 and 1976 stood out against the faded yellow covers.

Molly's anger and frustration began to give way to an overwhelming sadness. Why had they let her live like this?

Why had you? the internal scolding replied.

On the other side of the hall, another archway yielded similar results, and Molly wondered if she might have to fumigate the house twice. No way the fog of chemicals could pierce all this.

The sadness, the responsibility of dealing with it, pressed down on her. *How in the world am I supposed to handle all this?* There seemed to be no rhyme or reason to it. Unlabeled boxes lined walls and shelves. Clothes and shoes seemed intermingled with papers and books. Plastic milk crates filled with dishes and pots nestled heavily on top of mountains of black plastic garbage bags. Some of the bags had split to spill out actual garbage—old food cartons and cans. Clothes, blankets, and linens peeked through holes in others. Underneath it all, she saw corners and legs and edges of oak, cherry, mahogany, and hard rock maple.

Let's hope the fumigation works the first time. The longer this drags out, the longer you have to deal with them.

The hallway opened into a narrow butler's pantry. She paused, opening all the cabinets she could reach. One released a cascade of plasticware, which added a cacophony of hollow thunks to the air as it settled on the heaps and piles below. Molly shook her head. Less than twenty-five feet into the house, and she'd given up trying to decipher the contents of the mass around her. Her chest tightened with a deep sense of being overwhelmed. The whole thing felt impossible. "One rag soaked in kerosene and I could be out of here by tomorrow," she muttered.

Then Aunt Liz's words echoed in her head. *This is why I'm turning to you ... You are the only one who can help them. I hope you find it in your heart to carry out my wishes. And forgive me.*

"Aunt Liz, I don't know if I can." She stumbled over the corner of a box that stuck out from beneath a chair, and growled in frustration as she kicked the box. A scattering of flies and spiders repaid her anger, and she danced backward, trying not to fall.

In the kitchen, the grit of spilled food, ripped bags, and dirt ground under her bootie-covered shoes. The white stovetop was stained brown with burned grease, and smears of jam and mustard coated the refrigerator door. She opened cabinets, astonished to find one filled with clean dishes. More clean dishes stood in a drying rack, although the dirty ones in the sink had been there awhile. Probably since way before Aunt Liz died.

She opened drawers where she could, pulling the refrigerator door last. The stench shot through the mask and the Vicks and snatched her breath away. Molly swallowed hard and turned, bending over the sink, trying not to lose her breakfast. She inhaled through her mouth, then held her breath as she straightened, turned, and reached in to turn off the refrigerator.

Stepping back, she turned her attention to the basement entrance, near the back door. It opened easily, but Molly could go no farther; the stairs were completely blocked with boxes. She shook her head, not doubting for a moment that every room upstairs, plus the attic, looked the same. Her throat tightened as images of how her aunt had lived the last few years swamped her.

"Seriously, Aunt Liz, fire would be much quicker. And a whole lot easier." The thought was no longer a joke, no matter what her aunt had begged of her.

Molly left the basement door open, then pushed open the one window she could reach. She paused, looking around the kitchen, trying to imagine where she could even start. She leaned against the counter, bracing herself as tears stung her eyes. "Oh, Aunt Liz." She looked down, noticing for the first time the cloud of black spots that dotted her white-clad ankles and shins. Fleas.

No wonder Blossom bolted. I wouldn't live here either.

Abruptly, the sadness that had settled over her fled as a flush of anger returned. Her family's obsession with acquiring more and more possessions had led to this, had culminated in the misery of a sweet woman who could no longer say no to her family. To stuff.

It had to stop.

On the other side of the kitchen, an open door revealed a large room that Molly remembered as being Aunt Liz's formal dining room. Here is where that giant Tudor cup table had welcomed guests to elaborate dinners. Elegant women in tea dresses and hats had clustered here, while she and Mickey had peered in through a swinging door, mimicking the delicate manners and making childish jokes about tiny sandwiches and punch. Aunt Liz played the perfect Southern hostess.

Molly shook off the vision. Now the room seemed to be a combination bedroom and living room. A double bed pressed up against the back wall of the house held the rumpled covers and a scatter of magazines that must have occupied Aunt Liz during her last weeks in the house. Perpendicular to it and in front of some tall, overflowing bookshelves, a scuffed and lumpy microfiber couch faced an oversized, high-definition television. The coffee table in front of it held the remnants of at least six fast food meals, a stack of gossip magazines, and four remotes. As she moved into the room, a rat darted out of one of the food bags and vanished under the bed. Molly shuddered.

Lyric's nest. They lived in these two rooms, out of more than four thousand square feet. *Dear God!*

Behind the couch, a mound of garbage bags and newspapers looked more scattered and ragged than the other piles, and some of the nearby stacks had been shoved around and were partially collapsed. Molly shuddered, imagining this is where Liz had died.

Stay focused.

Molly pushed around the side of the bed, reaching for a chest of drawers on the far side. The bottom drawers already stood open, but she slid the remaining ones out. The top one stuck and she jerked hard. It gave suddenly, throwing Molly off balance. She stumbled, falling against the bed. The mattress slid away from her, and she fought to stay upright. Then, as Molly straightened, she noticed a blue strap sticking out from between the mattress and the box springs. Curious, she lifted the edge of the mattress and tugged the strap. A flat, zippered, leather bag dropped free. She propped it against the bed's footboard and grabbed the zipper pull. She yanked it back and pried open the bag.

"And what, may I ask, do we have here, Aunt Liz? Taxes? Old bills? Last week's grocery—"

Molly froze as she peered inside. Cash. Bank bundles of cash, at least eleven of them from what she could see. Hundred dollar bills. More than $100,000. And a spiral notebook with one word scrawled across the front: *Molly*. She set the bag aside and opened the journal. The first page contained only one paragraph, written in the same neat handwriting as the letter she'd left with Russell.

> *Mollybelle,*
>
> *There are dozens of other journals in this room, which I hope you will find time to read. But this one is the most recent and important. I've listed what I think are the most valuable items in the house, what they're worth, and who I think should get them. But in the end, it's up to you. Help as many people as you can. Use this money to get you through until it's all settled. I set it aside for you, because I know this process is going to take cash and that Bird and our kin are going to play you the devil until it's over. But you're strong. Take them head on, my girl. I will always love and believe in you.*
>
> *Liz*

So this is what they were so anxious to get their hands on. Molly's gut tightened as she understood a part of Liz's letter with a singular clarity:

Obviously, there was a method to their madness. Inheritance. I've noticed some things missing, but nothing major. They won't find what they're really looking for, and they won't until I'm dead.

Molly knew more than a few people who would do just about anything to get their hands on this kind of money. Some of them would even kill for it. She zipped the bag and slung it over one shoulder and left the room till later. Molly picked her way up the stairs, holding tight to the rail as she thrust aside and restacked boxes to make a path for the pest control workers. All four bedrooms on the second floor held the same proliferation of contents as the two on the first floor. The bathrooms had obviously not been used for anything but storage for a long while and one held a never-emptied litter box.

Blossom, where are you? Somewhere safe I hope. Liz really adored you. Please don't vanish on my watch. Molly smiled as she thought about how many pictures of Blossom took up space on her phone. Liz had perfected texting only to shower friends and family with shots of her orange companion.

Molly pushed on. Two of the bedrooms had small rooms beyond them, but she didn't attempt to reach them. By the time she opened the door to the attic, Molly was almost used to the smell, even though she felt hot and suffocated by the Tyvek. The smell hit her anew in the attic, stronger than ever, and an image of dead rats rotting in the heat made her pause. Still … it had to be done. With deliberate, measured movements, she cleared a narrow trail up the stairs. At the top, she hesitated again as she spotted daylight leaking in near the western eave. She stepped toward it, but stopped as an angry chattering bounced off the rafters. A squirrel, bushy tail flagging a warning, scolded her from the top of a box.

She stared at it. Squirrels in the attic. Of course there would be squirrels. Molly stamped her foot, and the squirrel flashed away, disappearing out the hole near the eave.

"Ms. McClelland!" A baritone voice from the front door sounded muffled as it found its way through the heaps and up the stairs.

Molly jogged down the attic stairs, then leaned over the second-story railing. "Don't come in here!" she called back. "I'll be there in a few minutes."

Molly tucked the tote bag under one arm, then marched down and out onto the front porch, where a dark-haired man in a red-and-blue uniform waited. When he saw her, he lifted the matching ball cap off his head and held it down to one side. "Ms. McClelland, I'm Taylor Eaton." He touched the label on his left breast pocket. "Cap's Pest Control. We spoke yesterday. I'm sorry we're a bit early."

Molly yanked off her mask and pointed at her ankles. The man glanced down, then took two quick steps backward. "Good heavens!"

"Tell me this will kill these too."

Eaton nodded, still watching her ankles warily. "It should kill everything living in the house. Vermin, anyway. You should wash those off. I saw a hose around the side of the house."

"Let's go." She trotted off the porch, motioning for him to follow. He scampered after her as she strode around the corner.

"Will it kill these, even under mounds of trash?"

He looked back up at her face, brown eyes wide. "Trash?"

"Hoarder. Hold this for me, would you?" She handed him the tote bag, which he took awkwardly, trying to juggle it with the other items in his hands. He finally tucked it under one arm.

Molly picked up the hose and turned on the water, showering herself hood to booties.

Taylor wiped his hand across his mouth. "Well … we've only done one hoarder house before. You have to remember this treatment was created to take care of termites, but it kills most everything else, including roaches and bedbugs."

"Rats?"

"Them too. The fumigation took care of everything in that house at the time, but if you don't clean it out, vermin have a way of finding their way back in. Especially once all their friends are dead. And quickly. Rats come looking to scavenge and rats bring—" He gestured toward her feet.

"Fleas."

"Yes, ma'am. Do you have plans once we remove the tents?"

Satisfied she'd drowned most of the fleas, she turned off the water. She pushed the hood back and tried to fluff her sweat-drenched hair. "They're delivering the dumpster day after tomorrow. You suggested we wait three to four days for all the chemicals to disperse."

Eaton nodded. "Yes, ma'am. We'll be back to aerate it starting Monday night, and we'll take the tent down Tuesday morning, but there may still be pockets in the house, if it's packed tight."

"Believe me, it is. I couldn't even get to most of the windows and cabinets to open them like you asked. And the basement is impassable."

"We'll run some air tests to make sure it's all dispersed, but you might want to wear a mask the first few days you work."

"You smell this house? I'll be wearing a mask for months."

He tugged at a stray curl over his forehead. "Ma'am—"

"Molly, please."

He smiled. "Molly, I was born without a sense of smell. Never could. A bit of an advantage in this business."

Molly smiled for the first time that day. "No doubt that'll be a comfort today, Mr. Eaton."

"Taylor." He handed her the tote bag.

"Thanks. Are you ready to start?"

"Sure are." He gestured toward the front yard. Molly returned to the corner of the house. Two large trucks filled the driveway. A large metal frame covered most of the first one, with tall poles supporting the long rolls of red-and-green tarpaulins on each side, while a plethora of ladders covered the top. Behind it, what looked like a shrunken tanker truck waited, an array of hoses running down the side and coiled on the back. Three men in identical uniforms gathered near the front of the trucks, smoking and pointing at different aspects of the roof. "It'll take us about three hours to cover the house, then the fumigation will start. Is the gas turned off?"

"It's all electric."

"Good. I just need you to sign some papers." He stopped, rubbing a leaf of the vines between his fingers. "These will probably be killed."

"That's fine. They'll have to come down anyway. The whole house will have to be repainted. And my guess is they're hiding some badly needed repairs."

Taylor shoved his cap back down on his head. "We'll try to save the roots." He headed for the driveway, giving orders to the three men standing near the trucks.

"Don't bother," Molly muttered, as she walked to the Explorer and tucked the tote bag out of sight next to her gun case under the seat. She peeled out of the Tyvek suit. A fine sheen of sweat covered her body, and the cooler April air hit her skin like a refreshing shower. She flopped the suit up on the hood, then went to the back of the SUV to dig a bottle of water out of her cooler, which she had resupplied that morning at the local convenience store. The cooler, like her camera bags, went everywhere with her. Life essentials.

Molly sat down in the shade of the open hatch and cracked open the top on the water. She felt tempted to turn it up over her head, but decided the wet t-shirt look might not be a good idea. She settled for fluffing the curls and shaking the sweat out of her hair. Then she gulped down half the bottle before she took a breath.

"Good golly, Miss Molly!"

Molly turned to see Finn striding up the drive beside one of the big trucks.

"Morning to ya!" He touched the bill of his John Deere cap, then handed her a towel.

She took it, but raised her eyebrows at it, then Finn.

He shrugged, a sheepish grin on his face. "I've had to wear one of those blasted suits before. Ya kinda wind up simmering in your own sweat."

Molly laughed. "You do at that." She began to dry her arms and legs.

Finn motioned with one thumb toward her yard. "You're starting to draw quite a crowd this fine day."

Molly looked past him, immediately glad she hadn't given herself a spring water shower. Neighbors, curious looks on their faces, had begun to wander in from all directions, their eyes warily watching as the pest control workers dragged the long rolls of tarps off the truck and began lining them up on all sides of the house. Taylor, who'd already climbed a ladder to the roof, walked around on the gables and valleys as if the steep pitches were a second home. He padded corners and eaves with some kind of tape, moving from one to the other quickly.

"I guess it will be a bit of a circus. Striped big top and all." Molly took another swig of water and draped the towel over one shoulder.

"And every good circus needs concessions."

Molly looked back at him, puzzled. "Beg your pardon?"

He snatched off the ball cap, clutching it in his hands. Obviously, this was a habit of his.

"Well, I was wondering, y'know, with the way this is a-going and all, after all, people watching a show get mighty thirsty, even on a day fine as this. You yourself ..." He motioned at the half-empty bottle in her hand.

"Want to open a lemonade stand?"

"Well ... actually, I've got this big ol' pickup perfect for tailgating. The missus and me, we take it to all the big games."

Molly laughed as the image of Finn selling ribs and beer out of the back of his truck came to her. "Fine. Just don't trash the lawn. And don't gouge on the prices."

"Whoop!" He shoved the cap back on his head. "No, ma'am!" He turned and jogged away in a half-limp half-trot, as if his left hip didn't work quite like it was supposed to.

She turned back to the house and watched, fascinated, as Taylor's men moved the rolls about, climbing ladders, tossing ropes, pulling the tarps up and over the house. It was an efficient and fast-moving effort, and the first of the red-and-green tarps headed for the cupola on top of the house before Molly finished her water. It unfurled, the stripes slipping over the gutters and to the ground like a heavy flag. Taylor, back on the ground, pulled long hoses from the second truck and headed into the house. Molly gave a hesitant grin as he entered the house for the first time, stopped, backed out, and shot a look at her over his shoulder. They nodded at each other, then he continued his work.

As the second rolled tarp ascended, an engine rumbled behind Molly, and she turned to see a massive, Alabama-crimson, dual-wheeled Ford pickup easing up Maple Street. She had to smile, some of the more pleasant memories of her childhood creeping back in as the truck slipped easily among the crowd that continued to cluster in her yard and street, the signature white A of the University of Alabama emblazoned on the doors. In the truck's bed, a slender blonde sat on a wooden crate, keeping a tight hold on an oversized grill. A long, thick plait swayed against her back as her body moved in sync with the truck. Her face held a lovely tranquility and soft smile. Molly got the feeling she had spent a lot of time in that truck bed. "Hello, Mrs. Eccles," she whispered.

Nothing said "small-town Alabama" to Molly like a community coming together over some event, drawn by food and fellowship. She missed this. Sure, she'd witnessed this type of gathering in other small towns, but she'd always been the observer, the outsider.

The crowd parted as the truck passed the driveway, some of them calling friendly jibes at Finn. With the driveway blocked, he turned it directly into her front yard, bouncing across the shallow ditch, about halfway between her drive and the house next door. He threw it into park, then hopped out. Together, the couple eased the grill down to the ground, then shoved four large coolers into place around it. Distracted, some of the folks began wandering closer.

Finn encouraged them with an impromptu sideshow patter. "Come on over, folks. The big top is gonna take a while going up and coming down. It'll be a fine day for something cold and something hot. We're gonna cook dogs, just two bucks. Burgers will be three. Drinks a dollar, too. Pull up a chair and we'll make it a party do."

A few of the neighbors gave him a friendly wave of dismissal, but others laughed or grinned, stepping a bit closer.

Molly chuckled. "Well, Aunt Liz, I may still be the outsider, but Molly's definitely back in town. And she brought the circus with her, big top and all."

6

Molly stared at the text from Russell, then shook her head. *Bird's headed your way with an injunction. Be there soon.* She swallowed the last bite of one of Finn's hotdogs, then reached down beside the lawn chair he'd offered her and picked up her Coke. Taking a slow sip, she looked up at the big top, now puffed out a bit with the air circulation inside. Behind them, the motors on the chemical truck hummed, pumping in the last of the pesticide.

The text confirmed her instinct last night about telling Bird and Kitty when all this would start. "Well, this is going to be fun."

"What's that you say, Miss Molly?" Finn dropped into the chair next to her and stretched his long legs out in front of him, crossing them at the ankles. He clutched a pair of tongs in one hand, and a smear of charcoal decorated his left cheek.

She turned the phone so he could read the text. Finn leaned toward her and squinted at the screen. He leaned back with a grunt, turning his attention to the house again. "He's a little behind his game today, Bird is. They'll be all done and wrapped up by the time he gets here."

"Probably because I told him the fumigation would start around two."

Finn laughed, then glanced at her. "Why in the world is that old sod called 'Bird' anyway? That can't be his real name."

Molly tucked her phone in her shorts pocket. "Nope. His real name is Thomas John. Got the nickname from his habit of climbing trees when he was a kid. Aunt Liz told me he would not stay out of the trees, even as a toddler. At first, just for fun. Later to avoid chores. Mama and Aunt Liz started calling him 'Birdie Boy,' and it stuck."

"Hmph. That why his oldest girl is Tommie Jane?"

"Yep. Bird was convinced she'd be a boy, so they didn't even pick out a girl's name. Just planned for the boy to be Thomas John Junior. Had to make do when she was born. RuthAnn was named for someone on Nina's side of the family."

Finn frowned. "Then how come Leland isn't a junior? Ain't he the oldest?"

Molly nodded. "He is, but I have no clue. In fact, he's the oldest of my generation. My brother is second." She paused, watching the tents pulse with air movement. After a moment, she stood abruptly.

Finn swiveled to look up at her. "What're you up to now?"

She grinned at him. "I feel the urge to take some pictures." Molly returned to the Explorer, opened the back, and unlocked the padded bag that held her equipment and pulled out her favorite Canon and a short lens. She attached the lens, checked the battery, and closed everything up. Then she turned her lens on the tent, the crowd, and the sky, snapping away as she returned to her seat. When she aimed it at Finn, he posed expertly with the tongs and a broad smile.

She laughed, then settled and turned thoughtful, the camera resting in her lap. "How in the world did Bird find a judge on Saturday?"

Finn swiped at his cheek with the back of his hand, demonstrating how that smudge got there. "That would be Judge Keeley. Poor craiter lost his wife last Thanksgiving, God rest her soul. Can't stand to be at home ever since. Goes fishing a lot with his courthouse buddies. But if he ain't fishing, he's down at the courthouse. Heard 'em say he even sleeps on his office couch sometimes. Wonder what grounds he used."

The answer came from behind them. "One I should have anticipated."

Russell's words caught them off guard, and both twisted in their chairs to look up at him. They stood, and Finn motioned toward the grill, where his wife flipped the latest round of burgers with a long-handled spatula. "Want something to eat, Russell?"

The lawyer started to shake his head, then hesitated. "Any hotdogs on that grill?"

Finn perked up. "Absolutely, my dear sir. Loaded?"

"Definitely. Peppers?"

"Got 'em. Coming right up." Finn headed for the grill, motioning the tongs at his wife.

"I didn't hear you drive up."

Russell pointed a thumb over his shoulder. "If you haven't noticed, you can't get a car past the intersection down there. Whole neighborhood is blocked off with people coming to see what's going on."

Molly took a quick shot of the line of cars stretching down Maple Street. "So what grounds did he use?" She motioned for Russell to sit, and she joined him.

"That Liz deeded you the house but not the contents. Finn's right. Bird found Edward Keeley in his office. He made a case that the will had not been probated, the contents still belonged to the estate, not you as a person, and that the pesticides might hurt those antiques, thus persuading Edward that the fumigation would have to wait until they were out of the house."

"But that's not true, is it? Doesn't the quitclaim deed specify personal property?"

"Doesn't matter. Bird argued that not everything inside belonged to Liz, which is also true, and that many things in the estate are specifically bequeathed to other people. His argument is that the fumigation could render them worthless."

"Which is not true."

Russell shrugged. "In my experience, injunctions are often issued in the name of 'better safe than sorry,' and the facts are sorted out later."

"Now what?"

"We wait. Edward said he'd have a deputy serve the injunction today, so Bird headed for the sheriff's office. In the meantime, Edward called me, and I phoned Greg Olson to give him a heads-up. Greg will escort Bird over here and serve the injunction, but he won't get in a rush with it."

Molly listened to all this, bemused. "Is this some kind of old boys network thing?"

Russell half-smiled. "Let's just say that if Bird wants to use the law to manipulate things in his direction, he should learn a great deal more about the law than he does. And he should learn to fish."

Molly laughed, a deep and genuine guffaw. "I forgot how things were done down here."

"Oh, it's pretty much that way just about anywhere, especially in small towns. It's the social oil that keeps things civil and civilized. Hard to give a man too much grief if you're going to bait hooks with him next weekend."

"I'll try to remember that." She paused. "Do you have a safe in your office?"

Russell glanced at her warily. "Yes. Why?"

"I found something in the house I need you to store for a bit. It's potentially a lot of trouble."

Finn appeared before them, a soda can in one hand, a bowed and overloaded paper plate in the other. "Here ya go, sir."

Russell grinned at Finn and took the drink, but his gaze returned to Molly, guarded, as he popped it open and sat it on the ground. He reached for the hotdog, took a big bite, and changed the subject. "Get to know any of your neighbors?"

She grinned at him. "Hard not to when the party's on your lawn." Molly nodded at the woman standing at the grill. "Sheila Eccles. Finn's missus. Met him twenty years ago when his University of Dublin debate team faced off with the Samford debaters. She says they still find debating exhilarating."

Russell chuckled. "I bet they do."

"See the lady in the blue tank top?"

"The one who looks like Kim Kardashian from behind?"

"Play nice."

Russell put the hotdog on the plate and placed one hand on his chest, palm flat. "Hey, I love the way Kim looks from behind. So who is she? Is that Linda?" Another bite and half the dog was gone.

Molly nodded. "Yep. Linda Allen. Widow. Lives next door, on the left side, with three kids, her brother, and an assortment of dogs and cats."

"Liz mentioned her on occasion. Liked her a lot."

"Linda's a sweet lady. Told me Blossom is still in the neighborhood and shows up at her house for food on a regular basis. She'll make sure the cat's taken care of for now." Molly paused, swallowing hard.

Russell leaned toward her. "What is it?"

Molly sniffed. "Did you know that Aunt Liz was part of a knitting and crocheting group?"

"No. Did Linda tell you that?"

Molly nodded, wiping a sudden spill of tears from one eye. "She said Aunt Liz came over to their house every Thursday evening. The women of the neighborhood gathered, as Linda described it, 'to knit and gossip.' Aunt Liz liked making caps and blankets for the premature babies at the Gadsden hospitals. And shrouds for the ones who didn't make it, so they would have something to wear when the parents said goodbye." She paused, swallowing hard. "I don't know if I could do something like that. I wouldn't be able to stop thinking about the babies." She paused again. "There's just so much about her I didn't know."

Russell squeezed her forearm. Neither of them spoke for a few moments, then the pump motors on the tanker truck grumbled slower and shut off, leaving an unexpected silence in the air. Molly turned to watch as Taylor checked a few things on the pumps and gave her a thumbs-up.

"That's it?" she called.

He approached her chair. "That's it. We'll wind the hoses back up and check the seals once more. We'll be back Monday morning to start the aeration and take down the tarps, which won't take that long." He gestured to his men, who had taken up residence on the far side of Finn's truck with hotdogs, Cokes, and three of the young ladies. Their sense of teamwork returned as they retrieved the hoses, double-checked the rolled and clipped seams, and posted warning signs on all four sides of the big tent.

A low-key community cheer went up as they got in the trucks and revved up the big diesel engines. The crowd parted and began disperse a bit as they edged their way through and out to the street, moving cars so the trucks could exit. As the rumble of the trucks faded away, the pleasant murmur of the milling crowd took its place. Some of the neighbors headed home, but others hung about. Two teen boys started tossing a football back and forth. Joined by others, a game of tag football broke out. A cluster of girls huddled, whispering and watching the boys. Moms chatted, bemused at the age-old ritual. The smells of charcoaled burgers and hotdogs lingered, even as Sheila and Finn showed signs of closing up shop.

Molly took several photos, tracking from one scene to the next, slowly aware that Russell watched her closely. She lowered the camera. "Yeah, this is nice. I admit. I miss this."

"It's a good neighborhood."

"Doesn't mean I'm staying. This is just the lull before the storm."

"You sure?"

"Believe me, Russell. I know storms."

He glanced around before asking, "What did you find?"

"A hundred grand in cash."

Russell choked on his soda. "Are you serious?"

"In a tote bag under the mattress. It's locked in the Explorer right now."

"Anyone see you come out with it?"

"Just the pest control boys. Why didn't she put it in the bank? She left a note and said it was for me to use on the house, but she had to know it'd still be considered part of the estate. I can't just start spending it."

"No idea. Maybe she thought since it wasn't part of the 'official' finances, it wouldn't matter. Or maybe she thought you'd be willing to keep it under the table."

"Then she didn't know me very well."

Russell leaned closer to her. "Liz could be strange about money, sometimes wise, sometimes ... not so much. She'd make big investments and not touch them for years, then turn around and play with penny stocks and keep large sums in the house. As a result, there's about five hundred grand in an investment account, and another eighty thousand in savings." He gestured at her SUV. "And now this."

Molly gaped at him. "She was a teacher! Where did she get that kind of money?"

"Like I said. Long-term investments. Back in the '60s she bought stock in Coca-Cola. Then in the '80s she bought Apple stock. Never sold either, despite all the ups and downs, until a few years ago."

"You think this was something she cashed out?"

He shrugged, paused, then shook his head. "No. I took over her finances, just as she started selling all her stock. She was too afraid of your family, and knew I'd keep her straight. In fact, she was terrified Bird would find out exactly what she was worth. I thought I knew everything, but I don't have a clue where that money came from."

An angry, hooting bellow from down the street echoed over the yards.

"Speaking of storms," Russell murmured.

"That sounds remarkably like a bull moose I once heard in Montana."

Russell snorted. "The moose would have better manners."

The bellow sounded again, much closer. This time it faded into a shout. "You can't do this!"

Russell stood and turned toward the approaching injunction party. Finn and Sheila wandered closer, as did some of the neighbors. The teens stopped tossing the football and closed in. Finn clutched a long-handled fork in a menacing manner. Molly stood slowly, glanced at Finn and Sheila, then returned her focus to her relatives. She raised the camera and took several pictures of their approach.

Bird marched up the drive, pointing furiously at the tent, his hand shaking wildly. Kitty and Lyric trailed him, their faces red from the effort of trudging up the street. Sheriff Greg Olson strolled in behind Bird, his expression placid and noncommittal.

Finn barked a laugh and stepped in behind Molly. "Ever heard Gillian Welch's song 'One Monkey'?"

Molly thought she'd swallow her tongue trying to keep a straight face. Instead, what emerged was a choked grunt.

Russell held up his hand, halting the party. Bird continued to sputter until he got out, "Show them, Sheriff." He rocked back on his heels and crossed his arms, a distinctly self-satisfied look on his face. "This tent has to come down. Now."

Greg offered up the injunction, and Russell took it, unfolding it slowly.

Molly raised the camera and took pictures until Kitty threw up a hand to block her. "Stop that!"

Molly lowered the Canon, eyebrows raised. "I promise it won't steal your soul."

Finn snorted. Molly realized that the crowd behind them had drawn closer, and she wasn't the only one taking pictures.

Russell cleared his throat. "I think you'll find, Mr. Morrow, that you're too late." He pulled his reading glasses from his pocket and perched them on his nose, scanning the paper.

"No. The judge said—I mean, that paper prevents—this has to stop!"

Russell folded the paper and handed it back to the sheriff. He took off the glasses and smoothly returned them to the pocket. "You are correct. That paper is worded quite specifically to *prevent* an action. However, once the action is underway, the injunction no longer has any sway. You'll need a differently worded injunction to get it to come down. And legalities aside, this kind of fumigation process, once it's underway, would have to be halted slowly and the house aerated properly. It's not as if we can just take down the tarps this instant. By the time you got another injunction, this will be complete anyway. Basically, what's done is done."

Kitty made a squeaking noise. "This is wrong!"

Bird scowled. "This is dirty. That judge did it that way on purpose. You gotta judge in your pocket?"

Greg cleared his throat. "Careful, Morrow. You don't want to be making accusations like that in front of an officer of the court."

Lyric whimpered. "Mama?"

Kitty made a shushing sound at her before turning her wrath on Molly. "You can't treat us this way and get away with it!" She took a step forward, but both Greg and Finn closed ranks with Molly.

"You, too, Kitty," Greg said softly. "Don't threaten her in front of me."

Kitty stopped, staring in amazement at both of them. "How dare you! She's a stranger! You don't know her, have no idea what she intends for any of this! She could mean to do much worse with the estate than we ever would. She's an outsider!"

Molly winced and her muscles tensed. She was an outsider now, but her roots in this place, as painful as they were, ran deep. She'd loved Liz, and, once upon a time, the people of this town. These people had destroyed more lives than just hers.

Greg didn't budge. "And I will enforce the law for everyone involved. If she breaks it, I'll arrest her. You as well. If you violate the law, I will arrest you, no matter how long any of you have lived here."

Russell's bass voice deepened and grew in volume as he pulled three legal documents from his coat pocket. "And this is legally Ms. McClelland's property, outsider or not. Hers to do with as she wishes." He handed a document each to Kitty, Lyric, and Bird.

Bird took his grudgingly. "What's this?"

"Restraining orders."

The level of indignation skyrocketed, as the three became incoherent, stuttering through their rage. Behind Molly, Finn muttered something that sounded like "manky gits." A low stir of curiosity murmured in the crowd.

Russell continued, his voice as even as a teacher explaining simple instructions. "You have provided ample evidence that you intend to continue to harass and badger Ms. McClelland, as well as trespass on her property, as you are doing now. These court orders preclude you or anyone representing you from coming within one hundred feet of the property or Ms. McClelland's person without her stated permission. Violation of these orders can result in arrest, fines, and/or imprisonment."

Bird ignored Russell, jerking his fist toward Molly. "You'll regret this! I promise you, you'll pay for this."

Greg cleared his throat again. "Morrow," he growled, "don't make me take action."

Bird glanced at him, then back at Molly. "This is just the beginning."

Molly's eyes narrowed. She'd had enough. "I have no doubt. Some things never change." Her words clipped hard in the air. She stepped toward him. "Twenty years ago *you* broke Aunt Liz's heart and turned my mother's to stone."

Her voice rose in volume with every sentence until her words echoed over the crowd. She jerked her hand toward him for emphasis and moved closer, forcing him to back up. Molly's entire body quivered as fury consumed her. "*You* left my brother—your own nephew!—bloodied and bruised. Your love of possessions ripped this family apart and put my mother in an early grave. It drove Mickey and me out of our home! Your greed cost me *everything*! You *destroyed* everything I cared about!" She jerked her arm toward the house behind her. "Greed did this. It killed the only decent person in this family. Your greed did all of it. But not this time, Thomas John. Not this time! This time I'll make sure Aunt Liz's wishes are granted. Not mine. And definitely not yours. *Now get off my lawn!*"

Behind her, a cheer, complete with applause, reverberated off the tented house.

Bird and Kitty, their faces almost purple with fury, turned and stalked away. Lyric hesitated, her eyes wide. She stared at Molly, unmoving, until Kitty turned and snagged her arm, dragging her away.

Finn shook his head. "Gah, that girl's a sandwich short of a picnic."

Molly watched the three as they retreated, the rage flowing out of her. She hugged herself to stop the shaking. "Either that, or I said something she's never heard before."

"You said something none of us have heard before."

Molly jerked around to see Linda Allen standing behind Finn. "What?"

"Why you and Mickey left so abruptly after your mother died. Was it really about Bird cleaning out your grandmother's house?"

Russell and Finn turned to Molly as well. "They should know," Russell said quietly, motioning toward the neighbors who had clustered around them. "They loved her too."

* * *

The crowd dispersed in bits and groups. The teens returned to their ballgame. Sheila gave Finn a quick hug and pushed him back toward the folks who followed Linda and Molly toward the small house to the left of the big tent. Kids flooded around the adults, rushing in and out of Linda's back door as if they all lived there, although Molly finally figured out that only three of them were actually Linda's offspring.

The kitchen—yellow, frilly, and sunny—smelled like cinnamon and peanuts, warm bread and fried okra. The house rang with the laughter of scurrying children, as a half dozen or so poured fruit juice and snatched cookies from a plate on the counter. Linda shooed them out the back door as the adults, mostly the four members of the "knit and gossip" group, along with Molly, Russell, and Finn, settled around a scarred wooden table polished shiny by use.

Molly sat her camera on the table in front of her and settled into a straight-backed chair. She toyed with the edge of a knitted yellow-and-brown placemat as the children scattered to the winds, the screened back door slamming behind them.

Linda winced. "I've tried," she said with a shrug. "But they forget."

Molly smiled. "I slammed a few in my time."

As the last of the children scampered out, Greg came in, dodging around a preteen boy in a football jersey. He nodded at Linda, then took up a casual stance near Molly's chair. Linda looked from Greg to Molly, who glanced once over her shoulder, smiling at the stoic sheriff.

Linda smiled brightly, then pulled a tray from a narrow cabinet, set it on the counter, and lined it with ice-filled glasses. "Who wants sweet tea?" All hands went up, and she took a brimming full pitcher from the fridge and filled the glasses. She smiled over her shoulder at Molly. "It's my grandma's tea. She always got the sugar just right." Linda placed the tray in the middle of the table, then settled in at the head as everyone reached for a glass.

"Molly," she said softly, "I know you don't know us from Adam, even though we may have some blood kin amongst us. My husband was a cousin, I think."

"David. On my daddy's side. Liz talked about y'all some." As Linda nodded, Molly glanced back down at the placemat. "Daddy died when Mickey and I were still little. I don't know many of his people. Most of them were from up on Chandler Mountain, near the lake, if I remember."

"Sure were. David and I moved down here when he got a job at one of the distribution plants."

"That's when you met Aunt Liz?"

"She was the first one to welcome us to the neighborhood."

"She didn't mind when the houses started going up around her?"

Russell took a sip of his tea. "I think she was glad for the company."

General murmurs of agreement circled the room. "We also got to know Bird about that time," Linda grumbled. "He kept insisting that we brought down the value of her house, since ours were smaller and cheaper."

Molly sniffed. "That's rich. I have a specific memory of Aunt Liz complaining to Mother that he was driving her crazy, wanting to know how she could afford that house on a schoolteacher's salary. Kept insisting she had a hidden source of income we needed to know about." She glanced at Russell, but he remained stone-faced.

Linda giggled. "Yep. One time we got to kidding her that she must be a kept woman. She thought it was a hoot."

Russell shifted uncomfortably in his chair, and Molly thought it might be a good time to change the subject. "My uncle has the word 'more' tattooed on his brain. He's always wanted more, was always scheming about how to get more, and if you had more he wanted to know how he could get some of yours."

"Why is he like that?" Finn asked. "Liz wasn't. You aren't. It's not from your family."

Molly hesitated. "I honestly don't know. Mama once said he'd been really hurt by someone, but she didn't go into any details. Truth is, I didn't care. To me, he was just always like that. It's who he was and we just had to deal with it. And he obviously hasn't changed. He cares more about things than people. That's pretty much what's killed our family."

Nodding soberly, Linda asked, "You said it drove you and Mickey away."

Molly took a sip, then leaned back in her chair. "Mama, Bird, and Aunt Liz grew up in the big farmhouse over on Cottonwood Road, the one my grandfather—their daddy—built."

"Where Bird and Nina live now?" Greg asked.

She glanced back at him. "Yes. And when my daddy died, Mother moved us back in there with my grandparents. Mickey and I mostly grew up there too. Mickey was eight. I'd just turned four. I really don't remember where we lived before that." She nodded at Linda. "I don't remember Daddy at all. Just pictures Mama had."

Molly realized she'd started to slump and straightened. This was harder than she'd expected. A deep ache began to build just below her heart. Too much past pain. "Aunt Liz already had her house, and Bird and Nina lived over at the foot of the mountain." Molly stared at her tea, swirling the ice around in the glass. "That old farmhouse was a great house to be a kid in. Strange nooks and crannies. Closets that seemed to go on forever." Her smile turned sad. "At least when you're five or six, they go on forever."

She cleared her throat and looked around at the people at the table. "Granddaddy got sick when I was fifteen. He died that July. His funeral was on the hottest day ever. Middle of a drought. The fight for his equipment started right away, since Gram had made it clear she wouldn't continue farming. It got ugly. Mama and Bird almost came to blows over it. It set them against each other for the rest of her life. When Gram died just a year later—"

Molly's voice clogged. She looked back down at her tea glass, watching twin drops of sweat slip down one side. Russell put his hand on her shoulder. She took a deep breath to shake off some of the pain. "Right. Yes. Gram died in her sleep. Mama called the funeral home, then Bird and Aunt Liz. Aunt Liz came over right away, and was there when the funeral home people came to get Gram's body. Mother, Aunt Liz, and I followed them back to the funeral home to make arrangements. We left Mickey eating breakfast, to wait for Bird. He was supposed to tell Bird which funeral home, what time we left, and to bring Mickey with him. They never showed. It took about three hours at the funeral home. Mama and Aunt Liz had a hard time picking a casket. When we got home ..."

The remembered pain choked off her words again. She turned to Russell, her eyes pleading for help. He reached out and covered her hands with his, squeezing them hard as he finished the story. "Bird and his boys, Leland and Bobby, had stripped the house almost bare."

A low gasp sounded around the room, and Finn mumbled something harsh and unintelligible.

Russell continued for her. "When they got home, Mickey was on the front porch. He'd tried to stop them, and they'd messed him up pretty badly. They took everything, even the things belonging to Molly and Mickey. Told Molly's mother that they could have them back only if she signed the house over to Bird."

"Blackmail," muttered Finn.

Behind her, Greg made a dark sound deep in his throat, and shifted to a firmer stance. He stepped closer to her, an ominous, protective presence, even in his silence.

Molly swallowed hard. "Gram knew the house was to be Mother's. She thought everyone else knew that too. We lived there.

It was our home. And she was the oldest, so the next of kin too. There should have been no argument."

"What did she do?" Linda whispered.

"She had no choice. She signed over the house. And even then they didn't return everything. Just the basics. Mickey joined the military. I only saw him twice before Mama died two years later. I haven't seen him since. I have no idea where he is. Mama was a nurse, but she'd only been working part time to help out while she took care of Granddaddy and Gram. We moved into this one-bedroom place down by the railroad." She looked up at them. "You know the houses owned by the Hammonds?"

"That line of shacks next to the tracks?" Finn demanded.

Molly had to smile at his indignation. "That was more than twenty years ago. They were not too bad back then. Just small. And noisy."

Russell squeezed her hands again and leaned back. "Why didn't you move in with Liz?"

Molly paused, her mind caught in memory flashes of that tiny house, where she'd slept with her mother and spent the winter huddled next to a space heater to finish homework. She shrugged. "I don't know. Not for sure. I know Aunt Liz asked her to, but I think Mama felt she'd never get Gram's house back if she did. She planned to find a way to get it at first, but never really had the will to pursue it. Her brother's betrayal just took it out of her. She stopped talking. She never laughed. She couldn't think straight." Molly's eyes clouded with tears. "I stayed with Aunt Liz a lot the last year because Mama was so tired all the time. The night I graduated from high school was the last time I saw Mama smile. Just after that, she caught something at the hospital she couldn't shake off. I guess her immune system was full of holes from the stress. She died in June. I called the funeral home, gave them almost all the money we had. I took the rest and caught a bus for Tulsa."

Russell scowled. "Why Tulsa?"

Molly smiled. "That's as far as the money would take me. I got a job in a diner, then started working my way through community college, then university. For a long time, I knew if I ever saw Bird again, I'd kill him. I didn't dare come back. But slowly the wounds healed." She paused. "Although I don't mind seeing him suffer a little bit."

Finn slapped the table. "After the run-ins I've had with the man, I'd like to see him suffer a lot. And I ain't even seen half what you have, dear Molly."

Linda got up and came to Molly. Startled, Molly stood as well. Greg, who'd moved even closer, stepped back. Linda grabbed her and gave Molly a hug so tight, Molly coughed and started to giggle. So did Linda, but when she held her at arm's length, tears glistened in Linda's dark eyes.

"You must be made of steel, girl."

"She is," Russell said.

"Mostly I'm just stubborn. I refuse to let that old bugger get his way again."

They all laughed, but as Linda released her, she shook her head. "It's more than that. And it explains a lot about why Liz ended up as she did."

Molly sat down again. "How so?"

"It became about holding everything and everyone close," Russell said evenly. "You remember your side of it. But for Liz, she lost her father, her mother, and her sister all within five years. She threw Bird out of her life as much as she could. You and Mickey left. Liz felt lost and abandoned."

Molly felt a twinge of guilt for the first time in twenty years. "I couldn't have stayed."

He nodded. "She knew that. She understood. But it didn't make it any easier on her feelings. In a way, her sister's death and Bird's betrayal laid the foundations of the hoarding. If she couldn't hold people close ..."

"She'd keep their things close," Molly finished.

"Exactly."

"She had Mickey's teddy bear," Linda said.

"She had what?" Molly's eyebrows arched.

"His teddy bear. She kept it on a shelf next to her bed. She said it made her remember good times with all three of you to see it there. It's next to a picture of you with a big white dog."

Molly pressed hard on her upper lip. "Jezebel."

"I beg your pardon," Finn said.

Linda laughed and punched him. "Not me, you old fool. The dog."

"I'm not old." He peered at Molly. "You really named a dog for the most evil woman in the Bible."

A laugh burst from Molly. "Gram did. It was a family joke. Granddaddy had a thing about white German shepherds. Bird knew where he could get one, but made Granddaddy promise to name it Sweet Pea, which was Bird's nickname for Nina."

Finn made an odd gagging sound. Linda slapped his arm. "Hush."

Molly laughed. "Granddaddy promised, but forgot to tell Gram. Or he *claimed* he forgot to tell her. Gram dubbed her Jezebel the minute Bird took her out of the truck. Mama later told me she thought it was a conspiracy between them to let Bird know how they felt about his future wife. Bird was ... not happy. He refused to say the dog's name. Never did, as long as that dog lived."

"What happened to Miss Jezebel?" Finn asked.

"Aunt Liz kept her for a while after I left, but Bird kept threatening to shoot Jezzie. That dog hated Bird. Growled and snapped at him every time he was around."

"A dog after my own heart," Finn said.

"Aunt Liz finally gave her to a farmer up on the mountain. She spent her last years chasing rabbits with a ten-year-old boy."

"A good way for a dog to go," Finn agreed, then stood. "And so should I. Miss Sheila will be most miffed if I don't at least help clean up at the house."

Molly joined him. "I should go as well."

Linda protested. "At least stay for supper. Fried chicken. There'll be plenty."

Despite the temptation, Molly shook her head. She picked her camera off the table and slung the strap over her shoulder. "I need to take care of some things. Lots to do before Monday." She gave Linda and the other ladies hugs, and they all filed out the back door, which slammed behind them, making Molly laugh. Linda shrugged sheepishly.

Russell and Greg followed her toward the Explorer. Twilight had settled over Maple Street, and the last of the sun cast long dark shadows over the lawns. Molly stopped, watching the neighborhood. The squeals and laughter of kids spread over the area. Some of the street lights had popped on, and clouds of night bugs knotted around the domes. Fireflies dotted hedgerows and bushes, and a light breeze stirred, bringing with it the sweet scent of honeysuckle.

"This is nice," Greg murmured.

"It is." She looked at him. "Thanks for this afternoon."

He nodded once. "Welcome back." He touched her arm lightly and headed back to his cruiser.

Molly opened her car door, but realized Russell still stood in front of the SUV, watching the kids. She grinned, but took the time to put her camera back in the bag before joining him.

"Sweet memories?"

"Liz loved this time of day. She'd sit on the porch and rock, listening and watching. It made her happy."

"It would most people," Molly admitted.

"But not you?"

She hesitated. "Please don't push."

He remained silent. "What do you have to do before Monday? Can I help?"

"Can you take that bag to your office tonight?" When he nodded, she went on. "It's clear that this is not a quick turn. I'd honestly thought this might only take a couple of weeks, then I could get back to my life. But this is going to take a lot longer, if not most of the summer."

Russell got it. "Your busy season. This is going to cost you a lot of money."

"Yep. Plus I carry the medical insurance on both my partners, through an LLC I set up. It won't break me. I do prepare for lean times. But it will mean seeking out some of the worst weather this winter, which is also not cheap, but it makes the most dramatic—and sellable—pictures. I also left my computer behind. I need to find a laptop, move to an extended stay hotel with wifi, and start making some arrangements."

"There's a StayLodge between here and Gadsden. Long-term rates and free wifi. And let me take care of the laptop. I know we've got a couple around the office we can spare."

"Thank you. I won't argue."

"If you'll meet me at the office tomorrow before church, say about nine, I'll get you set up."

"Perfect." She got the bag out of the SUV and removed the journal. She showed the first page to him.

"Yeah, that's Liz. If she was going to do this to you, she'd want you to be armed."

She closed it and dropped it on the front seat. "You want a ride back to your car?"

He tucked the bag under one arm. "No, I need to stretch my legs. See you tomorrow."

Molly watched him stride away, hoping she looked as good when she reached his age. She glanced left to see Finn tossing a baseball back and forth with a teenage boy whose red hair had the same wild look. Unlike Russell, Finn moved with a limp, although it didn't seem to hurt or slow him down in the least. An old injury? Sheila watched them from a perch on her porch rail, her face sweet and fair.

At the house in between, a young woman herded three preteens back into her house, while on the other side of the tent, Linda put two fingers in her mouth and blasted a whistle that would peel paint. Her kids responded with catcalls and teases, but made their way in her direction.

"Well, whoever ends up with the house will have good neighbors." She got in the Explorer and backed away from the tent. At the intersection, she checked traffic and started to pull out when she noticed Russell standing next to the big Mercedes in a parking lot on the other side of the boulevard. He paced, speaking rapidly into his cell. She circled around and turned in the parking lot, pulling up next to his car. He spotted her and threw one arm wide, then pointed at his front tire.

A huge gash sliced into the rubber near the rim. Molly stared as she realized all four tires were flat.

She parked and got out, just as Russell snapped his phone shut. "Can you believe this?" he bellowed.

Molly circled the car. One brake light had also been smashed. "Bird?" she asked quietly.

The fire went out of Russell. He sagged against the car and crossed his arms. "My money is on one of the grandsons, LJ or Eddie. Probably while Bird tried to get the tent down."

Molly's eyes widened. "Seriously? That's rough. And risky. There were a lot of people at the house. Someone could have seen them."

Molly paused and squatted next to one of the tires. She ran her fingers over the gash, which was about four inches long. Whatever had done this had been extraordinarily sharp and wielded with strength. As she stood up, a deep chill settled on her spine. "I expected them to come at me, but not this. Do you really think the people who support me in this could be in danger?"

Russell took a long breath and let it out slowly. "After all this started, Kitty let it slip to Shirley that Bird considered his sister's action a betrayal of the highest order. Treason, even."

"As in, 'this means war.'"

Russell nodded.

Molly shook her head, then ran her hands through her curls. "I swear, I just can't get past the part where this is over possessions. Things. Stuff. Objects that mean nothing in the long run. You can't get them in the casket with you."

"You're one of the lucky ones, Molly. Most people rely on their possessions. Security. Status. Comfort. A place to relax. Different reasons. But most people don't take it to the extreme. Bird has migrated to a whole new level of greed that not even the most voracious Wall Streeter could claim."

"Only he doesn't have Wall Street money."

"So he has to use other methods."

"No matter who it hurts." She pointed at the tires. "You call Triple A?"

"And Greg, to report it. Triple A is going to haul it to the Benz dealer in Birmingham, which is the closest. They'll have it back by tomorrow afternoon."

"So you need a ride home."

He shook his head. "To the office. A couple of my associates are there this afternoon finishing up some casework. We'll get the bag into the safe and go ahead and get you set up with the laptop. One of them can run me to my condo."

"I hope Triple-A shows up soon. It's going to rain again tonight." She looked down at the tire again. The four-inch gash seemed to be spreading. "This is going to get ugly, isn't it?"

"Mollybelle, this is just the beginning."

7

The ant wove a jagged, erratic path across the bottom step, in that way ants do, as if looking for food or water in every direction, all at once. It found the one drop that had not evaporated from the baking concrete and paused at the edge of it. Molly couldn't tell if it were drinking, or if so much time had passed since it had seen water, it wasn't sure what it stared at.

"Have some more." She shook her sweating glass and another drop fell, landing not far from the ant. "Better get it quick."

As if listening closely to the advice, the ant scurried to the new drop, pausing there. Neither drop lasted long, scorched to steam by the heat of the steps and the white-hot July sun. Molly clung to the edge of a shade cast by an old mulberry tree. The parched corn in the field next door crackled in a light, dry breeze.

Molly ran her glass of iced tea over the back of her neck, feeling the icy drops sliding underneath her dress. Trickles of short-lived relief. She raised her gaze heavenward. "No storm yet, but this heat could bring one on. He couldn't have died in winter? You had to take him in the middle of the hottest summer in years?"

"Squirt. Who ya talking to?"

Molly took a long drink of iced tea before deigning to answer her brother, who stood behind the screen door of the house. The sweet, frigid liquid chilled her throat, but not much else. "God. You gotta problem with that?"

Mickey snorted. "Like I thought. Talking to yourself again. What are you doing out here?"

"Couldn't stand the crowd inside anymore. Everyone wants to pat my cheek and tell me how sorry they are."

"Mama wants to know if you're ready to go."

"As I'll ever be."

"Gram's looking for her gloves. Then they'll be ready."

Molly downed most of the tea. "Gloves," she said to the ant. "Craziness in this heat." She turned the glass up and poured the last sugary drops on the step. "Here. Dessert."

She stood and brushed off the back of her skirt. She arched her shoulders, annoyed by the rivulet of sweat that slipped down her spine. Molly headed back into the house, pausing inside the screen door to let her eyes adjust to the dimmer light. In the spacious farmhouse, Molly could see straight through to the back porch, which looked like a bright beacon at the end of several darkened rooms. The west-side drapes were already drawn against the afternoon sun, tied back only enough to allow a breeze through the almost-lowered windows. The house buzzed with the sound of window fans and the dozen or more cousins who'd come to offer hugs and casseroles in exchange for a ride to the funeral.

"They aren't all going to fit in the car," Molly murmured.

"They just want to be seen arriving with the widow." Mickey sat, spraddle-legged, on the couch.

Molly frowned. "Why?"

He shrugged. "They think it'll put them in line for more stuff."

She brushed a fly away from her face. "Stuff? What stuff? Granddaddy died, not Gram."

"Doesn't matter. Gram isn't going to keep the farm going, so she won't keep all his things. I already heard Mother on the phone, taking offers on the tractor and the attachments, and fighting with Uncle Bird because she wants to sell it instead of giving to him."

"That's just wrong. He already has a tractor. A nice one. And Granddaddy's not even in the ground yet."

"Grow up, Squirt. People like stuff. They want it, they want more of it. And if they think they can get it free, they'll cluster around dead folks like flies on a hog."

"That just ain't right."

"Ain't a matter of right or wrong. Just is."

Molly rolled the glass between her palms. "I won't ever want anything that much."

Mickey stood up and locked the front door, then sauntered out of the room. "Then you'll be one of the lucky ones."

Molly followed him, his words stuck on repeat in her mind. In the kitchen, she dodged through a cluster of relatives so she could set her glass in the sink. She tried to escape out the back door, but a maternal hand grasped her arm. Molly waited patiently while her mother smoothed her black dress with her hands, then ran her fingers through Molly's unruly brown curls.

"I don't know why I bother," her mother murmured, her voice a bit shaky. "Your hair always does just what it wants to."

"And has for the past fifteen years."

"Just like your daddy. Do you have a brush in your purse?"

"Not carrying one." Molly looked over her mother's face, her heart aching at the sight of bloodshot eyes and blotchy makeup. "Mickey said you were selling the tractor."

Her mother paused and glanced over her shoulder, as if someone might hear, then cleared her throat. "I was thinking about it. I know you and Daddy spent a lot of time on that tractor, but we could really use the—"

"Sell it all."

Her mother froze, looking more closely at Molly. Concern narrowed her blue eyes. "Molly, honey, you never want to make such a big decision in the midst of grief."

Molly kept her focus on her mother's eyes. "If you don't, the vultures will pick Gram clean. She's so kind, she'll give it all away, even stuff she needs. Aunt Liz too. She won't stand up to them. You'll have to take over."

Her mother cupped Molly's face in her palms. "Don't worry. We'll take care of Gram. Family takes care of its own. That's what we do."

"Barbara asked her for some of the quilts this morning. Kept saying they were for Kitty's hope chest."

Her mother hesitated, then started to respond, but the door on the opposite side of the kitchen opened, and Molly's grandmother emerged, clutching a pair of black lace gloves. Aunt Liz followed her, teary-eyed and red-faced.

"Found them!" Gram exclaimed, waving the gloves. She looked around, searching through the sea of faces until she spotted Molly and her mother. "Regina, let's go now. Please."

The buzz of a disturbed beehive filled the kitchen as the cousins swarmed her, chattering softly. Gram accepted them graciously as she gently but firmly pushed her way to the back door. The crowd pushed by Aunt Liz, separating her farther and farther from Gram.

Molly and her mother exchanged quick glances, then headed that way as well. Outside, her mother grabbed Aunt Liz by the arm, then shoved their way to Gram. Dark looks and grumbles followed as the sisters entered the waiting limo. As the cousins vied for the remaining spots in the two black Lincolns the funeral home had sent for the family, Molly whispered a quick prayer.

"God, save me from this. Save me from stuff."

Molly jerked awake. The dream hovered with bright, harsh colors and twisted images, unlike the hot and gritty reality of the actual day, which still hung in her mind all too vividly.

The covers suddenly felt oppressive and smothering, the Southern humidity making the entire world feel damp. Molly flung them back, gulping deep breaths. She sat up and dropped her feet over the side of the bed. She reached for the lamp, needing to be free of the dark, and glanced at the clock. Only eleven; she'd barely been asleep.

"'One of the lucky ones.' Right." She stumbled to the air conditioner and turned it down two degrees.

She'd had the dream before, but not in a long time. She knew it had been brought on by her revelations that afternoon in Linda's kitchen. She prayed that everything before her with Aunt Liz's house would not make her continue to relive the pain of those last couple of years in Carterton.

For twenty years, Molly had put it behind her and healed. She had a great life, one carefully built and embraced. She didn't want it destroyed by two years from her teens.

Molly picked up her phone and typed in *Pls I need to hear from you. Pls. Hope we're okay.* She hit the key to text Jimmy, not caring what time it was. Her heart craved connection to the world she loved.

As usual, Jimmy heard, and he read between the lines. The returned text came through with few abbreviations.

> *Sorry. Lots going on but not much to tell. Swelling has lessened but not gone. Still in a coma. Her family's here. It's been hectic. I called the tv stations; they're cool. I've been working on the pictures and videos when I can. May have something to send them anyway. Taking care of y'all. Not mad. Just thinking.*

Molly smiled. The three of them—Jimmy, Sarah, and her—this was her true family. One of their own making. Siblings, with Molly the older sister, and the three of them looking out for each other. When Sarah's boyfriend dumped her a year ago, Jimmy offered to beat him up, only half joking. As they had all grown closer, Molly thought maybe Sarah and Jimmy would make a good couple.

Russell's call had, indeed, come at the worst possible time. They'd been shooting a storm, a supercell that had produced a fabulous F4 tornado, when debris struck Sarah. They rushed her to the hospital, and were still in the surgical waiting room when Molly's phone started ringing and wouldn't stop. After she finally answered it, she and Jimmy had fought—she wanted to ignore the summons; he insisting she go and get closure. Jimmy finally convinced her that she couldn't make Sarah well, that it was finally time to handle her family's issues, once and for all. Blood family.

But not her real family.

Sarah had to get well. She *had* to.

Her phone pinged again. *What about you? How's the house?*

Molly punched to reply and began one of her longest texts ever.

* * *

The rest of the night passed dreamless, and Molly slept until almost nine. After a shower and a vending machine breakfast, she called the StayLodge and made arrangements to move. She couldn't check in until three, but had to be out of her current room by eleven. Molly packed the few things she had in the room, secured her camera bag, checked out, and headed back into Carterton, hoping to find a restaurant or library that offered free wifi.

On the way, she spotted Linda Allen's minivan parked in the crowded parking lot of the red-brick Baptist church. On the other side of the boulevard, the Eccles' crimson pickup stood out among the cars massed around the white clapboard Methodist church. Most of the stores along the boulevard remained dark and closed, as did the tiny town library. A couple of restaurants posted hours that started at 11:30.

"Right. Sunday in the South." She did a U-turn in one of the breaks in the boulevard and pulled into a parking spot marked for visitors at the Methodist church. Almost every other spot had already been taken. The ancient marquee in front of the steps announced that the congregation had been founded in 1859, which made it slightly older than the town itself. Sunday school started at 9:15. Service at 10:45.

"So some things in Carterton haven't changed. Wonder if they still have coffee between 10:15 and 10:45." Probably. Molly remembered when she'd been old enough to ask about those peculiar times. Gram had explained that they'd been set in the late '60s when they'd shared the sanctuary with a black congregation that had lost their building to a Klan fire. *"We wanted to show that evil would not consume us. You have to take a stand sometimes, otherwise evil wins."*

The community was scandalized, but they persevered. With the new arrangement, the white folks would be gone by 11:45, and the black folks would take over at noon. The black church had been rebuilt and the congregation hadn't worshiped in the Methodist chapel since 1969, but the Methodists had voted to retain the new service times. Gram loved the reason for that as well. *"As it turned out, it put us at the restaurants before the Baptists let out. And we got home before the football games started."*

"Welcome to Alabama," Molly whispered, "where we stand against evil, fry up great chicken, and make football a third religion. Right after the Methodists and Baptists but before the Presbyterians."

Her phone rang and she dug it out of her clutch. Jimmy. Eagerly she answered. "What's the news?"

His gentle baritone couldn't contain his excitement. "I'm on the way over to the hospital. Her dad just called. The swelling is down, and they're going to try to bring her out of the coma."

Molly's spirit soared, and her eyes stung. "Oh, hallelujah! You'll let me know what happens."

"You know it. I'll call as soon as I can. They said it could take several hours before they know anything for sure."

"No problem. I'm moving into a hotel with wifi, and Russell has hooked me up with a computer. Not doing anything with the house today. It's still stewing in the pesticides. So I'll be around. Don't forget."

"Oh, I won't. Did you get some rest after the dream?"

"I did. Pretty good. Texting with you helped, I think. How are you doing? I know you're worried about Sarah. Getting any rest?"

Jimmy hesitated. "Molly, you'd have to see her to understand this, but she looks so peaceful. Like she knows she's going to heal just fine, and we're all crazy for running around like this."

"Maybe she does." Molly paused. "Do you talk to her?"

"I do. They think coma patients sometimes know what's going on. I told her you'd run off to Alabama to take on your uncle. You know that would make her laugh. Oh, and I told her that she and I—"

Molly thought for a moment the call had dropped. Then he cleared his throat and went on. "Listen, I need to mail you something. Could you send me the address at the hotel?"

"Sure. What is it?"

"A surprise. I'm about to turn into the hospital garage, so I'll lose you. Remember to tell me lots about tomorrow's unveiling. Miss you, girl."

With that, the call went dead. Molly leaned her head back and relief flooded through her. She stared up at the church steeple. "Thank you," she whispered.

Her phone rang again, and she lifted it quickly, thinking Jimmy might be calling back. She froze when she saw the caller ID, then answered slowly. "Molly McClelland."

Sheriff Greg Olson's voice was somber. "Molly, could you come to the station? Now."

She swallowed hard. "Has something happened to the house?"

"No. But we caught Lyric Filbyhouse trying to cut her way through the tarps."

Molly's elation over Sarah vanished in a poof. "Are you kidding? Does she not realize how dangerous that is?"

"Apparently not. Lyric has never been real quick on the uptake."

"Did she damage the tarp?"

"No. The deputies caught her before she got the knife in."

Molly felt confused. "Why do you need me? I really don't want to cross paths with Kitty. It's been a good day so far."

Greg cleared his throat. "That's just it. Lyric didn't want us to call her mother. She asked us to call you."

Molly's confusion deepened and her voice squeaked. "Me? Why me?"

"She won't say. Molly, this is your decision. You don't have to come. We can charge her with trespassing and violation of the restraining order and let the system work."

"What would happen to her?"

"She's insisting we don't call Kitty. She's not a minor so we don't have to. She'll stay in our holding cell tonight, then go before a judge tomorrow. It'll be up to the judge whether she's fined or held over, although she'd probably be allowed bail."

Curiosity began to edge out confusion. "What do you think?"

Greg hesitated. "Molly, to be truthful, I don't know Lyric well. No one does, not really. She seems slow, but that could be the result of Kitty's browbeating."

"In other words, you're as curious as I am."

"It is a puzzle, to be sure."

"Okay. What's the address?"

Molly plugged his answer into her GPS and backed out of the visitor's spot. Carterton had grown, but not so much that it took more than ten minutes to traverse the length of the town. The sheriff's department resided in a utilitarian concrete block building at the western edge, noted by one small sign near the parking lot entrance. The four green-and-white patrol cruisers next to the front door clearly identified what lay inside.

She entered a small lobby filled with hard plastic chairs and dusty silk plants. To her left, a young woman ensconced behind thick Plexiglas motioned her toward a heavy metal door to her right. She hit a buzzer to allow Molly into the main bullpen of the sheriff's department. The low hum of an active department greeted her, and a couple of the officers looked up and nodded at her. She recognized them as some of the men who'd stood guard on the house.

Eight desks clustered in the bullpen, five of them occupied. At the far end of the building, three empty cells waited patiently. In a glass-walled office on the opposite side of the room, Greg Olson sat behind his desk, typing on a keyboard with a rapid, two-finger style. He paused to peer at the screen, then typed more. As she headed for him, he caught her movement and looked up at her. He stood, motioned her to enter his office, and held out his hand as she did so.

She shook it. "I didn't think Carterton was the county seat. Why is the sheriff's department here?"

He smiled. "Pineville, the county seat, grew enough that they got a city police system. We were … inconvenient. It's better for us over here. They take care of the county seat and we take care of the rest of the county."

"Small town politics."

"Yes, ma'am."

"So where's Lyric?"

"I put her in one of the interrogation rooms. We want to record your chat."

"Isn't this a little odd?"

"Definitely. A lot odd. And normally we wouldn't grant her request. But, to be honest, it's made us more than a little curious. She doesn't want a lawyer. Or her mother. Just you."

"Turns things on its ear a bit."

"More than a bit."

"I definitely want it recorded. I don't trust any of them right now. And I don't know why she trusts me. Could you be in there as well?"

"I have to. Are you ready?"

"As I'll ever be."

When they entered the room, Lyric, who had been staring at her hands, stood abruptly and backed away from the table, startling Molly. "What's wrong?"

Lyric took a couple of deep breaths. "Oh, it's you. Good. I thought it might be Mama coming in." She appeared visibly relieved to see Molly. Today her hair was pulled back in a tight ponytail, and she wore dark jeans and a loose black t-shirt, which made her appear smaller than before.

"Sit down, Ms. Filbyhouse," Greg said evenly. As she did, he motioned for Molly to take the chair opposite Lyric. "We're going to video this interview for the protection of everyone involved." He moved to the corner, where a video camera sat, and adjusted the focus. He started the camera, then remained close to the door in a casual "parade-rest" stance.

Molly eased into the straight-backed metal chair. The block room epitomized the word "gray"—gray walls, gray table and chairs, gray floors. No windows broke up the solid bulk of the walls, and recessed lights were at least twelve feet overhead.

"Sheriff Olson said you wanted to see me."

Lyric clutched her hands together, fidgeting her fingers around each other. She stared at the table, but nodded, making the ponytail bounce.

"Why?"

Lyric stilled, her gaze still on the table. A few moments passed in silence before Molly spoke again.

"Lyric, why did you try to cut into the tent? That was incredibly dangerous. The pesticide gas is still in there. It could have poisoned you."

Lyric's words spurted out in a burst. "Did Bird really take your house and throw you and your brother out? Is his house your house? Was your house?"

Molly's eyes widened, then she nodded. "Yes. And my mother's. It was a long time ago, but you don't forget something like that."

"He tried to do it to me."

"What do you mean?"

Lyric glanced up, meeting Molly's eyes briefly. She looked down again. "We didn't know about you. That you would inherit it all, I mean." She stopped, rubbing her cheek with her shoulder, wincing. "We thought—" She hid her face in her hands.

"Go on."

The words came out in a rush, so fast Molly struggled to follow the girl's thoughts. "Mama's wanted me out of her house for a while now. She has a new boyfriend, so I'm kinda in the way, if you know what I mean. When Aunt Liz needed somebody to stay with her, Mama jumped at the chance. She thought moving me in with Aunt Liz would give me a place. Set me to inherit. We thought I'd get the house. We even talked to Aunt Liz about it, telling her that I would be the best to get everything, that I could take care of it, even though it's a really big house, but there's a lot of good stuff. But I overheard LJ—"

"Leland's son."

Lyric stopped cold, staring up at her. "What?"

Molly glanced at Greg, but he gave no sign. She looked back at Lyric. "LJ. He's Leland's son, right? I just want to get it straight."

Lyric looked puzzled a moment, as if she didn't understand the comment. "Yes. Leland Junior. Everyone calls him LJ." Lyric's eyes narrowed. "You really don't know us, do you?"

Molly scowled. "Why would I know who any of you are? When I left, your mother was eighteen and just married. Kitty is a distant cousin I only talked to at family reunions, like most of my cousins. Bird's sons were like Mickey and me. Leland wasn't married. Bobby had just joined the service. No one my age had children, and most of my cousins I knew by sight, but not personally. I've not talked to anyone except Aunt Liz in more than twenty years."

"Mama says you're lying. That Aunt Liz kept you informed. She wrote to you all the time."

"And I burned the letters when she talked about anything from here. Lyric, I begged her not to leave me a scrap. I would rather have walked hot coals than be here, and I'll be leaving as soon as I can carry out Aunt Liz's wishes."

"Do you know if I'm in her will? It would really help if I was."

Molly hesitated. This time, it didn't sound like one of Bird or Kitty's demands. For some reason, Lyric was really hurting. "To be honest, Lyric, I don't know. I haven't had a chance to look at everything she left, including the will. Some of her instructions are in the house."

Lyric looked down at her hands again. "She was good to me, Aunt Liz was. She didn't always like me, but she was good to me, to let me stay there. She knew what Mama was like, so she didn't push me out. I thought I might get to stay there after she died, maybe even inherit, but at least until things got settled. Then I heard LJ say they were going to 'pull a McClelland swap' on me when Aunt Liz died. Do you know what that means?" She peered at Molly from under her bangs.

Molly's chest tightened, and she tamped down the anger. Now was not the time. She gritted her teeth. "I suspect I do."

"I didn't know what that meant, but it sounded as if he knew Aunt Liz was going to die. Then she did. But before anything could happen, that lawyer swooped in and changed the locks and shut everyone out." She glanced down again. "I didn't even get a chance to get my stuff out."

"Is that why you tried to cut in?"

Lyric nodded once, staring at her hands.

Molly leaned back, still squelching the urge to take on Kitty and Bird in a parking lot somewhere. With this level of anger, she knew she'd win. She pressed her lips together and glanced at the stoic sheriff, who shook his head, just once.

"Mama doesn't know. I didn't tell her. She thinks he's on her side against you."

"Bird is never on anyone's side but Bird's."

"I just want my stuff. Daddy said I could come live with him, since Mama wants me gone so bad. He's down in Birmingham. But Mama said no."

"Lyric, you're over eighteen. You can live wherever you want."

Lyric looked up. "Really?"

Molly looked around at Greg, who nodded. "Lyric, what's his name?" he asked. When she told him, Greg left the room.

"Why do you think your mother doesn't want you around?"

Lyric shrugged. "She told me. Thinks I'm lazy. She doesn't want me to go to Daddy because it's Daddy. They've been divorced fifteen years and she still hates him."

"Do you have a job?"

Lyric shook her head. "Mama says I'm too stupid to keep one. No one would hire me because I'm fat and slow."

"Did you graduate from high school?"

For the first time, Lyric smiled. "Yes, ma'am. I did pretty good. I like to read. No one bothers you when you read."

"If you graduated, you should be able to get a job. Get your dad to show you how to fill out the applications."

Lyric brightened. "You think so?"

"You know that country star whose t-shirt you had on the other day?"

Lyric nodded.

"Didn't he drop out of high school?"

Lyric blushed, then smiled shyly. "Yes, ma'am."

"You'll do fine." Molly stood. "I'll be right back."

As she left the room, Greg met her in front of his office. "Her father is on his way. I explained the situation, and he couldn't get on the road fast enough." He paused. "She doesn't seem 'slow' to me, just unaware. You don't think anything is really wrong with her, do you?"

"No. More like she's been kept in the dark. Her mother's done a number on her, which doesn't surprise me. Nothing wrong with her that a good boost of self-esteem and a little praise couldn't help. And a few years away from Kitty. Ever get the urge to take a horsewhip to some parents?"

Greg sniffed. "Molly, my dear, you have no idea."

She ran her hands through her hair. "I can't believe it. A 'McClelland swap.' He's so proud of it, he brags about it. Still. Even his grandsons know about it. And none of them even acknowledge that any of it is illegal."

"Because they don't care."

She dropped her hands to her side, surprised. "What?"

He took her arm and guided her into his office. He gently pushed her into one of the chairs, closed the door, and sat next to her. "Molly, law enforcement in a town like this isn't as cut and dried as it is in larger towns."

He took one of her hands, and Molly found herself mesmerized by his focused gaze and firm, even voice.

"Investigations here often run on information. Who knows what and who is willing to share what they know. Physical evidence isn't always available. Men like Bird and LJ know that, and they believe their goals, their desires, outweigh everything else. The needs of others, the law. It's not that they believe themselves above the law. It's just irrelevant to them in terms of what they want to do. If the law interferes, they try to find ways to use it to their advantage or get around it. But it's not a consideration when they set out. Bird wanted your grandparents' house and saw a way to get your mother to sign it over. That he was engaging in grand theft and blackmail never even occurred to him. He wants Liz's house, and he probably worked with Kitty to get Lyric into Liz's good graces, hoping she'd leave the estate to Lyric because she felt sorry for the girl. He knew she wouldn't leave it to him. Thus he planned the same setup to grab the house. He would have found a way to blackmail Lyric out of it, knowing this child wouldn't have a clue what was legal and what wasn't. He set up the dominoes. Unfortunately for him, someone knocked the first one over before the plan was complete."

Molly, who had felt calmer as his words had flowed over her, felt slapped by his last sentence. "You think someone killed Aunt Liz?"

He remained silent a few moments before he continued, no expression in his face. "It appears to have been an accident. The coroner ruled it an accident."

"And there's no evidence to indicate otherwise."

"No."

"So it would depend on finding out what people know."

"Yes."

"Can I borrow a notebook and pen?"

Greg looked puzzled at first, then smiled. He released her hand and stood up and pulled a legal pad off his desk. He handed it and a pen to Molly. She and Greg returned to the interrogation room, and Molly pushed the pad toward Lyric.

"I want you to make two lists, Lyric. One is all the stuff you left in the house. Just what's yours. The second list should be a list of things you'd like to get from Aunt Liz."

Lyric shook her head. "But I don't know everything that Mama wants. Not really."

Molly handed her the pen. "No. I don't care what *Kitty* wants. I just want a list of what *you* want. I need to go through everything Aunt Liz left me, in terms of who should get what, but I'll keep your list too. I'll get what's yours to you, but I'll keep what you want in mind as well."

"Oh." Lyric looked thoughtful for a moment. "Can I put the pill bottles on here?"

"The pill bottles? What's in the pill bottles?"

Lyric shrugged. "No idea. But LJ told his brother that they needed to make sure they grabbed all the pill bottles. I knew that must mean something, or they'd never have mentioned them."

Molly had to agree with her logic, especially where that family was concerned, and it gave her the opening she needed. "Good thinking. And write down anything else you can think of that LJ said that might be important. You got this."

Lyric smiled at the compliment, then she looked up at the ceiling, lost in thought. Slowly, she nodded to herself, then started to write.

8

While Lyric wrote, Molly went to pick up lunch for the younger woman. She exchanged a fast-food meal for the lists, then left Lyric—and the information Lyric had shared in her formal statement—in Greg's care. She found a coffee-and-sandwich place that hadn't yet been hit by the Sunday lunch crowd and tucked her laptop under her arm, intending to settle in with a roast beef sandwich and their wifi.

Located in an old stone house near the train depot, Bailey's Garden Bistro had ancient hardwood floors, weathered barnwood paneling, and a wooden counter polished to a slick sheen by thousands of hands. The building had been a restaurant of some kind as long as Molly could remember, but her grandmother had told her it was once part of a large icehouse business. The storage area for ice blocks had been demolished in the early 1960s, when electric refrigerators finally put the last of the ice boxes on the back porch, even up on the mountain.

When the door closed behind Molly with a wood-on-wood squeak, a pierced and tattooed cashier looked up from her texting, and her greeting spoke of a better mood than Molly expected. "Morning, ma'am. What can I get ya?"

Molly scanned the blackboard menu behind the counter, amused by the flower-and-butterfly artwork that circled in and around the list of food. Someone had gotten bored. "Um …"

The cashier suddenly brightened, hopping off her stool. "You're Miss Liz's niece! Aren't you? I know you are. With that hair, you have to be."

Molly stared at her, admitting with caution, "I am."

The girl jabbed a fist in her direction. "Dude! You rock!"

"I beg your pardon?"

The girl bounced up on her toes, causing her jet-black pigtails to bounce. "You … you gave old Bird Morrow the smackdown he's had coming for years! Oh, my God, we are still crowing about that!" She whacked the counter with her palm, but her voice dropped to a conspiratorial tone. "We all hate him around here, but no one's had the guts to stand up to him. He's so freaking mean, him and his kin, all of them. Girlfriend, you killed it!"

Molly had the odd feeling she was being punked. She looked around, unsure of what to say. Fortunately, she didn't have to say anything. The cashier kept talking.

"Anything you want. Anything. On the house. On. The. House. Can I take your picture? Seriously, my friends are not going to believe you came in here to eat. Eddie and LJ have been bullies our whole lives. Whole lives! We're begging that you take them down too. Picture? Please?" She thrust her phone toward Molly.

Molly hesitated, then nodded. The girl scurried out from behind the counter, cell phone in hand. She threw an arm around Molly's waist and pressed their cheeks together, reversing her camera to take the selfie. She immediately typed in a quick message and sent the picture. She looked up at Molly again.

"I'm Amanda. Seriously. Anything you want."

Molly spoke gingerly. "A roast beef sandwich and an iced tea?"

Abruptly, Amanda was the cashier again. "Sweet or unsweet?"

"Half and half?" Linda's sweet tea had reminded Molly exactly how *sweet* Southern tea could be.

The young girl headed back behind the counter again, still grinning. "White or wheat? Cheese? Chips or fries?"

Ten minutes later, Molly had pressed her back against a wooden booth, computer up and running, when Amanda set a basket of sandwich and fries, along with a moist glass of iced tea, in front of her. When Molly nodded thanks, Amanda responded, "No. Thank *you*!" before bouncing back behind the counter and resuming her texting.

Molly took a bite and one more time read through the email she'd started for Jimmy. She'd summed up the events of the last two days and included the address for the new motel. She took a deep breath and continued typing:

Please let me know something soon. I know you will, and I hate that I keep repeating it, but it's murder not being there with you and Sarah, every step of the way. I know this makes me sound like a control freak . . . don't laugh. I can hear you laughing.

Truth is, I miss both of you. I know we argued over this, but I'm glad we're okay. Even though I now believe you were right to insist I come, I feel as if I've entered a foreign country. Even though I was eighteen when I left, I remember so little, I'm playing twenty years of catch-up. And it's not just the places and people. It's the way of life; the way of thinking about things. I know not everyone in this town is the same way, or even in my family. At least that's what Liz wrote. But it's hard for me to get my head around their motivations, the reason they act the way they do.

Like Lyric. She's almost twenty! Why does she put up with the way her mother acts? If she wants to live with her father and he wants her, why would she not go before now? It makes no sense to me. Aunt Liz once wrote me that my desire to rid myself of all things toxic had destroyed my sense of family. That there was a way to deal with toxic without running away. Maybe there is, but apparently she didn't find it.

Anyway, don't forget about me, your stranger in a strange land.

Molly hit send. She picked up her sandwich, glancing again at Amanda behind the counter. Bird was obviously toxic. The entire town knew it. Toxic and untrustworthy. Even the sheriff wouldn't turn his back on the man. Had they lived with Bird so long he had turned into a town fixture? Had he just been careful not to step over a line, or was Greg right about gathering evidence and information? Were the consequences of speaking out against Bird too great for the people who had to live here to chance it? She knew Greg would have arrested him given the chance.

She glanced at Amanda. Maybe being an outsider did give her an advantage no one else had. Maybe. Molly shook her head. She needed to focus on why she came into the bistro in the first place. Internet access. Rolling her shoulders to ease some of her tension, Molly turned her attention to searching "Ways to Clean Up a Hoarder's House." The details that emerged from the internet enlightened and worried her. Warnings about diseases spread by the rot and vermin. Suggestions for Do-It-Yourself cleanups and recommendations for agencies licensed and prepared to do it for a fee.

Molly weighed that option. Obviously, the quicker she rectified the situation, the faster she could get back to Jimmy and Sarah. She knew most likely no one would be in the office, but she sent an email to a cleaning agency in Birmingham and left her contact information.

Wouldn't hurt to find out.

But an agency would only clean. She still needed to deal with all the family possessions. After a few more bits of research, Molly opened a spreadsheet document and began to plan.

An hour later, she drifted back to the internet and opened her Facebook page. She grinned when she realized Jimmy had posted two of the latest shots from the Missouri storm. A sense that was almost giddiness enveloped her as she read through some of the comments. She was definitely in the right profession.

She sent Jimmy a quick private message to thank him for putting them up. She looked up and liked the page for Bailey's Bistro and wrote a quick recommendation. Her newsfeed, filled with the usual weather warnings, links to meteorological articles, and suggestions that she check out this or that system kept her attention for almost half an hour. As she shut everything down and prepared to leave, the bell over the door dinged, and a short, lean blond male sauntered in. His jeans, tight, torn, and oil-smeared, scuffed the floor as he walked. His formerly white t-shirt, equally filthy, hugged a muscular frame. Tangled hair sprouted from underneath a dark cap.

"Hey, Amanda."

The laconic drawl got a grimace from the server. "Hey, LJ. What are you doing here?"

Molly went on alert, every nerve on edge.

"She still here?" LJ asked. He glanced around, his gaze lingering on Molly.

Amanda froze. "Who?"

No games. Not with this crowd. "I'm still here, LJ." Molly slid her laptop into its bag, draped her purse across her body, and stood. "What do you want?"

He strolled toward her, a rolling walk, a thug wannabe, who was at least three inches shorter than Molly. His last step was abrupt and close, as if he expected her to back up. She didn't, and he put his left index finger against her shoulder, right over the collarbone. "What do I want? I want you to leave town and stop interfering in my family's business. You have no place here. That house is *ours*." He pressed the finger harder.

It hurt, but Molly refused to flinch. Instead, it added fuel to the flame building inside her. She stared at him, unmoving. "Have you ever seen what a board picked up by a tornado can do to a man's head?"

He scowled, confused. "What?"

"I have. It'll split the skull right open, dump brains right into your lap."

His lips curled. "What the—"

With a sudden jerk, Molly grabbed the finger against her shoulder and bent it backward. LJ hollered and dropped to his knees. She grabbed his jaw with her other hand and pressed hard as LJ's right arm braced against the floor. Molly put her face close to his, almost nose-to-nose. She pushed harder against his finger and heard the knuckle crack. LJ screeched. "Tell Bird it's *my* house. You keep messing with me, and I *will* burn it to the ground. Just like he does what he wants to with what's his, I will too. And you have no idea what's in *my* will. Stay away from me."

She thrust him away from her, and he toppled to the floor, clutching his hand. She grabbed the laptop case and strode out of the bistro. Once out the door, she ran for the Explorer, locked the doors, and backed away from the building. LJ exploded onto the porch, screaming something she couldn't hear. Gravel flew as she skidded out of the parking lot.

Molly's hands shook on the wheel so badly she didn't want to keep driving. She headed toward Gadsden, but when she reached the gas station at the edge of town, she pulled in behind it, out of sight from the road, and parked. Her mind spun in a hundred directions as she took long, deep breaths, trying to calm herself. In … hold … out. Repeat.

Why did I do that? She'd never done anything like it before. Hadn't even been sure what she planned to do when it started. Assault. It was assault. Technically she'd assaulted a young man. He could have her arrested. Press charges. Could she still get a restraining order on him? Wasn't he covered by the ones on Bird?

The thoughts felt endless. They raced in nonsense circles. She couldn't keep doing this. Couldn't try to fight fire with fire. She couldn't. She had to be proactive, not reactive. But how? How could she get in front of this?

Her phone dinged. Startled, she yanked it out of her purse. A text from Greg. *What? Why?* She opened the message.

You okay?

She stared at it. Did he know already?

Why?

Amanda posted a video on the town's Facebook page. You're going viral.

Nausea swept over her. No. Oh, no … Her fingers still quivered as she struggled to type a response: *How much trouble am I in? Do I need to come see you?*

You can come see me anytime. But you don't need to for any legal issues.

She gaped at his text. *Is he flirting? Now? No. Ignore it. Don't misread …*

I assaulted him. He'll press charges?

No. Given the comments, he won't dare. Not to me. You made him a laughingstock. But watch your back. Where are you?

Hiding behind the BP at the edge of town.

Good choice.

Heading to the feed store for supplies.

We'll meet you at the house. Stay on guard.

Will.

When no response came back, Molly dropped her phone back in her purse. Until that moment, she had no idea what she'd do next, but stopping in at the feed store made all the sense in the world. And the text chat had left her calmer and breathing normally again. *Can't hide behind a gas station forever.* She put the Explorer in gear.

Carterton Hardware and Feed had been in the same location since 1932, after the store down the road a bit, built in the 1800s, had burned. When the road through town had been paved in the late 1940s, they had graded through the small rise where the new store sat, leaving it to look out over the new road and the stores across the street like a castle on a hill. The road cut had been reinforced with sandstone and concrete, adding to the stately feel of the store's presence. Molly eased the Explorer up the hill and parked near one end of the building. For once, she hoped that something in Carterton had not changed in twenty years, and she opened one of the double doors leading inside.

Memories flooded back. The scent of the store remained a pungent blend of dog food, dried corn, and oil with a hint of rubber. The concrete floors were shiny black from age and thousands of boots and bare feet. As a kid, Molly had often run up and down the aisles barefooted, the floors cool on her summer-heated toes. Just called "the feed store" by the locals, it had always carried much more than the usual hardware and farm supplies. Fifty-pound sacks of flour lined the shelves, along with stocks of tools, overalls, work shoes, and seed packets. A freezer case at the front held homemade meat pies and ice cream. An ancient Coke case stood near it, the chest kind containing bottles that hung down from metal racks. Molly had begged Gram for a bottle many times, more for the fun of sliding one along the racks into the release mechanism and removing the bottle by giving it a great tug upward than for drinking it.

"Molly? Molly McClelland?"

Molly stared at the older woman who stood behind the horseshoe-shaped counter at the front of the store. Wiry, over-dyed brown hair had been forced into the curls of a 1950's hairstyle and a shift-style apron covered an ample bosom and balloon-like hips. A pair of reading glasses with cheetah-print rims perched on the end of her nose.

"Betty?"

"Lordamercy, girl. You're a sight for sore eyes. Get yourself over here and give me a hug." Betty Holcomb waddled out from behind the counter, an image frozen in time, unchanged from Molly's remembrances. A few more wrinkles. A few extra pounds.

Molly trotted toward her, and they grabbed each other in a hug Molly had been missing for twenty years. Molly closed her eyes and leaned her head on Betty's shoulder as the older woman rubbed her back. When they parted, Betty held on to Molly's forearms, peering at her over the top of the cheetah glasses.

"I'd heard you were back in town, figured it had something to do with Miss Liz's passing. Don't tell me she left you that nasty ol' house."

Molly didn't try to hide her surprise. "You knew about the house? About the hoarding?"

Betty tipped her head to one side in a half-nod. "Honey, everybody in the county knows about that house. And ever since the sheriff's men showed up to keep Bird and Nina out, rumors been flying about what kinda treasures she had buried in those walls and who she left it to. But, Lord, I never thought it'd be you. We all knowed how you felt about that, ever since what Bird did to your mama."

"It did come as a shock."

Betty let out a throaty laugh that bespoke of thirty years of cigarettes. "I bet it did! Come on back here and set a spell." Betty headed back behind the counter, motioning for Molly to follow. "These old legs don't like standing in one place too long." She slid one hip up on a tall wooden stool, then braced against the counter to complete the process. She gestured toward another stool.

"I am surprised you're open on a Sunday afternoon." Molly hopped up on it and looked around. "The store hasn't changed much."

Betty's smile held a bit of sadness. "Nope, unlike the rest of Carterton. We did update the inventory system. Open Sunday 'cause I need to cast a bigger net these days, what with the competition. And I don't much like being home alone." She paused, her voice dropping half an octave. "You know Whit passed on a few years back?"

Molly nodded. "Aunt Liz mentioned it in one of her letters. I'm sorry. He was always good to me."

"He thought the world of you, girl. Used to say, 'that Molly, cuter than a spotted pup under a little red wagon. Wish I could be her daddy. She needs one.'"

Molly pushed down an abrupt wave of sadness. "He pretty much was, you know."

Betty patted Molly's arm. "He hated what happened. But he understood, we all did, why you had to leave, you and Mickey. Didn't blame you in the least. But he sure did miss you both. We knew Liz tried to stay in touch, but we figured y'all needed to get away from all of this."

Molly tilted her head to one side. "Did she write Mickey as well?"

"Tried for a while. What about you?"

"You know he joined the military when he bolted from here?"

Betty nodded. "The Marines, if I remember."

"Yeah. Mama wrote him before she died, but I stayed angry with him for a long time, for leaving us both. No idea what happened after that."

"Liz had an APO address for him, and I think they corresponded for a while. Once his time was up, I'm not sure what happened. He visited a couple of times … then just … nothing. No more Mickey. I told her the military might help find him if she were next of kin, but she waved me off." Betty peered at her over the cheetah rims again. "You're his next of kin."

Molly shook her head. "Too late. And he didn't exactly try to keep up with me."

Betty sat a bit straighter and let out a long, drawn out sigh, one of an exasperated mother. "Stubboner than a deaf mule, the both of you."

Molly laughed. “Maybe so.”

“So did you drop in just to catch up, or …”

Molly hopped off the stool. “Not just. I need help getting that house taken care of.” She counted off on the fingers of one hand. “I need four of those tent-like picnic shelters—”

Betty pointed. “Pavilions. Very back of the first aisle.”

“Cleaning supplies and heavy-duty garbage bags—”

“All that’s midway down this aisle here. Make sure you include some baking soda. And some vinegar. They’ll help with the odors.”

“Gotcha. Some big boxes …”

Betty paused. “Oh, I’ve got some castoffs from the last shipment of overalls in the storage room in the back. Sturdy ones.”

“And some poster board and markers for signs.”

Betty shook her head. “Probably will need to get those down at the Dollar General. We try not to compete with them and the Walgreens on things like office supplies. Doesn’t do any of us any good to do so. But you’ll need a hammer?”

Molly raised an eyebrow.

“Not for Bird. For the tent pegs.”

Molly laughed. “Oh, yeah.”

“Tools are on that far left aisle over there. Although from what showed up on the Facebook, you don’t need much to take care of yourself.”

“You have a Facebook account?”

“Best free marketing there is. I’m on all the Carterton pages. And I always knew you were feisty, but heavens, girl. You took down the town’s biggest bully after Bird.”

Molly closed her eyes, the heat rising in her cheeks. “She shouldn’t have posted that.”

Betty’s laugh echoed off the walls, and she clapped Molly on the shoulder. “Are you kidding? We’re all loving it. That crew deserves to have their butts handed to them. Did you know the other one was out there too?”

Molly froze. “What other one?”

Betty looked surprised. “You didn’t know someone caught it on their cell? Several folks actually. They end with you shouting for them to get off your lawn?”

Molly sank hard against the counter. "No. I didn't. How bad is it?"

Betty tilted her head again, a quizzical look on her face. "Girl, it's not bad. This whole town is thanking God for you. Like I said, we all loved Liz. You have to remember, she taught at the elementary school for more than forty years. Most of the folks here had her for fifth grade. She was beloved like no one's business. Ever'one was worried sick Bird would steal her blind. That you are handing it back to them in spades has made you a local celebrity."

"But it may be putting me in their sights."

Betty sobered. "Yep. It will do that. But if anyone's up to it, it's you. You've already proved it."

"Not going to make this any easier."

Betty pulled her into another hug. "Why in the world should it be easy? This is a wound that's been festering for twenty years. Lancing it is gonna burn." She squeezed Molly one more time, then pushed her back. "Now. Where were we? Lawn chairs? We got some of the cheap ones in the back. About eight bucks."

"Betty, what would I do without you?"

"Pshaw! Stop. Do you need lawn chairs or not?"

"I think Finbar is going to loan us some."

"So you've met Mr. Finn, have you?"

"Oh, yeah."

Betty took off the glasses and tucked them into her ample cleavage. "They're good folks, Finn and Sheila. Grieved him a'mighty for Liz to go the way she did, before anyone could really help her. Just about broke his heart. Poor man wailed almost like he'd lost his own mama."

"So I can trust him?"

"More'n most. Oh, I think you already know who you can't trust around here, missy. Most of Carterton is not like your uncle and his sorry kin. Whoooo-ee!" Betty whistled. "If one of 'em gets arrested for murder, no one would be surprised."

"Murder? You serious?"

Betty paused. "Nah … probably not. Maybe. Anyway, no one around here will have anything to do with 'em. You know what happened to Mr. Russell's car, right?"

"Too bad no one got that on video." Molly suddenly shivered, imagining what might have happened had Russell arrived too soon.

Betty shook her head. "Even if they did, no one would snitch on them. LJ and his stooge Eddie are fearsome."

"Why haven't they been arrested?"

Betty shrugged. "What is it the cops always say? One thing to know it, something else to prove it. They always make it hard to prove anything. And even if people know what's happened, by the time it gets to the sheriff, it's all hearsay. So we all know ..."

"But nothing can be done."

"Yep. You need any help loading?"

"I got it. You ring it up, I'll load it."

Molly headed toward the first aisle, pausing at the Coke machine. She glanced back at Betty. "Still work?"

Betty's grin turned lopsided. "You know it, hon. Service guy comes once a month. It's become a point of pride for him to keep it working."

Molly laughed and turned down the aisle. She'd get the drink before she left. Thirty minutes later, the back end of the Explorer bristled with equipment. She paid, chunked a Coke out of the machine, hugged Betty, and headed toward the StayLodge, where she checked in and left most of her personal belongings. She stopped at Dollar General long enough to get the poster board and markers, then headed back to Aunt Liz's house.

She stopped in the driveway, staring up at the puffed out tent for a few minutes before getting out. A sheriff's car sat on the roadside in front of it, and after a few moments, Russell and Greg got out as she did, questions on their faces.

Greg spoke first. "You sure you're okay?"

Molly smiled. "I just spent an hour with Miss Betty. She makes all things right."

Greg chuckled. "That she does."

Molly looked Russell up and down. "I thought your car would be back by now, and you'd be off playing golf or fishing with a judge. You look more like golf."

Russell gestured to his polo shirt and khakis. "Too dressed up for fishing. But I forgot and left the clubs in the trunk of the Benz." He checked his watch. "They're probably delivering it to my condo as we speak. My garage guy will sign for it. What are you up to?"

"Putting a plan in motion."

"Yeah?"

She waved an arm toward the front yard. "After they take down the tent, the cleaning will start. I've contacted an agency in Birmingham, but I'm not sure they'll be interested. Anyway, we'll start by dragging everything out of the house that can be easily dragged. Obvious trash goes in the dumpster." She pointed toward the boxes sticking up over the tailgate of her SUV. "I'm going to set up four pavilions. One for things that need to be cleaned and returned to the house. Stuff that's good enough but not part of the inheritable distribution will be divided into 'Free' and 'Two Dollars.' The last tent will be for resting and refreshments."

Greg crossed his arms. "Your uncle will not be happy."

Molly shook her head. "Don't care. If they want to pick through kitchen utensils and old clothes, they can do it somewhere else. I'm sure there are families around here that need stuff like that more than they do."

"I'll still keep a man around."

"I appreciate that. I'm sure Bird has more patience and vigilance than I ever will."

Russell glanced at the equipment. "Want some help?"

"Absolutely!"

They went to work, and once again the activity on Liz's lawn drew the neighbors out of their houses. Two of the local teens joined in, and the five of them made quick work of setting up the pavilions. Finn wandered over, chatted for a bit, complimented her on her self-defense techniques.

She winced. "So has everyone seen that video?" Molly couldn't believe it had spread so fast through the town.

Finn nodded vigorously. "And they're loving it. Don't fight it, Miss Molly. You may get a lot of help because of it."

Molly licked her lips. "Then I'll be grateful."

He held up a finger. "Hang on with them signs. I got something that'll help." He headed home and returned with a grommet punch and fishing line so the poster board signs could be hung more securely from the front of the pavilions. He also negotiated rights to the refreshment tent, assuring Molly that anyone actually working in the house would be given free drinks and food.

"Ever thought about buying a McDonald's franchise?"

Finn scowled at her, shoving his cap back on his head. "Of course not. Making it real work would take all the fun out of it. Besides, Miss Sheila likes me home weekends. Hey, boy, let me help with that." He called over to his son, who was trying to hold one of the pavilions upright and still hammer the peg into the ground.

Molly felt Greg behind her before he spoke, his low baritone quiet, for her ears only. "You know, when Amanda started filming that, she thought she was going to catch LJ doing something vile. She had no idea she was about to catch Carterton's latest hero in the making."

"Oh, stop." She turned. His smile was kind, and a spark in his eyes made them shine. "I honestly had no idea I was going to do that."

"No, but it was a good move all the same. And it was obvious that you prepped for a fight, the way you packed up and tucked everything away."

"I was preparing to run."

He chuckled. "But you didn't. He expected you to back down. People always do when he goes at them like that. You didn't. That's what has people talking. No one has had the nerve to stand up to them."

"I'll probably pay for it later."

"Probably. They'll try."

She looked around the yard for a moment. "I don't want to keep fighting them, Greg. I need to find a way to get in front of this, and not keep reacting to them. Any ideas?"

He looked at her, his eyes pensive. "I'll put my thinking cap on."

"Please do." She crossed her arms. "So did you get Lyric off to her dad?"

"I did. And I don't know why what you said worked, but she was like a new person by the time she left, chattering to her dad about getting a job, and about some guy she's crazy about. I'd never heard of him, but she kept talking about him being so sweet and caring. Her dad was eating it up. Different from Kitty as daylight and dark."

"High school sweethearts gone wrong?"

"Way wrong."

She laughed, and he touched her shoulder gently. "Seriously. Thanks for helping with her today."

"You're welcome."

They fell silent a moment, just watching each other, and Greg let his hand drop. "I have to keep reminding myself you've only been in town since Friday."

"Me, too. Of course, I've got history here." She hesitated. "Just not with you."

"Not yet." He grinned.

She laughed and turned to check on the new setup. Greg stepped closer, resting his hand on her back, a comforting, protective gesture that made Molly feel secure and grounded.

For the first time, Molly felt as if she truly had a plan in mind to handle the house. She just prayed she wasn't deluding herself, but she couldn't quite shake the feeling that all of this would get a lot rougher before it got better. That feeling of being grounded wouldn't last. But it was a place to launch from.

That night, she had a brief email from Jimmy that underlined the idea that this was going to be one of the longest darkest journeys of her life.

> *The swelling is down; they've stopped the meds that kept her in a coma. But she's not waking up. They aren't sure yet why. You should also know that her father has called a lawyer. He plans to sue you. This has changed my prayers, but not much. I just want her to wake up, to come back to us, even as peaceful as she seems.*

Molly shut down the computer, lay across the bed, and stared at the ceiling. The flickers of a silent news station reflected off the ceiling and walls, a mirror of the chaos in her soul.

God, you promised you'd give us the strength to get through whatever life dumps on us. I hope that's still true. I'm going to need a lot of it.

Molly waited in the solitude for an answer, but even God was quiet tonight. Her mind had finally slipped into a doze when the sound of the first shotgun blast rocked the silence of the room.

9

Molly screamed, bolted up, and dropped between the two double beds in the room. She snagged her phone on the way down. Another blast from the shotgun sounded as the 911 operator answered.

Molly shouted, "Someone's shooting at the StayLodge!"

The third shot rocked her door. Pellets penetrated the wood, lodging in the wall behind it.

"They shot my door!" Molly dropped the phone. She grabbed her gun case off the nightstand. She popped it open, removed the Glock 9mm, inserted the magazine, and pulled the slide back to chamber a round. She braced her back against the nightstand and drew her knees up. She could still hear the operator calling to her, but she didn't want to let go of the gun.

She clenched it tight in both fists, listening, waiting for the next blast. In the distance, sirens wailed. A motor revved in the parking lot, then came the squeals of tires on pavement. A motorcycle.

Molly didn't move, every muscle tensed. When she heard the big V-8s of the sheriff department's cars roar into the parking lot and the shouts of friendlier voices, she lowered the gun, shaking hard. She shoved the Glock beneath the mattress, then wrapped her arms around her knees, trying to control the shaking. But she didn't stand until Greg Olson called her name through the door.

"I'm here!" She pushed slowly off the floor and stumbled to the door. She couldn't believe how relieved she felt to see him.

Greg's eyes widened with concern. "Are you okay?"

She nodded. "I'm shaking right down to my boots, but I didn't get hit." She looked at the door, which was riddled with shotgun pellets. "Not so much my poor door."

"Not just your door."

"What?"

"Are you all right to walk?"

She nodded, even though her knees still felt weak. Greg reached to take her elbow. When she stumbled off the sidewalk, he wrapped his arm around her waist, steadying her. They moved out into the parking lot, now awash in flashing red and blue lights. Three cruisers clustered in front of the motel, and an ambulance sat just beyond them, the EMTs out and on alert, waiting for a signal to move in. Most of the guests had started edging out of their rooms, peering around doors and leaning over the second floor rails.

Greg motioned to two of his officers. "Start the canvass. Find out if anyone saw anything. Check with the night manager about surveillance." They headed off, and he turned Molly so she could see the rear of her Explorer.

The rear glass lay on the ground, splintered. The back end of the SUV had been dimpled and pierced by hundreds of pellets. The cleaning supplies she'd bought had been scattered around, stomped and broken. Spray-painted across the blue tailgate were the words "Go Home or Die" in white.

Fear turned to rage, and Molly felt her heat rise from her gut into her face. "Son of a—" She cut off the word and turned to Greg. "You know who did this, right! Bird! LJ! One of their evil minions."

He nodded. "Did you see them?"

She barked a harsh laugh. "Ha! I was too busy cowering between the beds."

"As you should have been."

He studied her so closely, Molly wondered if Russell had told him she had a gun.

His voice was annoyingly calm. "You know you were right earlier. You need to get in front of this. You can't fight fire with fire."

"Revenge is best served cold."

"Molly." He drawled out her name into at least four syllables of warning.

She crossed her arms and looked at the back of the Explorer, a different idea easing into her head. "You wouldn't happen to know where I could get some spray paint this time of night."

Greg started to shake his head when one of the deputies spoke up. "I got a couple of cans in the trunk." At his sheriff's startled look, he shrugged. "Took 'em off some kids trying to tag the water tower last night."

"They still do that around here?" Molly asked.

"They try," Greg answered. "Seniors. Every year about this time. What are you going to do?"

"Answer their demand. Then start cleaning this mess up."

"Let us get some pictures first."

She nodded, then closed her eyes and stiffened her spine. If Bird had been in front of her at that moment, she might have beat his head in with one of the broken broom handles. Or, possibly, shot him. Greg was right. Neither was a good idea. But this underscored that she couldn't remain reactionary to their behavior. She had to find a way to get in front of all this.

Someone cleared his throat, and she opened her eyes to see a deputy holding out a can of red spray paint. She took it. "Perfect. Thank you."

One of the other deputies called to Greg from across the parking lot. "Sheriff! You gotta see this!" He jerked his thumb back toward the manager's office. Molly followed Greg as he strode over. The three of them crowded behind the front desk, where four small monitors displayed images from the cameras around the property. Two were aimed at the front desk, fore and aft, and one showed the back parking lot. The fourth one was pointed at the front parking lot, currently crowded with cruisers and bystanders. The monitor for that camera, however, had been rewound to earlier in the evening and showed a quiet parking lot. The time stamp was from before the attack.

Greg nodded at the manager. "Play it slow, Leon."

The slow-motion image showed a small blue, black, and purple motorcycle head into the parking lot and spin into a 180-degree turn, ready to pull out again. It carried two rather small and lithe people, dressed in all black and wearing ski masks. The rider slid off and sprayed the words on the tailgate. He tossed the can to the driver, then pulled a pump-action shotgun from a holster strapped to his back. He pointed it at the Explorer and pulled the trigger. The glass exploded. He backed up, pumped and hit the Explorer again. He stepped around the SUV, pumped the gun, and fired at the door of Molly's room. He holstered the gun, then started pulling the supplies out through the SUV's broken window and stomping and kicking them. After a few seconds, he mounted the bike and they sped out of the lot.

Molly sighed. "Obviously too small to be Kitty, Nina, or Bird. And you can't see a license plate."

The deputy snorted. "Don't need one. You recognize that bike, don't you, Sheriff? That's LJ's bike."

The manager looked up at him. "Leland Junior?"

Greg nodded. "Yep," he said slowly. He looked at Molly. "The same bike he reported stolen this afternoon after his encounter with you."

* * *

The shooting incident had taken less than five minutes to occur. The aftermath took more than three hours. The deputies made pictures, started the paperwork, helped Molly pick up the trash and tape a thick but clear plastic sheet where her rear window should have been. She kept the spray paint only long enough to draw a red line through the white words and write, "No!" over the end of the word "Home."

When she was done, Molly stepped back and studied the results.

Greg Olson walked up beside her. "Defiant much?"

She grinned. "Since I was fifteen." Still staring at the back of the Explorer, she asked softly. "Where are you from?"

He hesitated, glancing at her. "You so sure I'm not from around here?"

"You're Southern, but you are not from central Alabama. Around here they don't just flatten vowels, they squash them with an iron skillet and stretch them out in the sun to dry."

He snorted a laugh. "My folks were from Pell City, but Dad joined the army before I was born. I'm a military kid, lived all over. Folks around here say I don't sound like I'm from anywhere."

"So you sound like you're from everywhere."

"Something like that." He put his hand on her arm, turning her toward him, his face somber. Molly had an idea what might be coming, but she just waited. This was his call.

He glanced toward the door of her hotel room. "You have a gun in there." It was not a question.

"And a permit."

"I know. I checked."

"I figured you would. Did Russell tell you?"

He nodded. "You didn't shoot back."

"Nope. 911 is always the first choice. And nothing to shoot at. I wasn't about to put my head up and give them a target, just to take a look. They didn't come through the door. But I did pull it out. And would have pulled the trigger if they got in. I would have defended myself."

He waited. After a moment, Molly relented. "I have it because of what I do. I've mostly used it on snakes and rabid animals. Storms stir up a lot of unexpected activity. I've had to fend off a looter or two. Shot at a gator once, mostly to make it go away. I'm trained. Right now, I'm a single woman on the road alone. And I knew this situation might turn ugly." She looked back at her SUV. "I didn't know it would be this ugly. This quick."

"Try not to shoot Bird."

Molly peered closer at him. He was completely serious. "You think I would?"

"I do. I think you want to, more than you realize. Your anger about Liz runs close to the surface, and your rage about what happened twenty years ago keeps it fueled. That's why you reacted the way you did to LJ today. It's become almost instinctual."

She gestured at the truck. "They haven't exactly shown remorse for destroying our lives."

"You know what they say about revenge."

She cocked an eyebrow, a reminder of what she'd just said.

"No, I mean the one about digging two graves before you embark on it. Just keep in mind that he's not worth the cost. None of them are."

Molly focused on the back of her SUV again. "As I said. I have to get in front of this."

"You do. I've come up with an idea, but you'll need to talk it over with Russell. And it won't be easy."

"Sheriff?"

They both turned to the young deputy who approached. Greg motioned for him to speak.

The deputy cleared his throat. "Um … they … I mean, one of the patrols … they found the bike. It's in a ditch not too far from here."

Greg's lips pursed in disgust. "Let me guess. Near the Davidson cut-through."

The deputy nodded. "Yes, sir. They must have left the bike and hiked back over to the lake."

"Okay. Impound it. Call one of the Johnson brothers and have them haul it over to the garage. We'll look at in the morning." The deputy strode away, and Greg turned back to Molly. "It'll be useless for evidence, but we'll still go over it. They left it at a trail that cuts from the highway over to a lake near Bird's farm. Local kids use the lake for fishing, and they take the cut-through after school, then someone picks them up there. My guess is that they had a car waiting at the lake."

"I remember. And no traffic cameras."

"The only ones the city has are at the red lights in town. Some of the stores might have one pointed at the road. But if they had a car at the lake, they used the back roads to get away."

"So what's your idea?"

He reached for her arm again. "Let's get you settled in another room first, then we'll talk."

* * *

Molly sat on the passenger side of Greg's cruiser, staring at her childhood home. Now Bird and Nina Morrow's home. She wasn't sure that Greg's idea for "getting in front of it" would work … and she could already feel a painful twist in her stomach. Russell had been doubtful as well, but thought it might be worth a try.

Greg had picked her up for breakfast and talked her through how the morning might go once they got to Bird's. It was already nine, but there was not a lot of activity to show if anyone was awake. Molly could hear a tractor somewhere in the fields beyond, but doubted it belonged to Bird or anyone in his family. The land around the house remained a working farm, mostly because Bird rented out the fields and barns to neighboring farmers who kept them tilled and planted.

The sun rose behind them, shining on the house, and the mid-morning rays revealed a light dust in the air as well as a general ambience of decay. The house had not fared well under Bird's tenure. The porch sagged, the paint peeled, the roof buckled. Sprouts of grass burst from the gutters, making the house appear as if it had a bad haircut. The mulberry tree had grown, its canopy now completely shading the front porch, but the steps where she'd spent much of her childhood had pulled away from the house, canting to the left.

And the memories stung. Even the happy ones, times spent with Mickey or her grandparents, felt tainted, as if they had been spoiled by what came after. The house no longer represented any happiness for her. Just loss and an unrelenting ache.

This is going to be harder than I expected. Molly straightened her shoulders, however. A sense of determination to get this whole business over and done with pushed her on.

Greg touched her hand. "Ready?"

Bird strolled out of the house, wearing only jeans and an undershirt. He casually picked his teeth with a toothpick as he glared at them. Nina followed him out, looking equally unprepared for unexpected visitors. Her boxy housedress reminded Molly of something from the 1940s.

"As I'll ever be," Molly responded. "If we sit here in the car together any longer, the rumors will start."

Greg snorted. "Don't kid yourself. They already have." He paused. "There are also rumors about Leland."

"There have been rumors about Leland since the day he was born." She remembered those all too well, and had once felt sorry for her shy cousin. Two years older than Mickey, Leland had been born eight months after Bird and Nina had been married, which only added to the rumors. As a boy, he'd been dark and lean, in opposition to his parents and siblings, who were all blond, short, and slightly round. Bullies often used him as a mark, and for years, Leland had just accepted the taunts. Finally, one day he fought back, and the pestering scattered like autumn leaves.

"This is different. You might want to prepare yourself."

"How so?"

"He's not doing well."

Molly glanced at him, but he didn't elaborate. Instead, he opened the door and got out. She followed, hanging back just a bit.

"Y'all get off my property," Bird called out. "You ain't welcome here." He gestured at Greg with the toothpick. "And I don't want you arresting me because she's getting close to me. It won't be me violating that order. In fact, after what she did, you should be arresting her."

Leland pushed open the screen door and stepped out, letting it slam behind him.

Molly bit her lip to keep from gasping. She hadn't seen him in twenty years, but the change in him shocked her. Leland had always been lanky but wiry, with taut muscles, tanned skin, and a movie-star face. Now he was skeletal, his skin yellowish and taut, drawn thin across flaccid muscles. Purple shadows sat in hollows around his eyes, cheeks, and throat. He wore a tank top and khakis, and his shoulders, elbows, and wrists stood out like knots on a pine branch.

Molly winced as an odd thought hit her. *He looks like Mother before she died.* And the last images of Regina McClelland flashed behind her eyes, the same dark hair standing out against a yellowish, skeletal-thin frame, with muscles that could barely support her, as if she'd been consumed from the inside. *Oh, dear Lord. Leland's dying.*

He nodded at her. "Hey, Molly." His voice was rough and laconic.

She yanked herself back to the present and returned the gesture. "Leland."

"I hear you're as feisty as ever."

"I guess word gets around."

He gave her a weak half-smile and dropped into a rocker near the end of the porch as if all his energy had suddenly vanished.

The screen door slammed again as a sulky LJ came to stand next to Bird. A cross between the two other men, his cyclist's build was even more prominent in only cargo shorts. Blue eyes glared at her, the rage palpable in his face.

"Like Granddaddy said," he called out, his focus on Molly. "Y'all need to get outta here. Haven't you done enough?"

"We found your bike," Greg said to the younger man.

LJ straightened and turned to Greg, his eyes narrow. "Where?"

"Probably right where you left it."

"I told you that bike was stolen!" He took one step down off the porch, but Greg didn't budge. LJ stopped, crossing his arms. "I don't know where it was. When can I have it back?"

"Not for a while."

"Why not?"

"It was used in the commission of a crime. While that's being investigated, it'll remain in impound."

"A crime?" LJ twisted around to look at his grandfather, true confusion on his face. Bird remained impassive, but Nina shook her head and turned away, pressing a hand to her mouth.

Leland leaned forward, resting his elbows on his knees. "What kind of crime?"

"Attempted murder."

"What?" This time, LJ was genuinely stunned, and Nina turned around, wide-eyed.

Bird came off the porch with two strides, and he poked a finger at Greg. "You are not here accusing us of murder!"

"Daddy ..." Leland stood, a warning note in his voice.

"My grandson reported that bike stolen—"

"Daddy!" Leland's shout finally got Bird's attention, who backed off, running his hands back and forth over his head.

Leland focused on the sheriff. "Greg, tell us what happened, if you can."

As Greg explained, Molly watched the Morrows react. Bird's eyes widened and his jaw slackened. He glanced hastily at Leland, then LJ, then his wife, and back again at Greg. LJ sat and crossed his arms, hunching into himself. The rage dissipated from his face as he stared at his shoe tips, leaving something akin to miserable confusion. Leland, as he always had, took the news placidly, nodding occasionally. Nina developed a thousand-yard stare across the fields.

"Shooting the back of someone's vehicle is vandalism. Shooting into their door can give us a case for attempted murder." Greg stepped closer to LJ. "This isn't a prank, LJ. Not this time. This is jail time, when we find those responsible. Do you hear me?"

LJ nodded, the fight gone out of him. "She had it coming. But I had nothing to do with it."

Bird and Leland exchanged a long look, then Leland nodded. Bird turned to face Molly. He took a deep breath and braced both feet in a wide stance. "Look, I won't lie. I want you gone, and I'll do anything I can to make that happen. You have no right here, and no right to inherit. Liz had no right to do what she did. I'm next of kin. That house is full of our stuff—"

"Daddy …"

"—but you're blood." He held up a hand to stop any further protest, even though Molly had not moved. "Now I know what we did to Mickey, but he shouldn't have tried to stop us—"

Molly stiffened, and Bird pushed on, talking over her. "—but we never would have seriously hurt any of you. We certainly never would have shot you."

Molly crossed her arms, and her words were tight, forced. "You forced us out of our home."

"This house was rightfully mine. I'm the boy. Daddy had no cause to—"

"Molly, we didn't do this," Leland interrupted. He stood and took careful steps to the edge of the porch, although it clearly required a major effort. He wrapped an arm around one of the posts, leaning heavily on it. "Isn't there some compromise here?"

Greg looked at Molly. The ball was in her court. She looked at each of the Morrows in turn, still marveling that she'd come out of the same bloodline. Was there a compromise? There were certainly a lot of things in the house no one would have any use for. Finally, she settled her gaze on Leland.

"Maybe there is. Maybe." She uncrossed her arms. "Look, I'm sick of this fight. You say you don't want to hurt me. I don't want to constantly be on guard and angry with you. Can we call a truce?" She looked from Leland to Bird.

Bird hesitated, then nodded. "Go on."

"What's done is done. No going back. Let's go forward. I'm going to follow Liz's instructions as best I can—" This time it was Molly who put up a hand to stop protests. "But her specific bequests don't cover everything in the house, as far as I can tell. Let's start this way. Y'all be patient, and you get Kitty on board with that."

"Lyric could be an issue," muttered LJ.

"Lyric's in Birmingham with her father," responded Greg. At their startled looks, he shook his head. "Lyric is out of the picture for now. We have addressed her concerns."

LJ and his grandmother stared at each other a moment, then Nina shook her head once, an indication that this would be a topic for later discussion.

Molly went on. "I've set up four pavilions in front of the house. Once the tenting is done and taken away Tuesday morning, we'll start dragging everything out of the house for cleaning, sorting, and tossing. I'm also having a dumpster delivered. A lot of what's in that house is just trash." When Nina started to protest, Molly talked over her. "That's not an opinion. I'm not convinced Lyric *ever* threw away a McDonald's container."

Molly stood a little straighter, not entirely sure what she was about to say was wise or prudent. But they did have to find a way to get through this. "You want to come by every day, see what we're doing, that's fine. You can take anything in the 'Free' pavilion or the dumpster, and you can make a case for anything else you want. But you don't take anything else until the will is probated, and we've gotten through what Liz wanted me to do. When we're done and I put the house on the market, you make any reasonable offer. I won't turn it down."

"What about the restraining orders?" Bird asked.

Molly glanced at Greg, then back at Bird. "You keep the truce—no more attempted thefts, no more shotgun blasts in the middle of the night—I'll ask the judge to waive them."

Bird chewed his toothpick. "Y'know, some of that stuff is ours. Ya got no right to give it away."

Molly shrugged. "Then you shouldn't have left it with her. Should have brought it over here. If you've got a bill of sale, I'll hand it over. But I'm not taking any of you at your word. You've given me no reason to trust you beyond what I've already laid out. You gotta list? Bring it to the probate hearing."

They looked at each other, none of them wanting to acquiesce, but seeing few options. Nina stepped forward, her voice whispery. "If you find any pill bottles, don't throw them in the trash. I use them in craft projects at the kids' Sunday school. Can always use more."

Molly kept her face impassive. “I’ll keep that in mind.” She focused on Bird. “Do we have a deal?”

Bird sniffed. “As long as you keep your side of it.”

Greg took another step toward LJ. “This does not get the shooter off the hook. If you know who did this, it would be better for them to come down and talk to me about it.”

LJ shrugged one shoulder, but kept his eyes focused on his hands.

Molly and Greg returned to the cruiser but said nothing as he backed the car away from the house. Finally, as they headed down the road, Molly cleared her throat. “What do you mean, there are already rumors about us?”

10

The tent coming down wasn't quite as much a circus as it was going up. Good to his word, Taylor Eaton and his crew opened the tent Monday evening, installing huge fans to begin moving out any remaining chemicals. Although no odor came from the chemicals, the smell of the sealed-up house created a perimeter of decayed reek that stretched over several houses. Molly apologized to her neighbors, but they waved her off with some good-natured ribbing. Finn even commented that it was worse than when old man McNally fertilized his fields with chicken manure ... but not by much.

Still ... they all kept their distance, and most left for school or work about the time that Taylor's trucks rolled in the next day. Molly wandered about, documenting everything with her Canon. But Tuesday morning by ten, the sides had fluttered to the ground, and the boys had begun the meticulous task of rolling up and packing away all the tarps. Taylor took a few final readings, then gave her a checklist to follow, and with an awkward sideways hug and good wishes, he and his team boarded their trucks and rumbled away.

Molly stood in the yard, again looking up at the house. Every time she did, she saw something else that needed to be repaired or replaced. Liz too had been dismayed by the condition of the house, listing in her letters all the ails that she had no energy to address: *My painted lady has withered and wrinkled. She needs a facelift and a makeover.*

"Indeed she does," muttered Molly, turning the camera on problem areas. The vines covering the porch's latticework had shriveled and faded from the pesticide, accentuating the house's sad, wounded look. "Better days," she promised. "We'll see that you have better days coming."

The signs on the pavilions swayed in a light breeze that also caused some of Molly's curls to bounce and whisk about her face. It was a good day to begin such an endeavor, with sun reflecting off high cirrus wisps. April could be unpredictable in Alabama, so she was glad that the forecast gave hope of almost a week of sun, light breezes, and mild temperatures. Another Tyvek suit from Greg waited in the Explorer, but for now, she just stood and took it all in, occasionally letting her sharp artisan's eye aim her camera.

Memories flooded over her, most from before the Great Rift, as Aunt Liz called it. While the old farmhouse no longer held happy memories for her, the Victorian certainly did. Molly and her cousins tearing through the house, which rang with squeals and shouts. Aunt Liz's laughter and her "Now, children, slow down," delivered in a completely nonserious and teasing voice. Liz loved having people over, even on rainy days when the kids would roughhouse upstairs or invade the attic while the adults talked downstairs. Although if there was a whiff of secrecy from the adults, the kids knew how to gather on the stairs at just the right spot where they could hear but not be seen.

That's how Molly had found out about Bird's greedy antics, which had started in his teens. She heard the news about at least four pregnancies among the cousins, and that Leland's younger brother Bobby would be joining the army. Those babies were all grown with kids of their own now … and Bobby stayed overseas after his time in the service. He'd seen too much of the world outside Carterton. He'd married a Frenchwoman, and his family lived in Paris. Bird had, of course, disowned him.

Then, another memory peeked through, making Molly's eyes widen. She must have been seventeen, after the rift, spending the night with Liz during one of her mother's night shifts. Liz had thought Molly asleep, but an unexpected visitor had come to the house, and Molly snuck out to eavesdrop. Soft voices had remained indistinct, but when Aunt Liz walked him to the door, Molly caught a glimpse of the handsome black man in a three-piece suit. Molly had been shocked by their kiss.

Molly grinned. "Russell. Did you know I was there? Is that why she sent you away so quickly?"

The low rumble of car engines and the sound of tires on gravel pulled Molly from her reveries. She turned and her eyebrows arched as three sheriff's cruisers pulled up, and six officers got out, including Greg. He sauntered over to her with a cocky grin on his face.

"What are y'all doing here?" Molly asked.

"My day off, and I told the boys I was coming over to help." He motioned toward the others. "They volunteered. We even brought our own Tyvek suits."

She snorted a laugh. "Haven't they put in enough hours at this house?"

He leaned closer and stage-whispered, "They also recognize that the faster the house is cleaned up, the quicker they can stop the extra patrols. And who knows? They may wind up on a viral video."

Now Molly's laughter was genuine. "Okay! I get it." She turned to the others. "I need to do a quick walk-through first, take some pictures, then I'll start divvying up the tasks. I'll make sure we get lunch." She looked back at Greg. "There's a case of water in the back of the Explorer. We can set it out under a tree so it won't get too hot." She motioned at the SUV stationed out of the way under one of the ancient oaks. "I'll order pizza, sandwiches, and drinks from Bailey's in an hour or so."

She gestured for him to follow her to the Explorer, where she pulled out her Tyvek suit and tore open the package. As she stepped into the suit, she asked, "Have you heard anything about the bike or the shooters?"

Greg shook his head. "No. We've looked at surveillance recordings from a couple of stores in the area, where their cameras pick up the road, but nothing yet." He paused to help Molly shrug the suit up over her shoulders. "And I suspect we won't until someone who knows them steps up."

She paused to pull the bottle of Vicks out of a pocket in her shorts. She wagged it at him. "Thanks for this, by the way. I'm hoping I won't need it much longer."

"Keep it. We keep one in our cars at all times."

“Thanks.” She smeared the ointment under her nose, dropped the bottle back in her pocket, and zipped up the suit. “So you think we may never know who the shooter was.”

He paused and studied the house for a moment. “I wouldn’t go that far. A lot of folks in this town loved Liz, and they love this house. And they aren’t all that fond of Bird and his ilk. The comments on those videos of you put an exclamation point on that. My guess is someone will overhear something whispered to someone else, and the whispers will fly around town like a crow looking for corn. Some secrets are just too sweet to keep.”

Molly grinned. “Life in a small town.”

“It has its good points and its bad.” He paused. “And LJ is not the only grandchild.”

“I thought Bobby was still overseas.”

Greg sniffed. “He is. But remember RuthAnn and Tommie Jane are still here. They have seven kids between them, and all of them idolize Bird. Their patriarch.”

“Ah. I forgot about the girls. They were still in elementary school when I left.” Molly’s heart ached. She hated to admit she’d had hope for the girls. “I had thought that after watching what happened with Mama they might have escaped the family curse.”

“Tommie Jane tried. She got a scholarship to Alabama, but Bird made her turn it down. Told her she’d be disloyal to the family to leave. She and her husband run a Dollar General in Attalla. The kids stay with Nina and Bird during the summer. RuthAnn’s boy Eddie is as bad as LJ ever thought about being. They hang out a lot together.”

“You think it might have been Eddie on the bike?”

“Maybe. He’d certainly know where LJ keeps the keys. And he’d feel loyal enough to him that he might take revenge for what you did. Young men and humiliation aren’t a good mix.” Greg straightened as if the subject were closed. “Is there anything you want us to do while you do the walk-through?”

She nodded toward the side of the house. “There are tables for the pavilions over there, along with three or four tarps. Could you get your guys to set up the tables and spread the tarps on the lawn close to the house? They’ll be the initial dumping area. And as soon as the dumpster gets here, anyone who doesn’t care to brave the house can start taking down all that latticework and the vines.”

He nodded and took the Tyvek package from her and pulled out the mask, booties, and gloves, holding them out. She pulled the hood up and pushed all her hair under it, then tucked the booties and gloves under her arm and draped the mask over her wrist by its elastic band. She snagged her camera and turned toward the house. Greg walked with her until she stopped on the steps. "Wish me luck."

He shook his head once. "Between God and your sense of determination, you, my dear, do not need luck."

Molly stared at him a moment, an odd twist of joy swelling in her stomach. She wasn't sure about the God part, but she gladly recognized the blessing in not having to do all this alone. She pushed the thought—and the feeling—aside and nodded, whispering. "Thank you."

On the porch, she double-checked the booties, then pulled on the gloves and mask to make sure she had no exposed skin. Taking a deep breath, she pushed open the door.

She half expected the ominous sound of skittering claws. Only a hot, oppressive silence surrounded her. No rats. That was a good sign. After a few steps, she checked her legs. No fleas. No roaches. Nothing.

But everything else remained the same. A stench that made her eyes water despite the ointment under her nose. The overwhelming, unending piles of memories and rubbish. Antiques stood alongside the broken remnants of dime-store furniture. Squaring her shoulders, Molly took the first pictures—left, right, down the hall, and up the stairs. Then she moved forward carefully. She had made a mental list of what she had to do first, and she would tackle them one by one.

Flip the main breaker to turn on the electricity so they could have lights and hot water, but keep the HVAC unit off. They would have windows and doors open for days. No need to waste power. The same with the fridge and freezer. Everything inside would need to go, and both appliances scrubbed and disinfected. Check Aunt Liz's room for journals and pill bottles.

She took photographs of the kitchen and as far down the basement as she could poke the camera. She moved on to Aunt Liz's room, taking several shots of every tableau in the room—the bed and shelves, Lyric's nest on the couch, even the strewn containers where she suspected Finn had found her aunt.

The room felt eerier than it had before, although Molly wasn't sure why. Maybe because she knew more about what had gone on in here. She picked her way to the bed. She paused, gazing over the shelves behind it, most of them stuffed with books, magazines, bills, file folders, and junk mail. But as Linda had said, in a clear spot near the head of the bed, one of the shelves held a raggedy and ancient teddy bear and a picture of Molly and the white shepherd, Jezebel.

They were both within easy reach of the bed, and Molly reached for the bear. Ten inches tall, the bear had matted fur, a torn ear, and a missing eye. Its loose joints made it flop. She stroked it with affection.

"Good morning, Mr. Bromby. I didn't expect to see you ever again." Her muffled voice sounded flat.

In a weak attempt to mimic Mickey's bear voice, she growled, "Me either, Miss Molly. It's been too long."

"It has. Any idea why Mickey made you an English butler kind of bear?"

"Too many reruns of *Family Affair* most likely."

Molly laughed softly at the old family joke, that Mickey always identified with Mr. French, who was too proper and always put upon by a gaggle of children. Leland was the oldest of the cousins, but Mickey had come along only two years later. The rest of them had been closer to Molly's age, and Mickey had too often gotten stuck babysitting.

Molly set Mr. Bromby back on the shelf. "I'll pick you up later," she whispered. "I promise."

The picture, however, elicited a less tender reflection, a fleeting memory of the day it had been taken. A family gathering at the house where Bird now lived. A Sunday, blistering hot, maybe July or August. Mickey had taken the picture, trying out a camera he'd gotten for his birthday. Both of them had fled the arguments in the house, which tended to happen anytime Bird and their mother were under the same roof.

"Smile, Squirt!"

"No."

"Don't let them get to you. They been doing this since they were kids. Mama and Bird ain't never got along."

"How do you know?"

"'Cause I'm older and wiser than you. And I always will be."

"So where are you now, Mickey?" she whispered. "I could really use some help here."

Molly shook her head, pushing away any wishful thinking. Whatever. She'd done it on her own for a long time. Why should now be different?

She took a close-up of the picture and bear.

"Now, move on, Molly."

Right. The journals. Under the bed. Molly pulled the covers up on the bed and knelt beside it, taking a deep breath before tackling what lay beneath. She dug a mountain of old food containers, crates of books, and two suitcases from under Liz's bed before she spotted the two boxes shoved up toward the head of it and covered with old magazines and mousetraps set with cheese long since dry and useless. Molly tugged them out, then gingerly tripped all the traps and put them aside. She sat the boxes on top of the rumpled blankets. One held journals, one pill bottles. The journals were the most recent, with dates on the front from a few months before Aunt Liz died to a few years ago. The most recent one must be the one she'd found with the cash.

The pill bottles were mostly large supplement containers. Vitamin C. Turmeric. Echinacea. Molly assumed they were all empty, but the box weighed a bit more than she'd expected, so she shook a few. Nothing. Then … one rattled. She opened it and peered in to see only cotton. Gently she pulled out the cotton to see what remained inside.

Entwined in the cotton was a diamond pendant on a thin silver chain. It sparkled as Molly turned it over in her hand, and an image hit her, one from a photo of her aunt taken many years ago. Liz, dressed to the nines for a church dinner, this necklace shimmering around her throat. Her mother had kept a framed five-by-seven of it near her bed. She'd often used it as an example of what they could all be.

"You look just like her, Molly. If you'd just brush that hair. Isn't she lovely? We could all look like that." Her mother meant it as encouragement, but at thirteen, it had made Molly resent her aunt. Beautiful and kind or not.

It had never occurred to that young Molly that the necklace was real. Clearly, it was—and worth a small fortune.

Molly dropped the necklace and bottle on the bed and grabbed another bottle, digging the cotton out. Then another. And another. More jewels, earrings, loose stones tumbled into her hands. Diamonds, emeralds, sapphires. A dragon's hoard. No longer a *small* fortune.

Molly stopped breathing. A surge of rage at Nina Morrow shot through her like a bolt of fire. She wanted to scream, to roar in frustration and anger. She grabbed the footboard of the bed and squeezed, the fury shaking every muscle. The grief—of losing Liz, her family, the curse that pure greed had laid on them—rolled over her in waves, and Molly sank to the floor, tears flooding her eyes and cheeks. She sobbed, her gasps for air coming in deep, endless rolls. She jerked the mask off, and dug the heels of her hands into her eyes, trying to make it stop.

"Try this."

Molly jerked back with a yelp, staring up at Greg. Tyvek covered and impassive behind the mask, he held out a large handkerchief. "You were taking too long."

She swallowed hard and accepted the handkerchief, wiping her eyes and mopping tears from her cheeks and neck. She blew her nose quickly, and looked up at him over the cloth, eyebrows raised.

He shrugged. "I knew you'd either found something horrific or had gotten hurt." He glanced at the splay of jewelry on the bed. "I had no idea it was both." He picked up one of the empty bottles and turned it over in his hand. "Nina's pill bottles. So much for Sunday school craft projects."

She squeezed her nose and lowered the handkerchief, swallowing again. She tucked the cloth away into one of the suit pockets. "Help me up."

He held out his hand and pulled her upright. "There's more going on in that head than any of us suspects."

She nodded and slipped the mask back on. "You did warn me about Nina. I guess I thought I was immune by this time."

"You'd have to be dead to be that numb. You've been gone twenty years. That's time to let wounds scar over, feel not as painful. You're ripping a lot of things open. It'll probably get worse before it gets better."

"So much for having a truce."

He shook his head. "A ceasefire is not peace."

"True dat." She started gathering jewelry and shoving it back in the bottles. "Can you lock these in your trunk? The Explorer is too open now. I'll grab the journals."

"You got it. Ready to give us marching orders?"

"I am. Carry on."

After the two boxes were tucked away in Greg's cruiser, Molly stripped off the Tyvek and slipped a t-shirt over her tank top. Returning to the porch, she addressed the deputies gathered around her. They had spread the tarps, and several sections of latticework had been ripped down and stacked to one side of the house. She stood on the porch, feeling much like a general about to do battle. And maybe, just maybe, she was.

"Thank you, all of you, for coming. I appreciate you more than I can say. We are going to tackle this front to back, first floor to attic. We need staging areas for the furniture, which will be the rooms on the first floor, mostly these two front ones." She pointed to either side of the house. "The first tasks will be to empty these two rooms of broken furniture and anything NOT furniture. If a bag is obviously garbage, drop it in the dumpster. If you can't tell what it is, place it on that far tarp. Boxes too, although those will need to be reviewed before going in the dumpster." She gestured toward a 20x20-foot tarp on the right side of the house. "That's where the dumpster will be. Broken furniture, catalogs, newspapers, and phonebooks, don't even ask; just dump. Be ruthless. I certainly will be.

"The middle tarp is for uncertain items and boxes that need to be sorted. The last tarp is for things that clearly need to be cleaned and put in the pavilions or back in the house. This will include things like knick-knacks from shelves, books, photos, stray dishes, etc. If the ones who started on the latticework want to finish that, have at it. But no one, NO ONE, goes into the house without a Tyvek suit. For now, the risk of disease is still too great.

"We'll want to stop by three, since anything not in the dumpster or 'Free' tent will need to be set back inside for lockup. Does anyone have any big garage or industrial fans I could rent?"

"I do!" The voice came from the side yard, and Molly stepped down off the porch to see Linda Allen and Sheila Eccles walking up. They both carried buckets full of cleaning supplies.

An unexpected sense of relief flooded through Molly as she trotted toward them. The neighborhood was still on board. *Why would I doubt it?* She greeted both with a quick hug. "Thank you so much. You really have the big fans?"

Sheila grinned. "We do. Finn keeps them for tailgating. Those parking lots get hot."

Linda lifted one of the buckets. "I know we can't go in the house, but if y'all will fill these with hot water, we'll start cleaning what they bring out."

And with that, the biggest cleanup operation Molly had seen outside the aftermath of a tornado began. Two of the officers helped Sheila carry four fans, which were set up in the house in an attempt to bring fresh air into the effort. The dumpster arrived just after noon, and as the latticework thudded to the bottom of its pit, Molly ordered pizzas, sandwiches, and gallons of sweet tea and Cokes. The food pavilion became the break room, and everyone worked, nibbled, and worked some more.

Nina and Bird arrived around one o'clock, but they didn't approach the house. Bird backed the truck into the yard, but he and Nina got out with fast-food bags, perched on the tailgate, and watched. Molly started to approach them, but Greg stopped her, holding her arm near the elbow and pulling her close enough that no one else could hear his words.

"Truce," he said. "Not peace."

She stared over his shoulder at Nina, who glared back. "So I can't strangle her?"

"Ill advised."

"I'm tempted to give her a box of empty pill bottles."

"Don't bait the bear."

"Wonder where Kitty is."

"And don't borrow trouble either. Maybe she's just somewhere sulking."

"Plotting, more like it."

"You have a suspicious mind."

"Realistic. Why is it that the rest of us are sweating like iced tea in the sun and smell like three-week-old gym shorts, and you still smell like Old Spice and soap?"

His laughter "did her heart good," as her mother used to say. He released her and stepped back. "Because I've been on the second floor with a fan."

"You're still in Tyvek."

"Good genes."

"Ha! Find anything interesting?"

He watched her face closely. "This was in a book. I don't think it was a bookmark." He handed her a folded twenty-dollar bill. "So I'd suggest you check all the books."

Molly glanced at the house. "Which reminds me. Where *are* all her books?" She pointed at the front room on the left. "That used to be her library. Floor to ceiling shelves crammed with books. The shelves are there. The books are not. I can't believe she would have gotten rid of them."

Greg shrugged. "Maybe she had to sell them?"

Molly shook her head. "No. She would have sold the jewelry first. They have to be somewhere in the house. Maybe the attic?"

"I'll keep an eye out. I'll start bringing down some boxes for the sorting pile later this afternoon. I've just been moving things around and trying to decipher what's what. When do you want to start in Liz's room?"

Molly looked at the ground. She'd thought about this, about what Liz would want done with her personal things. But there was also a hard reality to consider. "Liz would want her clothes given to charity, but the chances are they are not fit for it. Between the infestations and the chemicals ..." Her voice trailed off. "I just can't ... yet."

He put his hand on her arm. "Don't worry. There's time. You're already tackling a lot. And there's no telling what else you'll find in there. You see to everything else that's going on. The room will keep." He paused. "And the longer you're at this, the easier it'll be."

That sounded like personal experience, but Molly didn't press. Now was not the time.

As Greg returned to the house, Molly ran back and forth, answering questions and giving directions, as everyone fell into an efficient routine. Bags and boxes were brought out of the front two rooms and tossed into the dumpster or poured out on the tarps. Molly quickly decided what went into a trash bag or to the "clean it" tarp. She kept the camera busy as well, taking dozens of pictures and making sure she had everyone's name.

With most of the cleaning still to come, Molly gave Linda cash and asked her to go to Carterton Hardware and Feed and bring back more water, bags, paper towels, and new boxes for the items to go back in the house. Glad to have something to do, Linda left and came back with supplies … and three retirees who'd been hanging out with Betty, wondering what was going on up at "Miss Liz's house." Molly got them Tyvek suits and put them to work immediately, emptying furniture drawers into trash bags for the sorting pile.

Eleven people can make quick work of even the tightest-packed rooms, and by two o'clock, everything was out of the foyer and front rooms except the furniture. Three of the officers began lining up the furniture in rows of similar size, with tables closest to the doors. Two other deputies got the unpleasant duty of bagging up all the food in the kitchen, while two others used brooms in an attempt to sweep out at least a decade of dust and debris.

No dead animals yet, at least. Taylor had warned her that the bigger ones—rats, squirrels, moles—would probably try to get out and head for the attic or the basement. She definitely wasn't looking forward to those areas.

Linda and Sheila stayed busy washing picture frames and ceramic souvenirs, vases, keepsake plates. Linda took over the Hummel angels, bathing each one gently, drying them with a soft piece of muslin, and boxing them tenderly. Tears dripped down her cheeks the entire time. When Molly hugged her, Linda whispered hoarsely, "I just miss her so much."

Molly had one of the deputies return the angels to the bottom of the now-empty secretary, then helped Linda move on to a set of Depression-era glassware in an opaque blue pattern, which Sheila immediately suggested they hide from view. She and Linda stored those in a box and asked Greg to put them in his trunk as well. More items for Russell's office. Molly documented it all, her camera never far from hand.

But far more went into the dumpster and the "Free" and "Two-dollar" table than into hiding. As those two tables filled, Nina and Bird wandered over and began to pack up everything on the "Free" table into sacks and boxes they had brought with them. Molly paused to watch them, and Bird shook a spool of frayed ribbon at her. "You're giving away some good stuff."

"Help yourself," she said quietly.

He paused near the "Two-dollar" table and picked up a small set of drill bits. He turned it over in his hands, an odd look of confusion in his eyes. He opened it, and looked up at Molly suddenly. "These were your daddy's."

Molly took a step closer. "You mean Granddaddy's?"

Bird shook his head. "No. Not *my* daddy. *Yours.* Will McClelland. You didn't know?"

Molly felt cold and crossed her arms. "No. I don't remember him at all."

Bird scowled. "Not at all? Regina didn't talk about him?"

Molly shook her head, uncomfortable and unsure where this was going.

"Good man. A carpenter. Logger." He held up the drill bit case, a question in his eyes.

"Take it." The hoarseness in her voice startled her, and she cleared her throat. "No charge."

He nodded and put it in his box.

"When can we get into the house?" Nina asked.

Never. You'll never see the inside again. Molly turned to her. "A couple of days, maybe. Inside is a health hazard right now. I'm not letting anyone in without a protective suit. Too risky."

Bird looked over the tables again. "We'll be back tomorrow."

Linda put a hand on Molly's shoulder as they watched Bird and Nina drive away. "You okay?"

Molly patted Linda's hand. "Yeah. Thank you." She turned to face her new friend. "I don't know why. It just never occurred to me that Bird would know anything about my father. But they were close to the same age. Small town. No reason he wouldn't."

"If you ever want to go up on the mountain, talk to some of his kin, I'll take you."

Molly smiled. "I appreciate that. Maybe someday."

Linda gave her a quick hug and went back to cleaning. A war of emotion churned inside Molly. Years of bitterness battled with the notion that Bird had sounded almost human. Caring, even, about a man who'd been dead for more than thirty years. Molly rolled her shoulders. *Not now. Too much to do.* She turned back to it.

By three, Molly began the wind-down of all the work. Everyone was growing weary, but a huge dent had been made in what needed to be done. Two rooms were cleared and staged. And, as Liz had promised, papers taped to the back of some pieces of the furniture listed names and phone numbers in Liz's handwriting. All the latticework had been stripped from the house, opening it up to full sun and the glorious April breezes. Denuded of the claustrophobic vines, the house looked almost welcoming again.

Linda and Sheila still had dozens of items left to wash and insisted on staying until the last item had been sorted, cleaned, and returned to the house. Molly finally shooed them home as school buses drove through, depositing kids who bolted out their doors only to stop and watch the activity at the house. Eventually they wandered over and snagged the last of the pizza. The adults started arriving home from work around four, and they drifted about, looking at the tarps and tables, as the rest of the workers peeled out of sweat-drenched Tyvek and downed water.

Items from the "Two-dollar" table, mostly souvenirs and vases, disappeared as well, as soon as Molly explained that the money would go toward cleaning supplies and food for the workers. When one little girl became enchanted by a musical figurine of Cinderella, Molly gave it to her readily.

Finally, Molly locked up the house, locked the camera in its case, grabbed a bottle of water, and leaned up against the Explorer. The last folks drifted away, and Greg came over to lean next to her. He wasn't quite as free of sweat or scent as he had been earlier, but a whiff of Old Spice still lingered.

He cracked open a bottle of water and took a long swig. "Russell's on his way."

"You call him?"

"He called me. He tried you without luck."

"Ah. I locked my phone and purse in the glove box. I really need to get that back glass replaced. Any idea what's up?"

Greg shook his head and drank more water. "Nope. But he sounded seriously disturbed."

They fell silent for several minutes, both just resting and watching the house. Greg finished his water, capped the empty bottle, and set it on the back bumper of the Explorer. He crossed his arms. "Did they tell you?"

Molly knew what he meant. He'd been right about the rumors, and Linda and Sheila hadn't been working fifteen minutes before they brought them up, along with Greg's history in Carterton. "That your wife died?"

He looked at the ground. "Yes. How did it come up?"

"I asked why you had run for sheriff three years ago. Most people don't enter politics halfway through their careers. Especially to run for sheriff." Molly paused, unsure how to continue. "I'm sorry."

He remained still. "I'd been a cop for twenty years before we moved here so she could take care of her folks. I retired to help. After … I had to go back. To do *something*. But I didn't want to be a deputy. I wanted some control." He paused. "I guess that's very telling."

"Tells me you're not made of stone. There's a few folks around here that think that."

One side of his mouth jerked. "Then they should stay out of trouble."

Molly hesitated. "Speaking of …"

"Like I said, I have no idea where Kitty got off to, but my guess is you were right. She's somewhere plotting, and it may have something to do with why Russell wants to see you."

"Mm."

They fell silent again as Finn waved at them from his yard and began to lope in their direction.

"So do you think he knows everything about everybody in Carterton?" Molly asked.

"Probably. People like to talk to Finn. I've done it myself. Talk to him for five minutes and you discover you're revealing all your life's secrets."

"A handy man to keep around, if you're the sheriff."

"Why do you think I know someone will eventually spill it about the attack on you? If it were football season, we'd have the info by this weekend, from his tailgate partying. This time of year, we'll have to wait for a cookout or a church picnic."

"You seem very certain."

"I've only been sheriff three years. I've been in Carterton a lot longer."

Molly raised a hand as Finn crossed into her yard, peering closely at the dumpster, tarps, and pavilions. "Want some water?"

Finn waved her off. "I'm good, Miss Molly!" When he'd closed the distance between them, he continued. "Miss Sheila said y'all got a lot done today."

"We made a good start." Molly pointed at the dumpster. "But that's only about a quarter full. Lots to go, especially once we hit the attic and the basement."

Russell's Mercedes pulled into the drive and he got out. Impeccable as ever in charcoal gray, his expression and stride were pure business.

Molly stepped toward him. "So what's wrong now?"

Russell took a deep breath but hesitated, glancing at Finn and Greg. Molly dismissed his concern with a shrug. "Whatever it is, it'll be all over town by morning, especially if Kitty is involved."

His brow furrowed. "How did you—?"

"She's been missing in action today." Greg crossed his arms. "We knew she had to be stirring up something somewhere."

"She's filed an injunction in an attempt to keep you from distributing property not named in the will."

Molly squinted. "But the will hasn't even been probated! She can't know what's in the will. And what's not. I'm not even completely sure."

"She doesn't have to know. The injunction is inclusive of the property in the house that is, quote, 'unnamed.' Since we have the will, the burden falls on us. You'll have to provide an inventory to the court as part of the probate. Her point is that you won't be able to provide a complete inventory. She plans to prove she knows of things in the house that you don't, since they aren't named in the will. If she can, there will be grounds to contest the validity of the will."

"That's garbage." Finn yanked his cap off and hit it against his thigh. "She can't do that, can she?"

"She can try." Russell closed his eyes and rubbed his forehead, as if to push out a headache. "She can get it in front of a judge. What happens after that depends on the judge she gets and the case she makes in court. And how far along you are with the clean-out when she gets to the judge. One of her arguments is that Lyric lived with Liz and was promised certain items. She also claims that there's a new will that may be hidden in the house, and that if you find it, you'll destroy it."

"So, essentially, she wants a look at everything that comes out of the house."

"Essentially. And I've heard through the courthouse grapevine that she and Bird plan to contest the will when it is probated."

Molly sniffed. "No surprise there. Any word on the probate?"

"That was the second thing I wanted to tell you. It *may* be set for a week from tomorrow."

"That's quick," Greg said. At Molly's questioning look, he patted her arm. "I've seen them take as long as two years."

She looked back at Russell. "But you said, 'It *may* be set.'"

"We were lucky," Russell offered. "All the potential heirs responded quickly. Most are in this area. Which brings me to number three, which is a puzzle. We're in search of a young man named Frederick Davidson. He's a distant cousin, but he's mentioned in the will. Which is odd because he lives in Sevierville, Tennessee. I've never heard Liz mention him. We didn't get a response to a certified letter, so I called his workplace, then his landlord. But he didn't pay the rent at the first of the month and no one has seen him."

"Well, that *is* weird," Finn interjected. When they all looked at him, surprised, he held out both hands as if the answer were obvious. "You're talking about Freddy, right? Freddy Davidson. Good-looking young chap, about twenty-five or so? He came down here to look for a job, in Birmingham, Gadsden, maybe. He's a driver, beverage and beer trucks, that sort of thing. Liz let him stay here a few weeks. He went home right before Liz died." He paused, looking at each of them. "You didn't know?"

"No." Greg straightened. "Go on, Finn."

"Well, that's what's weird. Lyric said he went home. He just up and left. But you go home, and you don't pay rent, the landlord is gonna know where you are, y'know? No one just vanishes, not this day and age."

11

Molly twisted around in the sheets like a rotisserie chicken. Nightmares—mostly about tornadoes ripping apart homes and families—plagued her until almost four. She dozed another hour, but finally, she got into the shower to blast away the last remnants of sleep. It was time to start the day.

She got dressed and checked her computer to find a brief email from Jimmy, updating her on Sarah's condition. It was the first since Sunday, despite her daily emails to him. This one was short and abrupt. Sarah was responding to pain stimuli, which was good news, but still not awake. Her father was still talking lawsuit.

Get in line, bub. Molly definitely couldn't worry about that now. She was more concerned about the tone of the note. Jimmy had always been the mediator of the team, friendly and optimistic. This note was curt to the point of being rude and had been sent in the middle of the night. Definitely not like him.

But her own reassuring words in response did not come. She felt blocked, numb, as if she shouldn't respond at all. A week had passed since she'd seen them, since Sarah's accident. But it felt like a lifetime. Molly knew part of her numbness came from exhaustion. Brain fog from lack of sleep and too many long hours dragging around house trash. Yet she felt as if a curtain had dropped between them. Not just a lifetime ago … a life. She still wanted to return, wanted to be with them. But the past she had so carefully packed away had returned to her full force. And it now stood between them. But she had to say something.

Finally, Molly typed,

Good news about Sarah. No worries about dad. Will sort that out later. But how are you? Are you resting? Call me sometime if you want to talk. Evenings are best right now. More time to talk. Thinking about you. M

The words felt false, as if she were just pretending. But they would have to do. Just as she hit send, her phone rang. She yelped. *Who in the world?*

Greg.

She answered the same way she'd greeted Russell. "What's wrong?" *This is becoming a habit.*

"Get to the house. Now." And he hung up.

In less than ten minutes, Molly turned onto Maple Street, but she was blocked from the house. A chaotic scene of flashing red and blue lights, shouts, and running first responders spread out before her. Working lights on tall poles had turned night into day. Two fire trucks—one on the street, one on her yard—anchored hoses snaking across hers and Linda Allen's lawns to the pine grove behind the houses. Smoke billowed across the neighborhood in clouds thick with soot and ash.

Molly leaped from the Explorer as soon as it stopped, coughing as the smoke rolled over her. Her skin prickled and her chest tightened as she fought to make sense out of the pandemonium. *What's burning?* Her gaze darted from the flames in the grove to the house. It seemed to be safe, no blazes on the roof or sides, but bellowed orders echoed through the air as the fire captain directed the team leaders to different positions. The teams dashed from one spot to another, adding to the confusion and madness. The whole neighborhood was outside, families clustered in their ash-dotted nightclothes, holding tight to each other, faces wan and shocked. Wide eyes looked from trucks to firefighters … to the fire that still burned in the trees behind Liz Morrow's house.

Molly ran toward the main blaze, looking again from it to the house, and she spotted a clear line of burnt grass that ran between them. Stunned, she stared at it a moment, then searched desperately for Greg, calling his name as she darted between firefighters and sheriff's deputies. He found her, snagging her from behind. She spun, screaming over the mayhem. "What happened? What happened?"

He searched her face, and for a split second, Molly knew he'd wondered if she'd set the blaze. But whatever he saw in her face apparently told him otherwise.

He raised his voice as well. "Started about thirty minutes ago. One of the neighbors was up with a sick kid and smelled it. Called 911. Two deputies were close, got there quick. It's mostly contained now. It never threatened the houses."

She pointed at the burned line on the ground. "Someone set it!"

"Probably, but too soon to tell for sure."

"How else would it start?"

He shrugged.

"I didn't do it, Greg. I swear to you."

Something in his eyes shifted, an acknowledgment. "I know." Near the blaze, someone called his name. "Wait here," he said, and trotted off.

Molly hugged herself, feeling as shocked as her neighbors appeared. She looked from the fiery copse of trees, and again traced a three-foot-wide line of blackened grass toward the house.

The house. Aunt Liz's house.

Desperation rolled over Molly, even as the madness around her began to subside. Hundreds of images flooded through her, a vertigo-inducing kaleidoscope made up of more than thirty years of good times and bad, fights and parties, storms and recoveries, her mother's last days and long chats with Aunt Liz. The names on her aunt's papers popped into her head, a roll call of good people who deserved better than the hand they'd been dealt by life … or her family.

Molly did not want this house, but it had been part of her for a long time, and in just over a week, it had put yet another anchor in her, grounding her to this town and to this family. She hated it and she loved it. And she certainly didn't want to see it burnt to the ground, despite her earlier declarations.

I have to make this right. Aunt Liz gave me what I need to end it all. Make it right. I have to. No matter what!

A hand rested on her shoulder, and Molly turned, screaming. "They tried to burn my house!"

It was Linda. She arched back at the declaration, but then she nodded, compassion in her eyes. She wrapped her arms around Molly. Molly leaned heavily against her, dropping her head to Linda's shoulder. As they held each other, Molly felt others surround them, adding their own arms to the circle.

No one spoke, not even as the group began to break up. One by one, the neighbors drifted away, back to their now-safe homes. The fire doused, the firefighters gathered their equipment, preparing to leave. Linda and Molly finally released each other, brushing ash off each other's shoulders and hair.

"I have to get breakfast for the kids," Linda whispered.

Molly nodded and squeezed her friend's arm. As Linda walked away, Molly turned her attention back to the house. The sun had breached the horizon, casting long, red-gold rays up over the pines. Smoke lingered, darkening some of the rays to purple and umber. The gables and the spires of the house rose far above the houses around it, the resulting shadows flowing over the ground with peaks and dips. With its peeling paint, dead overgrown vines, and solid structure, the house was both magnificent and shabby.

"I can see why Aunt Liz loved you," Molly murmured.

"Why do you think someone would want to burn it?" Greg's voice came from behind her.

She turned. "I don't know. It makes no sense. Everyone involved with this desperately wants this house and everything in it. The only person around who doesn't want it is me, and I swear to you, Greg. I did *not* do this."

"I believe you. But that leaves only one obvious motive."

Molly nodded. "There's something in that house they don't want us to find."

* * *

"What better place to hide something than in a hoarder's domain?"

Russell, Greg, and Molly sat in one of Bailey's Garden Bistro's booths, discussing the fire over omelets and bagels. Russell's question hung in the air a moment, until Greg countered. "But if you want to keep it safe and hidden, you're not going to destroy it. You'd find a way to retrieve it."

"Say, for instance," Molly continued, "during the chaos caused by a fire that appeared to threaten the houses, but your deputies arrived too fast."

Russell toyed with his omelet. "Which means we may never know why it was set or who set it?"

"Unless they *were* trying to destroy it," Greg said. "What better timing than just after you've threatened to burn it in a viral video? They destroy what they need to and you get the blame."

"That's a truly insidious thought," Russell muttered.

"We're speculating in circles." Molly reached for a packet of strawberry jam. "We don't know enough."

"Indeed. So I'll put the patrols back on the house tonight. If they did intend destruction and not just distraction, they'll be back."

"And I think I'll move into the house as soon as it's clean enough."

Silence hung in the air as the two men looked at each other, then at Molly. She focused on the jam, opening the packet and squeezing it onto her bagel. Russell spoke first. "I thought you didn't want anything to do with the house."

Molly shook her head. "I don't. But I don't want anything to happen to it either. This process is obviously going to take a while. I can't keep staying in a hotel, and Greg can't keep using the deputies as security on a private residence. It makes sense." She looked up at them, looking from one to the other. "Right? Makes sense."

After a moment of stunned silence, they both nodded. Then Russell chuckled softly. "She's getting under your skin."

Molly grinned shyly. "Maybe. A little. Doesn't mean I'm not going to sell it. But maybe."

Greg grinned. "Yeah. Right."

Russell finally took a bite of his omelet. "You made good progress yesterday. How long do you think it's going to take?"

"A least a half a day per room, just to drag everything out. Probably three days each for the basement and attic." Molly broke apart the bagel and popped a piece into her mouth. "Five rooms downstairs, seven on the second floor, so two to three weeks to get everything out. I did hire a cleaning service out of Birmingham that specializes in this kind of stuff. They start at the end of the week. The three guys, Betty's friends, who helped yesterday are in it for the long haul. And whoever volunteers. I'll start going through Liz's journals, and I'll start divvying up the furniture as soon as I can get an adequate list. So I'm hoping to be mostly done in a month."

Russell cleared his throat. "And the other stuff you found?"

She paused, a portion of bagel halfway to her mouth. She put it down. "That'll have to wait. I don't know enough about it, where it came from. I do hope there will be something in the journals." She glanced at Greg. "What are the next steps where the fire is concerned?"

He shrugged. The shadows around his eyes seemed harsher than earlier, and Molly wondered how much sleep he'd gotten. "That line to the house was definitely spurred by an accelerant. The fire captain is sending a sample off to see if they can tell what it was, but it smelled like gasoline. I'll check with the local stations, see if they remember anyone buying a large amount in cans, but I'd lay odds they siphoned it out of a car or a tractor. Some of the farms have their own tanks as well. I'll talk to a few folks, especially the ones on the other side of that grove. But the kids come and go through there all the time. Even if they spotted someone, they might not think anything about it."

He paused for a sip of coffee. "To be honest, I don't have a lot of hope that evidence is going to prove anything."

"Like the shooting."

He added more sugar to his coffee and stirred it slowly. "We'll have to wait until someone gets nervous enough to talk. And I won't be surprised if the two incidents aren't related."

"I just don't understand what they hoped to gain. Did they want to burn the house or not? Or did they think a threatening fire would stop my work on the house? If they think that, they don't know me very well. And if they did want to burn it, maybe it's less about what they want than what I might find. All of the above. None of the above. I don't know." She dropped her fork back on her plate in frustration.

Greg gave a single nod. "But you might want to brace yourself for Bird. He's never going to think you didn't set it, especially after the shooting. You're just tired and want it over with."

She pushed aside her plate. "I have thought about that." She considered yesterday's conversation over the drill bits. "Maybe. He saw what we got accomplished yesterday, and he knows I plan to carry this out." She shrugged again, and ignored the looks that Greg and Russell exchanged.

Greg put a hand on her arm. "Molly, what are you thinking?"

Bird. She was thinking about Bird, picking up every item off the tables, studying each one as if it were made of gold. There had been a curiosity in his expression, more than just avarice.

She shook her head. "Nothing. Just tired, like you said." She straightened. "If Bird wants to come at me, let him. It's not like I've not already dealt with his blustering. If life were easy, I wouldn't be chasing tornadoes for a living." She smiled at Greg and put her hand over his. "Bird's just a different kind of storm front."

12

Molly stopped mid-sentence, as her breath caught and a chill slid down her spine and into her legs. She stared down at a pile of garbage bags and overstuffed duffels.

No. Please … no. I don't believe it. A spear of rage shot through her. *How could they …?*

"Are you okay? Molly?" Dina, the cleaning service's team leader, stood in the doorway of the attic. Her voice sounded flat, muffled by her Tyvek suit and mask.

Molly thrust her arm out behind her, palm facing Dina. "Stay there. Don't come any farther." She blinked and focused on the pile again, still hoping that what she saw wasn't … really …

A hand. A human hand. A human hand in the act of decomposing.

The cleaning service team, four eager young women who started work on the front rooms of the first floor without hesitation, had arrived that morning. Satisfied that she'd made the right decision in hiring them, Molly had taken a break from the cleaning and sorting zoo to give Dina a tour of the house. When they'd reached the attic, Molly had picked her way farther back than she had before in order to give them both a better idea of exactly what cleaning the attic would entail. She had just shoved aside a stack of quilts when the hand flopped into view from out of the next mass of stuff.

Molly leaned over and tugged the topmost bag away from the heap. The rest of the man lay sprawled between layers of bags. *Dear Lord, what have they done?* She let out a long breath. *Well, now we know.* Here was the source of the odor they couldn't clear, and quite possibly the reason for the shooting and the fire. He'd been there awhile, like the storm victims she and her own team sometimes found, days after everyone else had left. Like those people, this man had been abandoned, left behind to rot.

But this man had not died from flying debris or collapsing buildings.

Her anger sagged into sadness and she backed away. "God, help us," she whispered, and turned to Dina. "Do you have your phone with you?" As usual, Molly had locked hers in the Explorer.

Dina nodded and pulled open a velcroed pocket. She held it out to Molly, who took it, pulled down her ever-present mask, and dialed Greg's number from memory. When he answered, she said, "This is Molly. I'm in the attic. I think I've found what they were trying to burn." Finn's words echoed in her mind. *Good-looking young chap, about twenty-five or so* … "And I think it may be Frederick Davidson."

As she described what she'd found, Molly watched Dina's face go stark white, and she knew her own face must be just as pale. She listened to Greg's instructions, then hung up and handed Dina the phone.

Dina was ahead of her. "We need to vacate the house."

Molly nodded. "Everything has to come to a full stop until they can investigate and—" She hugged herself. "I can't imagine how much evidence we've already destroyed."

Dina shook her head. "Probably not as much as you'd think. We haven't started with the chemicals yet, and this entire house is a giant exhibit of tainted evidence. He was murdered?"

Molly nodded and pointed to her chest. "Gunshot. At least one of them."

"Figured." Dina squeezed Molly's arm. "We clean up a lot of crime scenes. The forensic stuff is never like it is on television." She nodded toward the body. "I'll bet he wasn't killed up here. Even if they find something downstairs … it'll be a mess, and it'll have nothing to do with you or your attempts to clean out the house. Just remember … if you hadn't been doing this, he wouldn't have been found at all."

Molly understood what Dina was trying to say, but it didn't really help. She motioned for them to head downstairs. Dina turned and led the way. Just before she shut the attic door, Molly looked back. "Sorry," she whispered.

Molly's steps slowed as she descended the stairs. They had been making such great progress since Wednesday morning's fire. After the shock of the blaze had worn off, everyone pitched in with a new sense of urgency. Neighborhood teenagers brought friends after school, and the retired guys she'd hired showed up with their wives. The cleaning and sorting sped up to a new level, and they had cleaned out not only most of the first-floor rooms but also the front stairs, the kitchen, and three of the upstairs rooms by the time Dina and her crew arrived Friday morning. Molly had closed off Liz's room; she wanted to be more involved in that one.

The front lawn had become a scene of organized chaos, with a half-dozen or more people washing and sorting the hundreds of items. Molly directed where each piece went with an energy she didn't know she had. The two-dollar tent had raised almost four hundred dollars. Bird and Nina had showed up each day to rake clean the "Free" table, but Bird no longer bothered with the dumpster. Nina still kicked around it some, but Bird spent more time on his tailgate, just watching, saying little.

Not even about the fire. Unlike Greg's prediction, Bird had been unusually somber on Wednesday, even asking once if she'd heard anything about it. When she'd mentioned that to Greg, he'd remained silent, although she knew he had to be adding it to whatever other information he'd gathered over the past few days. There'd been no sign of LJ or Kitty. Kitty's injunction had hit a wall with the judge, and the truce Bird had made with Molly had been seen as a betrayal. But Molly wasn't counting her out of the picture … not yet. The will's probate date had, in fact, been set for next Wednesday, and Molly knew in her gut that Kitty would be there.

But now all their progress had come to a screeching halt.

Dina quietly rounded up her team. They left, with Molly promising to call when they were allowed back in the house. Molly pushed back the hood on her suit, twisting the mask in her hands as she called all the workers to the front porch. They clustered slowly, and even Bird slipped off his tailgate to wander over, a quizzical look on his face. Nina remained in the dumpster but stopped digging to watch. This is what they wanted—for all work to stop—and Molly observed them closely as she spoke.

"Folks, we're going to have to stop work immediately." A low buzz moved through the crowd, and she held up her hands. "Please. I don't want this, but we have to vacate the premises. Something's—"

Her voice broke as she watched disappointment cross most of the workers' faces. They all, in some way, had an ownership in what they were trying to accomplish. Many had known Liz for years; this was their way of honoring her. Just in the past few days, as more workers had arrived, it felt as if all of Carterton had an interest in retrieving the house from its ruin. Thursday had been tremendous, as residents from different neighborhoods had stood next to each other, becoming friends.

Linda stepped up next to her. "What's happened? Just spit it out."

Molly straightened and took a deep breath. *Linda's right. Get it over with.* The words came out in a rush. "We've found a body in the attic. A man who's been shot. The sheriff's department will have to take over, to investigate. We have to stop right now and leave it all."

Disappointment turned to shock as speculation shot through the crowd, the buzz building to a frenzy. It was Sheila Eccles who first put two and two together. She stepped closer to Molly and called out. "Is it Freddy?"

Everyone fell silent as Molly looked at Sheila, who explained quietly. "Finn said he was missing."

Bird, a fierce look on his face, stepped forward. "Can't be. Lyric said Freddy had gone back to Tennessee. She'd know, right?" At Molly's raised eyebrows, he hunched his shoulders. "I mean, they were, you know, sweet on each other." He looked around at Nina, who was as void of expression as anyone Molly had ever seen, staring only into the sky. "Right?" Bird asked her. Nina gave no response. Bird turned back to Molly, his chest and neck turning red, his voice insistent. "It's not him. It can't be."

Molly's eyes narrowed in confusion and she glanced at Linda, who looked equally puzzled. *Why was he so upset that it might be Freddy?*

Greg's cruiser pulled up in the drive, and two other cruisers parked on the street. A van, painted with the sheriff's logo and the words "Crime Scene Unit," pulled in behind Greg. Greg got out, his expression somber, his eyes locked on Molly. She got the message.

She turned back to the crowd around her. "This is it, folks. I'm sorry. But we have to vacate. Officially, the house is now a crime scene, and we have to let them do their work."

Sheila looked down at the wet rag still clutched in one hand. "If there's even any evidence left."

Molly stepped forward, gently herding people away from her. "Ya never know."

"You'll keep us posted?" Sheila asked softly.

"I promise. Y'all will know anything I do."

Molly stopped beside Bird, who hadn't moved. Instead, he was staring at the attic windows. Behind him, Nina crawled out of the dumpster.

"Bird," Molly said, "we have to move away from the house. They have to set up a perimeter."

His voice came out harsh. "It can't be Freddy. It can't be."

"Bird ..."

"No! He was a good kid. Good to Liz. Helped her out. Helped us out on the farm some. Worked with LJ." He looked at Molly, and his cheeks grew even redder, his eyes wet. "Weird that he got sweet on Lyric, but they were a lot alike, y'know? Not all there. It ain't him."

"Bird!" Nina said sharply. "You talkin' too much. Let's go. Ain't nothin' we can do here." She tugged her husband by the arm, pulling him back toward their truck.

Molly watched them leave, and she was still staring as Greg approached her. "What was that all about?" he asked.

She shook her head slowly. "No idea. But it was very ... peculiar. He was extremely upset ... to the point of tears ... that it might be Freddy."

"Everything about those two is peculiar." But he turned to watch the black pickup leave, his brow furrowing.

"No doubt about that." Molly looked at the house. "So now what?"

Greg turned back to her and squared his shoulders. "First, you show the crime scene techs and me where you found the body. Then you—and everyone else—have to stay clear of the house for a few days. We'll put up tape for a perimeter."

She glanced around at the stacks of stuff on the tarps and in the tents. "No chance I can finish some of this?"

"Nope."

"What if it rains?"

"Rain's not due until next week. You're the weather expert. You think it's going to rain?"

Molly pursed her lips. She wouldn't lie about this. "No."

"You can't be hanging around while we work. Nice try though."

She sighed. "Worth the attempt."

Greg pointed at the house. "Let's go."

Molly had no desire to return to the attic, and she shifted from one foot to the other as Greg and two techs suited up. When they were ready, she pulled up her hood, replaced the mask, and led the way. As they headed upstairs, she looked back, watching the techs glance around at the semi-cleaned rooms, and the ones on the second floor that had not yet been touched. Their eyes seemed to get wider with every step, and Molly understood how overwhelmed they must feel. The shock of her first look at the house still lingered in her mind, even though it felt like ages ago. "But less than two weeks," she muttered as she stopped at the door on the second floor that opened onto the attic stairs. She looked over her shoulder. "The odor gets worse from here." They all nodded, and she pulled the door open and flipped on the light.

She paused again at the top of the stairs, opened the door there, and pointed at the pile where the body lay. "It's over there. You'll have to be careful where you step. Several of the piles are on top of stacks of magazines. Easy to slip and fall." She watched as they gazed over the heaping mounds that stretched across the attic, from one end to the other. The windows, filthy as they were, still allowed long streaks of sunlight to trail across the furniture and random piles of clothes, books, and linens. Dust motes danced in the rays, still stirred up by Molly's earlier visit.

"No one should be left in a place like this," she whispered. "How could they?"

Greg put a firm hand on her forearm. "Molly, go back to the hotel. Let us work. We'll be here for a while."

"I want to stay."

"You cannot. I'll come see you when we get a break. Go."

Molly scowled, but turned and headed down the stairs. *I don't want to leave!*

As she trotted out of the house and down the steps, she had to dodge a crime scene photographer taking shots of the house, the yard, and the neighborhood. Strands of yellow crime scene tape already bordered the yard, although her Explorer was still inside the perimeter. When she reached it, she yanked open the back of it and leaned on the tailgate, stripping off the Tyvek suit. She'd almost gotten used to wearing the hot, airtight suit, but it was still a relief to peel out of it and let the cool air dry her skin. She tossed the suit in the back and pulled a bottle of water out of the cooler. She swigged almost half of it, her eyes still on the house. The urge to continue work, no matter what, dogged her, and she finally looked away, closed the rear of the car, and got into the front.

She pulled her phone out of the glove box and checked it, frowning at a voicemail from an unknown number. She selected it.

"Hi, Molly, this is Leon, over at the StayLodge. You have a package here at the office. You can pick it up anytime."

Molly deleted the message, curious as to who would be … ah, Jimmy! He'd said he was sending something. She put the Explorer in reverse and one of the deputies lifted the tape to let her out. Ten minutes later, she rounded the sharp curved hill in front of the StayLodge and pulled up in front of the office. Leon threw up a hand in greeting as she entered, a little *beep-beep-beep* sounding as she opened the door. She paused and looked back at the doorframe. "That's new," she said, grinning.

"Hmph!" Leon snorted. "Your attack made the owner nervous. He had the thing put in the next day. Making me crazy, beeping all the time. Worse than a smoke detector with a dead battery."

She laughed. "You'll get used to it."

He handed her a large manila envelope over the counter. "Or go mad trying. Sorry. It's been here a couple of days. I've been off, and our temp is beyond lazy."

She tucked the envelope under her arm. "No problem. Thanks!"

"Have a good evening."

She got back in the Explorer and moved it closer to her new room, now on the second floor. The one downstairs had a new door and a new camera pointed to the lot in front of it, but she didn't want to move again. She and Leon had struck up an easy friendship since the move, and she knew he'd look after her stuff while she was gone.

In the room, she dropped the envelope on the desk and sat down, opening it carefully. She pulled out a stack of binder-clipped papers, which had a handwritten letter on top. As she read it, her heart and mind soared, then sank.

Dear Molly,

This is a good news/bad news packet, and I hope you won't take what I'm about to say too hard. Believe me, it's not easy to write.

The good news: Attached are two emails and a contract. After you left, I worked on your pictures and Sarah's videos from the last storm. Not much else to do waiting around the hospital. I sent them off to a bunch of folks. One was a national adventure magazine. They're doing a story on storm chasers next spring and want to interview you and publish a couple of your pictures. The contact number is on his email. The money he mentioned is pretty good, but you know how it is: get it in writing. Sarah's videos got picked up by two local stations. Her dad signed for those. Not a lot of money, but enough to help out with the co-pay here. The insurance has been great so far. Thanks for keeping it on us. I know it's been a stretch for you to do it sometimes.

The contract is for you. A job. A long-term one for a St. Louis station. You'd be a regular weather correspondent and storm chaser for them. Contact is a guy named Hunter Bradley. There's more detail in his email. I sent them the pictures and some of the videos Sarah made of you describing the storms. The money is good not great, but I hope you'll think long and hard about it … because obviously Sarah and I won't be with you.

I didn't want to do this by mail, but you know me. I'm lousy on the phone. I'd get all tongue-tied. And I started to do it by email, but that didn't seem right either. Call me when you get this, and I'll give you more detail.

You see, it's now clear that Sarah's going to be here a long time. Even if she woke up tomorrow, she'll have a long recovery. THIS IS NOT YOUR FAULT. I know you. You cannot blame yourself. Sarah is an adult and made her own choices.

But the bottom line is that I'm not leaving her. When she wakes up, I'm going to propose. And my money is running out. I've never saved a lot, and staying in a hotel ate my cushion. I've been applying for jobs, and I've accepted one at a TV station. I start next week. Editing videos; it is what I do best. I've moved to an apartment.

You can handle that contract on your own. Absolutely you can. But I didn't want you to take it thinking we're going to be a part of it.

They need to know your decision by the first of the month.

Sarah and I love you. You know that. But it's time we went our own way.

Jimmy

Molly thrust the packet away from her as if it would make the bad news go away. Her heart felt so tight, she thought she'd pass out. She couldn't get her breath, and she began to shake.

No. He can't do this!

Molly pushed away from the desk, stood up, and leaned over it, fighting the dizziness, the nausea as a flush of heat coursed through her. *Breathe, Molly,* she scolded herself. *Just breathe.*

She gasped, sucking in a deep lungful of air. The tears came then, unbidden, a flood that streamed down her cheeks and neck. She straightened and looked at herself in the mirror through blurry eyes.

"What is he doing? He can't! We're family!"

No, you aren't.

Friends. Business partners. But no matter how Molly felt, not family. Not to Jimmy. Not to Sarah. Just business. Molly stepped back, stumbled, and sat down on the floor with a thud, the blow racking her spine. The tears became sobs, and she leaned against the end of the bed as she let her grief out, anguished thoughts circling in her head.

He can't … but he had. She was not the "big sister." Just a boss. A partner.

This is why Mama passed out.

The thought came unbidden, but it rang true. The overwhelming grief she'd seen that day in her mother. The sobs, the inability to catch a breath. The soul-wrenching sense of betrayal.

And that *had* been family. Blood family.

"Family takes care of its own. That's what we do."

Her mother's words. And Aunt Liz's. They learned that from Gram … had to. It was just like her grandmother to put family first, no matter what. Even when Bird did not.

Molly released a long sigh, then pushed herself up and headed for the bathroom. She pulled a half-dozen tissues from the box in the wall. She still trembled from the rush of adrenaline, but she dried the tears and washed her face.

Her mother had pulled herself together and gone on. With life. With work. So had Aunt Liz. They did it. So could she.

But she could not face talking to Jimmy. Not yet. She sat back down at the desk, took a few deep, calming breaths, and carefully composed a text.

Got the package. Can't talk right now, but wanted to let you know. Congratulations on the new job. I'm proud of you. Always. Glad you are there to take care of Sarah. Always said you two were a cute couple. Will look over contract. Thanks. Will call soon.

She reviewed it twice before finally hitting send. In a few moments came a return text, short, thankful, and contrite.

Thanks. Hope you're okay, not too hurt. Sorry to send it that way.

She responded. She would take the high road with this, no matter the disappointment and grief.

No problem. Will all work out for the best. Talk later.

No response, which was a good thing. Molly wasn't sure she could be pleasant much longer. She still felt numb, gobsmacked, but fury lingered just at the edges.

And Leon won't like it if you start smashing up the furniture.

She snorted, humor pressing through as she thought of the older man's reaction to one of her temper tantrums. She hadn't thrown a really good one since arriving in Carterton, although the scene with LJ came close. Not many people could handle them. Sarah had always hid. Jimmy tried too hard to calm her down and usually wound up making it worse. Mickey could handle them because he had a similar temper.

I bet Greg could handle them.

Hm. Molly thought back to that first day. While she had read Kitty and Bird the riot act, Greg had stood to one side, bemused … and more than a little pleased. He'd liked that she'd taken charge. And his reaction to her confrontation with LJ had been more concern for her in the aftermath than LJ. Or LJ's finger.

Greg Olson did not find her intimidating. This was new.

This was a good thing.

Molly rolled her shoulders to work some of the tension out. "Okay, you can't sit here mourning all afternoon. Or thinking about Greg Olson. You have things to do."

She reached for the contract and took off the binder clip, setting Jimmy's note to one side, upside down. This was going to hurt for a long time. But she would not let it derail her. Pain could be dealt with.

I know that well. After all, I have a lot of practice. So stop it with the self-pity. Get on with it.

And she did. She found an email address for the magazine and emailed, requesting a time for the interview. She reviewed the station's contract, then emailed Hunter Bradley, looking for some follow-up information and perhaps a phone conversation about expectations.

Then, the rest of the afternoon, she worked with Liz's journals, and only occasionally did she glance at her phone, suddenly realizing that more than responses from Jimmy or the emails she'd sent, she wanted to hear from Greg. Instead she tried to focus on her aunt's words, especially the journal from the leather bag. Only a few entries covered the pages of that one, stopping right before Liz died. The last three hit harder, bringing Molly to a halt.

==

March 2
Peggy, poor child, lost another baby over the weekend. This is the third. No trouble getting them. She just can't hang on to them. And she so wants one who might be normal, only I'm not supposed to say normal. Not sure anymore what I'm supposed to say. But without disabilities. She worries what'll happen to Edward when she gets too old to take care of him. Thinks only one "normal" brother isn't enough. Just hope she doesn't ruin her health—or her sanity—trying.

==

March 12
Molly, I hate to be addressing these to you. No telling who'll wind up with them. Hope you do. But it's getting weird. Something's happened, something bad. I don't even want to talk about it. Still don't believe it happened right here in my house! I'm such a wimp! I hope you don't hate me for what I've done. I hope you can get it all cleaned up.

==

March 13
Bad day. Afraid to sleep. It'll be over soon. They are afraid of me. Of what I know. Mollybelle, watch your back.

==

Molly closed the journal and shut her eyes. Maybe the journals hadn't been the best idea, given her current mood. The next day, March 14, Liz had died, buried in a mass of trash in her own home. And right now, Molly desperately wanted to hang Lyric … Kitty … LJ … whoever was responsible … from the closest tree. Finally, she calmed down enough to call Russell with a request that caught even him off guard.

"I want to see Aunt Liz's autopsy report."

13

Molly pushed on with the journals, stopping occasionally for a break and to make lists—one for Greg regarding the journals, a separate list of questions for Russell concerning the autopsy, and a preliminary list of names she wanted to compare with the material in the will and the names on the furniture. Russell had promised he'd have the autopsy report for her the next morning, and they agreed to meet in his office at nine. By the time her text alert sounded, Molly needed another breather.

Pick you up at 6. Will buy dinner.

Molly looked at the phone, then texted Greg back: *I'll be ready.* She'd already taken a shower and changed clothes when one of the earlier journal entries had truly gotten under her skin. It shouldn't have bothered her, but her nerves were still raw from Jimmy's note. The shower had helped calm her down, but she was glad Lyric was out of reach and Kitty strangely absent. Hanging them from a tree for what they'd done to Aunt Liz still appealed to her.

At six, she answered the door to find Greg standing there in jeans and a polo shirt. It was a great look for his lean frame, and she found herself grinning in appreciation. He looked only slightly sheepish in return. "Had to change from the crime scene anyway. And since I'm off duty, I thought I'd check out a look other than the uniform."

"It works on you. Although the short hair still says, 'Cop.'" She grabbed her purse and walked with him to the parking lot, where she stopped, wide-eyed, when he unlocked a black Dodge Charger.

He feigned surprise at her reaction. "What? Sheriffs have private lives."

She whistled. "That's one hot car. You could chase down a few miscreants in that."

He chuckled and opened the passenger door for her. "It's fast, but it doesn't have the power of a patrol car."

She slipped in and buckled her seatbelt as he walked around. As he got behind the wheel, she whispered, "It even still smells new."

He whispered back. "Air freshener."

She laughed, grateful for the easy banter between them. It had been a tense few days. "So what did you find at the house?"

He put the car in reverse. "It was Freddy. He still had his wallet in his back pocket, but we'll confirm with fingerprints. He'd been printed for his job, and he had been picked up once in Tennessee for suspicion of pandering—"

"Pandering? Are you serious?"

He shook his head. "A misunderstanding. I talked to a police chief up there who said that Freddy was … a little naïve. He always believed the best in people. He knew this girl who convinced Freddy to drive her to a couple of hot-sheet motels so that she could pick up some Avon orders."

Molly stared. "He believed her."

"Every word. Even tried to convince the cop he was wrong about arresting her."

"Bird said that Freddy was sweet on Lyric."

"That makes sense. He'd believe her to be wonderful, and she'd love that, every scoop of it. I've asked her father to bring her up here tomorrow morning for an interview."

"Y'know, I kinda hope she has nothing to do with this. That someone else told her he went home."

"You're not getting soft on me, are you?"

She waved away the notion. "Nah, I still want to string her up for what they did to Aunt Liz. But I do think she needs a break if it means getting her permanently away from Kitty. Anything else major at the house?"

"Just one. After the coroner removed the body, we were examining the area around it, and we found another stash of jewels."

Dismay shot through Molly. "Not another one! I seriously didn't know Liz had so many tucked away. Russell could have helped her get a safe deposit box if she thought they might be taken." Greg remained silent, and Molly's curiosity piqued. "What?"

He shook his head. "I'm not sure, but I don't think these were Liz's. They were in a small metal briefcase, and some of the loose jewels were wrapped in fabric and secured in small bags. Two of the necklaces didn't look like anything Liz would wear. I don't think they're hers."

"You think they're stolen?"

"I do. I sent photos to buddies I know in Birmingham's Burglary Division and Gadsden's Property Crime Department. If anything this substantial's been reported, they should have it."

Molly absorbed this information, with a nagging thought in the back of her head. "Would a case like that survive a fire?"

Greg didn't hesitate. "Yes. It's built for that."

"I'm starting to have second thoughts about staying in the house."

"I don't think you should stay there until it's empty and sterilized with bleach."

"Speaking of—"

"Not for a few more days. We have a team there around the clock, but it's still going to take some time. We need to finish processing the area around the body … and I want to take a second look at where Liz died. Have you cleaned that area?"

"Not yet. I was saving it until I'd gone through more of her journals. I have a feeling there's more in that room that I need to search for with care. Not just start lugging stuff out." She paused. "But I have asked Russell to pull the autopsy report. I'm meeting him tomorrow at nine."

Greg took this in. "What do you hope to find in the report?"

"Not sure, really. But I've seen where Finn found her. I guess … settle some of my curiosity." Molly suddenly realized how this must sound to him. "I mean, I know you investigated—"

"We did." His tone was a bit tight.

Hush, Molly, you're going to trip over your own tongue. She waited.

Greg slowly smiled. "Don't worry about it. Truth is, the coroner looked at the scene and immediately decided it was an accident. So did I. There was blood on a table she'd hit on the way down. She had become fragile. EMTs had already been to the house a half-dozen times because she'd fallen. To tell you the truth, we had no reason to think otherwise. It never occurred to us that someone would want Liz Morrow dead."

Molly felt a stab of pain. "I didn't know all that."

Greg glanced at her. "All what?"

"About her frailty. Her falling. She had written that she was ill …" Her voice trailed off and she stared out the window. "But I didn't realize …"

"Molly," Greg spoke quietly. "I don't think she let anyone know how bad it had gotten. Not Finn, not even Russell. And Lyric and Kitty were just biding their time."

"I still want to hoist them up the nearest pine tree."

"Get in line. I think about half the county has some grievance against them. I even have a report from Nina reporting Kitty for stealing eggs!"

"Oh, how I love small-town life. Stolen eggs. Jewel thieves. Murder."

"It keeps me on my toes."

Jimmy is from a small town …

Molly blinked back the thought and turned her face toward the passenger window. Not now.

But after a moment of silence, Greg asked gently, "What's wrong?"

She waved away the question. "Nothing."

"Molly …"

"It's not about here."

"Didn't ask if it was. But you definitely went somewhere else right then. Somewhere painful."

Molly felt a twinge of annoyance as she looked around at him. "Are you psychic now?"

"No," he replied slowly, "but these windows are reflective at night. You can stare out the window all you want. I can still see your face."

A laugh burst from Molly. "You're wicked."

"True. But concerned. Talk to me."

She told him about the packet from Jimmy. "I heard right back from the magazine. The interview is set for Sunday afternoon. It's a good opportunity, and they've already agreed to buy a couple of the pictures. Would help pay for some of the stuff I'm doing here. The job? Maybe."

"Is the job something you want?"

Molly looked back out the window. "I don't know. It's becoming harder to make any kind of living—much less a really good one—as a freelance storm chaser. It would allow me to keep doing that, but I'm not thrilled with being anchored in St. Louis. And I have to admit it hurts that they won't be with me. I thought … I guess I thought that our partnership was more than jobs to them. We're friends. We've been through a lot. For it to just … end." She shrugged. "It's a lot to think about with everything else going on."

"Change is never easy, even when it has to happen."

Molly heard the pain in his voice, and spoke softly, "What was she like?"

He didn't miss a beat. "Sweet. Kind. Pretty much my opposite."

"How did you meet her?"

He grinned. "College. Juniors. I was in criminal justice and she was an English major. We both took psychology. Married before the year was out. Her parents didn't like me much. The military brat. A cop. But they got over it."

"Good for them."

"Ha! They fully expected to have to support us. But I got a job right away, and we did okay."

"What was her name?"

"Anna. Anna Marie." Greg's face softened, and he fell silent. They rode without speaking a few moments, then Molly turned her head as the Gadsden city limits sign disappeared over her shoulder. "Wait … Where are we going?"

Greg's grin was mischievous. "I thought you might be tired of the Waffle House and the Bistro. Top O' the River has the best catfish in the area. Creole shrimp. Broiled crab."

Her mouth watered. "Sounds like heaven."

"They even have fried dill pickles."

Molly stared at him, not entirely sure he was serious. "Um. Pass."

He laughed. "You don't know what you're missing."

* * *

Molly slept solidly for the first time in days. She blamed the catfish, which had pleased a palate definitely weary of fast food and sandwiches. She'd even tried the fried dill pickles, pronouncing them a taste that had to be acquired over a long period of time, which made Greg laugh.

And she liked making him laugh. From the first day they met, he had been her best source of hope and information. He'd encouraged her, and he'd told her more about her family than anyone else could. He was responsible for her current truce with Bird …

Bird. The old man had called her late last night to ask in a harsh whisper if the body was really Freddy. When she confirmed it, he'd hung up on her.

"'Curiouser and curiouser,' said Alice." Molly peered into the mirror as she attempted to put some kind of control on her curls. Her gut told her Bird's drawers were in a twist because he knew something about Freddy's death. She'd mention the call to Russell and Greg later.

Giving up on her hair, she fluffed it, slipped on a headband, and headed out. She'd never worn a lot of makeup—her job didn't exactly demand it—but since arriving in Carterton, she'd abandoned it entirely. It was kinda freeing not to worry about how her face looked every time she left the room.

She got in the Explorer and turned the key. Nada. "Come on, baby. You have to start. I can't afford a new car right now." Molly waited a few moments and tried again. There was a hesitation, then the motor turned over. She let it run for a few moments, running her hand across the dash. "I know I've asked a lot of you the last couple of weeks." She thought about the storm she'd left behind, when she'd almost tipped it over and had to use the four-wheel drive to plow out of mud. "Um, the past few months." And then there were the storms she'd photographed over the last seven years.

"Okay," she confessed. "Years. But you're too much of a trooper to give up now!" With a grin, she put the SUV in gear and backed out of the space.

Molly was a bit wary of turning the Explorer off when she got to Russell's building but had no choice. "Be good," she whispered as she got out.

Immediately, she looked around for Kitty, but the parking lot was relative-free. She headed into the building, thinking about the astonishing events that had taken place since the last time she'd been here. She took the elevator up and entered Russell's office to find it exceptionally quiet. "Right," she said. "Saturday."

"Molly?" Russell called from down the hallway.

"It's me!"

"Lock the door and come on in here!"

She did, to find Russell seated at his conference table, several books and file folders set in neat rows in front of him. She thought she recognized Liz's folder, but she couldn't be sure. Legal folders tended to look alike.

"What's all this?"

He stood and pulled out a chair for her. "Sit. I have the report for you, but I thought we'd go over how Wednesday will proceed, if you have time. Have you ever been through a will probate?"

"Nope." Molly sat.

Russell did as well, and slid a thin folder toward her. "Before you look at the autopsy report, know that it could be rough. Do you want to look at it in private?"

She shook her head and pulled the folder closer. "No, but I have some questions you may find awkward to answer."

"More awkward than you asking if I had slept with my client?" A smile lit his eyes.

Molly relented. "Well, I hope not. Thanks for getting this."

"No problem. Autopsy reports are public record in Alabama. The rest came as a few favors." He nodded at the folder, and she pulled her list of questions out of her purse. Taking a bracing breath, she opened the folder.

He had gathered everything she wanted to see: the autopsy report, the official police report, the officer's notes, signed by Greg, and the EMT's report. She wasn't entirely sure what she hoped to find—more like she'd know it when she saw it.

At first, everything seemed straightforward: an older woman—who'd fallen before—had gotten up from her bed at about two in the afternoon. She was found wearing her nightgown. She had tripped and fallen again, hitting her head on an accent table. On her way down, she had grabbed for a stack of books, magazines, and boxes, which had collapsed on top of her, the weight apparently causing her to suffocate. Her live-in caregiver, Lyric Filbyhouse, had not been home at the time. She returned around four.

Molly stopped and added a question to her list: *Where was Lyric at the time?*

A neighbor, Finbar Eccles, who had been trying to reach Elizabeth Morrow on the phone for more than an hour, had come over to check on her and found her body. He called 911 and performed a rudimentary attempt at CPR.

The EMTs arrived, but it was clear Ms. Morrow was deceased. They called the coroner and retreated until needed further. The sheriff, Gregory Olson, arrived shortly after the EMTs. He surveyed and mapped the scene, took photographs, and waited for the coroner.

Molly paused and searched through the file for Greg's map. It was neat, thorough, and a fairly accurate representation of the way the room looked right now. She went back to reading.

The coroner had arrived, pronounced Ms. Morrow's approximate time of death, and had given instructions for his team to remove the body to the morgue in Gadsden. Since she had died at home under complicated circumstances, an autopsy would be done. The home was released to Mr. Russell Williams, the deceased's attorney, who had arrived shortly after the coroner.

Molly looked up. "How did you get there so fast?"

"Greg called me the minute he got the 911 from Finn."

"Prearranged?"

"Yes. Liz had left the information with him after she called 911 the second time due to a fall. She wanted to make sure he would not be obligated to call the next of kin first."

"Who would be Bird."

"Correct."

Molly turned the page to the autopsy report. The clinical descriptions on a blank outline of a human figure helped ease the impact that this was about her aunt. Official cause of death was suffocation, but Molly read each detail carefully. The bruises from previous falls. Four broken ribs, probably from the collapsing boxes or CPR, or both, along with an old, long-healed fracture of the tibia. No signs of sexual assault. The blow to the head caused by a hard, pointed object, which had obviously been the corner of the table.

There was a significant amount of dirt and debris on her back and in her hair. The bottoms of her feet were coated in mud.

Molly stopped. *Mud?* She made a note. The house was filthy, but not enough to coat her feet. Then, as Molly came to the bottom of the page, she froze, and every nerve snapped to attention. Ms. Morrow also had a significant amount of dust and goose down in her nostrils, probably from having just gotten out of bed.

Molly sat very still, finally looking up at Russell. Her face felt hot, and her hands trembled as she turned the file around and pointed at the note. He read it, and at first he shook his head. "I don't know what—" He broke off suddenly as realization hit and his eyes widened.

Molly said it, even though she didn't have to. "Aunt Liz was allergic to feathers. She's never slept on a feather pillow or under a down comforter a day in her life. The only feather pillow in that room is Lyric's."

14

"They killed her, Russell."

"Molly, we cannot go accusing them of this."

"They knocked her down, and when she was unconscious, they pressed Lyric's pillow over her face until she suffocated. Then they covered her up in her own garbage."

"Molly—"

Molly had been pacing Russell's office with long, loping strides ever since she realized what the down in Liz's nostrils had to mean. "They killed her. I don't know if it was Lyric or Kitty or Nina or one of those rotten grandchildren, but one of them killed her!" She pointed at the report, still lying on the table. "I swear I'll hunt every one of them down and beat them till they confess!"

"Molly, stop it!"

She halted, chewing her lip. "Russell, I swear—"

"Don't say it, Molly. Don't say it out loud again. Don't think it. You blurt this out in front of someone, and you'll be in far more trouble than they will be. You cannot be dragged into thinking about revenge. They are not worth it!"

"But Liz is!"

"I know. Believe me. I know." His words were low, dark, and choked.

Molly felt some of her fury drain away. His words, those two words, carried with them the weight of love, loss, and regret. Two words.

I know.

Molly ran her hands through her hair, pulling free the headband, and she shook her fingers as if to fling away spiderwebs. "Okay. So what's your plan?"

"Sit, please." When Molly dropped reluctantly into the chair, he spoke slowly. "First, we have no hard evidence she was murdered."

Molly jerked her finger at the report.

He relented. "Fine. We have no hard evidence as to who killed her. That house was an open-air landfill. People came and went whenever they pleased. Finn said that Freddy worked odd shifts. Lyric and Kitty both were in and out, as were most of the grandkids. They wanted something special for a party? No worries. Aunt Liz won't miss it."

Molly crossed her arms, hugging herself. "So what do we do?"

"First, we call Greg and Judge Keeley. Tell them our suspicions, see what they say. I'm fairly sure that finding feathers in her nose will not be enough to overturn the coroner's ruling on cause of death." He paused. "But it might be probable cause to have her exhumed."

Molly leaned over the table toward him. "Are you sure? Wasn't she embalmed?"

"Yes. But if they pressed the pillow over her hard enough to kill her, there may be other traces in her lungs the coroner didn't find. We'll have to talk to him." Then, after a moment, he shook his head. "Do I want to do it? No. But with Freddy's death, there's already proof that someone's willing to kill over what's in that house. It's not a great leap that Liz's death might not have been accidental."

"What would a second examination prove?"

He gestured at the description. "What's missing in this report?"

Molly didn't understand and shook her head.

"She supposedly died under the weight of boxes and books that fell on her."

Molly straightened. "But the only bruises were old ones, from previous falls."

Russell nodded. "Exactly. Liz was frail. She bruised easy. She used to tell me that she'd bruise if you looked at her funny. So why were there no signs of impact on her skin? In some accidents, bruising doesn't show up until after death. But an exhumation would confirm the lack of injury." He sighed. "Pure speculation. We need to talk to the coroner."

Molly shook her head. "Let's hope Greg and the judge can come up with something so we don't have to do that."

He closed the report. "What were your other questions?"

"Where was Lyric when this happened?"

"Supposedly out getting food. It was about two in the afternoon."

Molly thought about it for a second. "Where was the food from? New York?"

Russell scowled. "What?"

"Finn had been trying to call Aunt Liz for more than an hour. He got there around three, called 911, started CPR. The EMTs showed up. Greg showed up. The coroner showed up. Only then did Lyric return, after four. Seriously, how long does it take to get takeout in a town not much larger than a Super Walmart?"

"Obviously, something we need to ask her. And?"

"Why were Aunt Liz's feet coated in mud? She supposedly had just gotten out of bed. Two in the afternoon. In her nightgown. Feet covered in mud. Does any of that make sense to you, knowing Liz as you did?"

Russell leaned back in his chair. "No. None of it."

Molly closed her eyes, suddenly exhausted. Nothing about this made sense. Her entire body ached with grief and anger, frustration and a determination to find answers. She just didn't know how to start.

Greg. Start with Greg.

He is with Lyric right now.

Molly's eyes snapped open. "We need to call Greg. Now."

* * *

Molly strode back and forth through the sheriff's bullpen, but the pacing did little to dampen her irritation. Russell sat at one of the empty desks, making notes on a legal pad. The one deputy in-house seemed torn between keeping his eye on Molly and Russell and the occupied interview room, where Greg had been interviewing Lyric Filbyhouse and her father for almost two hours. When the sheriff emerged, the young deputy eagerly took his place in the room and shut the door.

Greg, carrying his own legal pad full of notes, motioned for Russell and Molly to follow him into his office. Inside, Greg shut the door as Russell sat. Molly stood. "Well?" she demanded.

Greg shook his head and dropped the pad on the desk. "Nothing helpful."

Molly crossed her arms. "She has to know something!"

Sitting down, he peeled back a couple of pages. "She's a mess. When we started out, she was crazy to talk about Freddy, what a good man he was, how he'd been great to her—"

"But—" Molly started.

Greg held up a finger and continued talking. "How he was visiting friends in Tennessee but had a good job here and would be back, and they were going to get married next summer and finally get away from Kitty ..." His voice trailed off and he looked up at her, then Russell.

Russell sighed. "She didn't know he was dead."

Greg shook his head. "Nope. And I believe her. The kid is a superhero in her eyes. She started talking about him taking her to Vulcan Park in Birmingham, then it evolved into this odd adventure story that became more unbelievable, until her father realized she was talking about a movie they'd both seen." He looked from Russell to Molly. "That took a full half hour."

"Dear Lord," she muttered.

"Indeed. When I did finally get her focused on what was going on at the house, she kept insisting that Freddy had nothing to do with whatever LJ and his buddies were up to."

"What does that mean?" she asked.

"No idea. She did keep repeating that Kitty should just adopt LJ since she liked him better than she liked her own daughter."

"That poor girl," Russell said. "Kitty has done a number on her."

"No doubt about that," Greg agreed. "I did get her to admit that Liz never used that down pillow. Said it gave Liz hives."

Molly looked at Russell. "Told you."

Russell dismissed her with a wave. "It's still not evidence of murder."

"No, it's not," Greg said. "But it does create suspicion where none existed before." Before Molly could speak, he pressed on. "When ... WHEN ... we gather enough, it'll be ammunition to put before a judge."

Molly gestured in the direction of the interview room and her voice caught, her throat tight. "Did you tell her?"

Greg paused. "Yes. About fifteen minutes ago. She hasn't stopped crying since. And with that news, her father realized that Lyric could be in some serious trouble. He stopped the interview and asked for a lawyer."

Russell straightened. "I could recommend a good one. She won't cost much. And I know a couple of the legal aid folks."

Greg nodded, and Russell stood, straightened his suit, and left the office. Greg remained silent, watching Molly as she crossed and uncrossed her arms, shifting her weight from one foot to the other. The war inside her felt as if it were tearing her apart. Her entire being ached, and not a single thought would focus in her mind. "I don't—" she started, then stopped, wiping her mouth with one hand, pure frustration making her tremble.

Greg waited.

She thrust her arms down by her sides, her fists clenched, and it all came out in a rush, in one breath. "I don't know what to do. Or how to feel! I should be angry at Lyric, but she seems more a victim than villain. We have no evidence on anyone else. There's a dead body in my house, some kid—a good kid!—I didn't even know existed and now he's dead. Shot, maybe somewhere else in the house. There are a thousand requests for stuff out of the house—and not just Bird or Kitty or any of them. Liz left journals that are part memoir, part conspiracy theory, part recipe book, part family history. People are shooting at me, trying to burn me out. Sarah's still unconscious and Jimmy's ended the partnership, and I have a job offer in St. Louis, but they have to know by the end of the month, and I don't think I can finish here by the end of the month. I literally don't know which way to turn!"

Greg simply observed her, still waiting. Molly's rush of energy drained away, and she slumped in the chair.

Greg came from behind his desk and sat in the chair next to her. He took one of her hands in his. "Molly, you're trying to photograph the storm, the supercell, the vista, instead of the farmhouse underneath it."

She looked at him, slowly absorbing what he was saying. The heat of his hands sent reassuring warmth through her. "I'm trying to take it all in at once."

He nodded and leaned forward, focusing on her face. "And you can't. You want to see the end of the story when you haven't even made it through the middle yet. Stop. Don't just read the journals for information. Read them for bits of understanding. Start making lists—you're good at it. But compartmentalize. Don't jumble what's going on with you and Bird with what's going on with the house or what's going on in Missouri. Or the attacks. Or Lyric and Freddy. Or Liz and Freddy. Break everything down. Look at one thing at a time. Make a plan of action and stop getting derailed by sudden hits of inspiration. None of this is going anywhere."

"So … focus on the journals while you finish with the house. Don't think about the crimes right now."

"Exactly. First and foremost because that's *my* job."

"That's why you get the big bucks."

He smiled. "Such as they are." He released her hand and leaned back in the chair. "Freddy's body has been removed, but it'll be at least another twenty-four hours before we're done. I'll keep you posted. Now you and Russell go away. I'll wait for Lyric's lawyer, then get back over to the house."

They stood, and Greg returned to his desk chair. Molly hesitated at the door. "How do you do this? Do you do it all the time?"

"I like puzzles. Mostly I like people."

"People are the reason I chase tornadoes." And Molly left his office, pulling the door shut.

15

August 10, 2010
Gene's kids delivered the remainder of his household goods this morning. Most of it, gratefully, fit in the attic. Some went into the front parlor. Ashley kept thanking me and making noises that they'd be back to get it out as soon as they could, but I know she's lying. Wouldn't meet my eyes. I don't know why they don't sell it. Goodwill it. Something. They all know Gene won't be leaving the facility. Buddy kept saying things like, "This was Grandma's, and it's been in the family for a long time." Like I'd think that Hoosier cabinet had been bought last week ...

==

Christmas Day, 2010
I called Buddy and Ashley to wish them a Merry Christmas. They didn't answer the phone. I left a message. Gene's been gone a month now. They never answered my letter either ...

==

June 12, 2011
Buddy and Ashley have moved to Montana. I called Tate (Ashley's sister), but she has no interest in the stuff either, even the Hoosier cabinet. And it's worth some money. I checked it out on

eBay. But Tate's sorry they just dumped the stuff on me. We talked for a long time, and she told me the missing pieces of the history on the Hoosier and some of the other pieces. I think I'll write them up and tape them inside the pieces.

==

July 4, 2011
Happy Birthday, America! Great cookout today. Some of the family showed up, but mostly the neighbors. Finn's been a big help lately. My sugar's getting worse, so I'm trying to lose some weight, but boy can Linda cook a fantastic red-white-and-blueberry pie! Yum. Stole a second piece for later. Roy hung around later, asked if he could store some stuff in the basement. Yeah … whatever. Everyone else is doing it, why not him …

==

February 3, 2012
Tried to clean some today. The clutter in the front rooms is starting to get to me. Snow on the ground, so I was stuck here. Made some progress, but it's hard to clean when you don't feel like you can get rid of items belonging to other people. I got Buddy's address from Tate. I sent him a letter asking permission to sell some of the items. No response yet …

==

February 18, 2012
Carter Jackson stopped by today, told me he could definitely move some of this furniture down at the auction house. No word from Buddy.

==

September 5, 2012
Betty June died last week. Her daughter stopped by today to ask if I could keep some things while they finished cleaning out the house. Somebody tell me why I can't ever say no to these people …

==

Taping butcher paper to the walls of her hotel room, Molly began constructing a grid of items, origins, and possible contacts for all the major items in the house. Russell had already told her she'd have to provide an inventory of anything of major value in the estate to the court before any of it could be sold or distributed. Any items that had been sold or given away so far were minor pieces not worth enough to be inventoried.

The journals had turned out to be a wealth of information, and Molly had been able to break the entries down into three major categories: everyday events, items being moved in, family stories. Almost every entry related in some way to one of those topics. As she broke down each journal and translated the information onto the charts, an odd history of what had happened to Liz began to emerge.

Thomas Morrow and Rebecca Jenkins Morrow, Molly's grandparents, each had two siblings. Those siblings had seven children between them, plus the three Thomas and Rebecca raised—Bird, Liz, and Molly's mother, Regina. That second generation—the ten cousins—had created the most trouble, borrowing from their parents, swapping possessions faster than underwear, and all of them apparently more interested in what a piece of furniture stood for in the family history than what it took to take care of it. Nobody wanted to keep them; nobody wanted to get rid of them.

So Liz, the family genealogist, suddenly became the keeper of all things family history, whether it was a letter from a great-grandparent or a highboy dresser. Over the course of eighteen months, three families had abruptly dumped almost entire households of furniture and boxes on Liz, asking her to "keep it for a while." Only they never came back to get anything. And their kids certainly didn't. Ashley, Tate, and Buddy were Molly's age, more interested in moving to Montana and living in a tiny house than dealing with family furniture. But they were still too connected to a sense of "family history" to get rid of anything.

Molly crossed her arms, staring at her charts. "Heaven forbid you sell Grandma's buffet, even though you didn't want it in your house. No wonder one of America's fastest growing businesses is storage facilities."

With a house overloaded, Liz found cleaning next to impossible. So more stuff, trash, and the detritus of everyday life piled up around her. She'd tried the auction idea—she'd sent three large items, which had brought in a nice bit of cash—but Bird and some of the others had created such a ruckus, she had no energy to continue. That's when Liz began to plot Molly's involvement. Starting in late 2013, almost all the journal entries were addressed to "Mollybelle."

Molly finished another journal entry and made a note on the butcher paper. "Liz, you old dog, you set me up a long time ago, didn't you? No wonder you kept sending me so many letters." She drew an arching line between two family events from the journal, then sat back at her desk. The next few entries were of the "everyday life" type—grocery shopping, menu planning, a trip to the hairdresser—Liz left nothing out. Then came the entry that made Molly's eyebrows arch.

==

August 12, 2014
Ah, Mollybelle! A sweet day! I heard back from Mickey. I had written him about my plans to set everything up for you to handle once I was gone. He doesn't write much these days, which I can understand. I do hope you two can meet again someday, so he can tell you why he's not part of this. It's just not my place, or I would have told you long ago. He has asked for your address, but since you don't really have a physical address, just the phone number and email, I don't know if he'll reach out. Or if he can. But I

gave them to him. Anyway, I had explained, and he completely approves. He thinks that if anyone in this family can deal with this in the way I want it to happen, it'll be you. He said you had great moxie. I always liked that word—moxie. It's so you.

==

Molly pushed the journal back. *What in the world had Mickey done? Prison? Overseas, like Bobby? What?* Whatever had happened, he'd never reached out to her. But, *could* he reach out to her?

Stop it. This will make you crazy.

Her phone beeped. She scooped it up to check the text from Greg, which made her pause almost as much as Liz's entry.

Church tomorrow? I can pick you up at 10.

Molly stared at it. *Church? Is he kidding?* Molly set the phone aside, staring idly at the labyrinth of names, possessions, and events on the butcher paper covering her wall. Church had always meant family, and she hadn't been inside one since her mother's funeral. For her, church had nothing to do with God. God was in the storms, the power of His creation. Molly marveled at what God had brought forth on a regular basis.

But church? No.

She picked up the phone, and typed her reply. *Thanks, but I'll pass tomorrow. Need to get ready for the interview.*

But she paused before she hit send. *No. Don't lie to him. Not him.* She backspaced and retyped the last sentence. *Thanks, but I'll pass tomorrow. Not ready for church yet.*

She hit send. That was absolutely the truth. But she also doubted that she'd ever be ready. Molly pulled a journal toward her and kept reading. Greg did not reply.

* * *

At 9:00 a.m. Sunday, just as Molly took the last bite of her power-bar-and-Coke breakfast, a knock on the door startled her away from the latest journal. She scowled. She wasn't expecting anyone. Molly checked her phone for texts, to discover she'd missed one while she had showered. From Greg: *I'll be there around 9.*

Still, Molly checked through the peephole, just to make sure. Greg stood there, quite handsome in a three-piece navy blue suit. She ran her hands through her hair in a vain attempt to smooth the curls and pulled open the door. "Wow. You clean up nice."

A twinge of red flashed on his cheeks. "Thanks."

"I'm still not going to church this morning."

The red spread and his eyes widened. "Oh. No. I didn't think …" His voice trailed off and he cleared his throat. "The forensics techs are finished with the house. I thought you might like a ride over, not be alone the first time. We have plenty of time before church."

Molly felt her own flush of heat, not quite sure why. "Sure. Let me get my phone and purse." Greg waited at the door while she grabbed them. As they settled into the Charger, she asked tentatively, "Anything you can share?"

He hesitated for a moment, his eyes focused on the road. "He was shot twice with what looks like a 9mm. That's the pathologist's preliminary estimate. She found entrance and exit wounds on both. The techs didn't find the bullets, but they didn't really know where to look. If we can find where he was shot, that would help, but 9mm guns are as plentiful in this county as snakes. Unless it's been used in a crime, ballistics won't be on file."

He paused as he turned onto Maple Street. "I talked to Freddy's boss. The kid was a virtual saint. Always on time. No conflicts. No arguments. Customers loved him. He wasn't, as Bird would say, 'slow.' He was just a sweet kid who liked people."

"So this isn't about him."

"My guess is he saw something or got in someone's way."

"When do they think it happened?"

Greg hesitated again, just as he turned into the drive. He put the Charger in park and turned off the ignition. He finally looked at her. "It's hard to pinpoint, given the decomposition, but he thinks it's about the time Liz died. Maybe before."

Molly felt an icy calm settle over her. "You think they were killed at the same time."

"Yes. And I need you to promise me something."

"What?"

"We're releasing the house to you, but you know there's no way it's been completely processed. With the condition it's in, that's impossible. What I want you to promise me is that if you see any sign, any inkling of another crime scene, you stop, clear the house, and call me."

"What am I looking for, besides blood?"

His mouth twisted. "Normally I'd say anything that looked odd …"

Molly coughed. "But in this case, that might be a little difficult."

He looked back at the house. "I don't know. You seemed to be getting a feel for the place. And you're the one who's questioned the lack of bruising on Liz. You're used to spotting patterns in ever-changing clouds. My guess is that if something is off, you'll spot it. How's the work with the journals going?"

The change of subject startled Molly, and she stumbled over the first few words. "Uh, good. I'm finding … speaking of patterns … I'm finding a method to Liz's madness. I only started with the ones from a few years ago. I suspect that the older ones will be an intriguing look at Carterton. But these mostly chronicle what happened since people started dumping stuff on her."

She looked out at the house again. "You know, for more than twenty-five years, I've tried to understand the need for collecting possessions. I know what psychologists say. I know all the theories." She tapped the side of her head. "I get it … here. Intellectually. Maybe. Sort of." She tapped her chest. "But here. I don't think I'll ever truly understand."

Greg shrugged and opened his car door. "You're wired not to."

Molly followed him, and they headed toward the house. "What do you mean?"

"Molly, everyone is unique. God wired us all in different ways so that we could use our gifts in ways He intended. You see patterns. Developing storms. Liz's method of surviving. You have an artistic eye with a camera lens. You are outwardly focused. That's why you can do this."

Molly peered at him as they stepped up on the porch. *How does he know I have an artistic—? Wait.* "You looked me up?"

The twin spots of red reappeared in his cheeks, but his face remained stoic. "You're a stranger in my town. Of course I looked you up."

"What did you think?"

"You're a great photographer. A risk-taker. Odd sense of humor, but you do chase tornadoes for a living. Are you going to open the door or not?"

Grinning, she pulled out her key and opened the door.

Not much had changed, but Molly hadn't expected it to. The forensic techs had mostly confined their work to the attic. The front rooms, their raw wooden floors and tattered wallpaper looking sadder than ever, echoed as they walked through, looking at the lines of furniture. Molly ran her hand along the edge of one table.

"This table has been in the family since 1880. Liz wanted it to go to one of the nephews. I've got an extensive inventory for the probate on Wednesday, but there's still a lot of work to do."

"What about Liz's room?"

Molly shook her head. "It's been a little hard to tackle that one. But I'll start today."

Greg checked his watch. "I need to—"

"It's okay. I've got everything I need here to start. I don't have to go back to the room. Maybe pick me up after?"

He nodded. "We'll get some lunch."

"And I have that interview this afternoon. So I won't get much done here today. We'll start fresh tomorrow."

Greg left, pulling the front door shut, a solid sound that bounced around the walls. The house was definitely well built. The windows still stood wide open, and a light breeze stirred the tattered and dirty lace curtains on the windows. With most of the downstairs garbage removed and lots of fresh air circulating through the house the week before, much of the mustiness had cleared, and with Freddy removed, the remaining odors weren't as toxic. Molly decided that she could forgo the Tyvek suit. But a lingering scent of decay and rot still tickled her nose.

Get to work. You'll get used to it.

Molly headed for Liz's room and opened the door slowly, standing in the frame. After she'd pulled the journals out from under the bed, Molly hadn't spent much time in here. Now she gazed around the room slowly, trying to take all of it in.

The room measured almost twenty by twenty, big enough for a bed, dresser, couch, recliner, large screen television, and two walls of shelves. And ceiling-high stacks of magazines, newspapers, books, boxes, and storage bins, looking like cumbersome columns towering over everything else. Two of those columns had collapsed, allegedly killing Liz, and their piles still lay scattered over what little floor space remained. Molly skirted those to get to the shelves behind the bed.

"Hi, Mr. Bromby." She gingerly picked up the bear, cradling it in both hands to keep it from flopping around. "You must have kept Liz company for a long time." Molly frowned. "How did she end up with you anyway? Last time I saw you was—"

In the house by the tracks.

She looked up at the picture of her with Jezebel. That had been next to her mother's bed.

Molly scanned the shelves, her gaze lingering on each object for only a moment, as a deep dread grew in her gut, spreading as she took in the bed, the stack of twenty-year-old magazines in a corner of the room, the table in the corner. The bed had been her mother's. Regina's. Aunt Liz always slept in a huge four-poster antique bed that she'd found at an auction. In a bedroom on the second floor. The table had been next to their couch.

Molly moaned. Almost everything in this room had been left behind when she left for Tulsa. "Oh, Aunt Liz! I am so sorry!" She sank down on the bed. "Did we start this? Did *I* start this?"

Something brushed her leg.

Molly jumped high and left. Her screech echoed through the house as she looked down into golden eyes and a fluffy orange coat. Molly finally inhaled, even though her heart still raced. She put a hand on her chest. "Blossom?"

"Merroow." The orange tabby leaped up on the bed. Molly offered a hand for the cat to sniff. Which he did, then head-butted it affectionately.

She stroked him. "Where have you been? You haven't been hiding out here, have you? If you have, don't go eating any of the dead stuff you find. It won't be good for you. Nasty stuff." But he would. Molly knew she couldn't leave him in the house. She wondered if Linda could keep him. She'd been feeding him as an outdoor cat, but now that the house was open a lot, Molly knew he'd find his way back into his home.

She picked the cat up, and he nuzzled into the crook of her neck, purring. "Hope Leon likes cats," she whispered. "If I couldn't save Aunt Liz, at least I can save you."

After a few moments, she put Blossom down and set to work. Back in the front yard, she found a box of rubber gloves left behind when they'd had to walk away, and she set to removing boxes and bins from Liz's room. She grabbed an empty box from the yard and packed up the few things Lyric had requested—some gossip magazines, a journal, sparkly pens, a few clothes. Finally she reached for Lyric's feather pillow, which had been tossed onto the foot of the bed.

She paused, staring at it, thinking about the down in Liz's nostrils. She knew the argument could be made that the house was filthy, feathers probably floated in the air as a matter of due course. There were other items stored in the house that contained down: they'd already dropped two moldy down comforters into the dumpster outside. One of the rooms upstairs had a stack of pillows in the corner that reached to the ceiling. Still …

Molly tugged the pillowcase smooth, looking closely at it. Nothing, just the usual smears of makeup—Lyric wore make-up?—and rings of saliva stains. Molly slowly flipped the pillow over. More makeup. More spit.

And a heart-shaped rust-colored stain, right in the middle.

Blood.

16

"It could be Lyric's. She could have scratched herself."

"Yes."

"People do that you know. Scratch themselves in their sleep. I've done it."

"Yes."

"But you don't think so."

"It has to be tested."

"Down feathers in her nose. Her blood on the pillow. But it still wouldn't be enough."

"No."

"No idea who held the pillow."

"Exactly."

"I hate this. And I want the house back."

Greg and Molly stood in the front yard, watching as forensic techs scurried in and out of the house again, this time removing everything from Liz's room, including the boxes Molly had already pulled out.

"You were right to call me back."

One of the techs paused on the porch and raised his arm at Greg. "Sheriff?"

Greg nodded and started toward the house. When Molly followed, he stopped her. "Not this time. Stay here."

"I hate this."

"So you've said. I'll be out in a minute. What time is your interview?"

"Three."

He checked his watched, nodded, then headed into the house.

Molly crossed her arms and hugged herself. "I hate this," she whispered. "Liz, what in the world happened here?"

The sound of a muffler-deprived Impala drew her attention to Maple Street, where Kitty's car chugged to a halt, dieseled a few times, then fell silent. Kitty shoved her way out of it, then headed toward Molly. Molly strode toward her, not wanting Kitty to get far into the yard. "What do you want, Kitty?"

"What's mine! What's Lyric's! Someone called me and said strangers were taking stuff away. You said you wouldn't get rid of anything without telling us." She waved a hand at the forensic techs, who were packing boxes into a large white van. "What are they doing?"

"Collecting evidence."

Kitty stopped, staring at Molly. "Evidence of what?"

"Murder."

Kitty ran a hand across her mouth. "So it's true. I just thought you were being cruel. Freddy's dead?"

"Yes."

Kitty twisted back and forth, looking from the house to Molly, around the neighborhood, behind her, back to Molly. "No, this ain't right."

"It's not. But it's happened. They removed his body, and they've been going over the house. More evidence was found today. What do you know about this?"

Kitty stilled, her eyes wide. "Me? What would I have to do with it?"

Molly made her voice as monotone as possible. "In and out of the house all the time. Your daughter lived here. She and Freddy were seeing each other—"

"Liar!" Kitty screamed. "She and LJ—" Her voice broke, and she backed away from Molly. "You're a liar!" She spun around and marched back to the Impala, gunning it forcefully as she turned it around in Linda's drive and sped off.

"What was that all about?"

Molly jumped at Greg's voice, then let out a long sigh. "Kitty being Kitty. I'm not even sure what she was talking about, except that she apparently didn't know about Lyric and Freddy. I'll have to think about it. What did they find?"

Greg watched the Impala disappear around the corner, his face somber. "Bullets." He held up a small paper evidence bag and shook it. "Four of them. And more blood. I'm on my way to the lab. I'll need to drop you off."

Molly's heart raced, as did her words. "Bullets? Where? In Liz's room? Where? Where was the blood? Four? I thought he was only shot twice."

Greg released a long exhausted sigh. "Freddy was. The walls of Liz's bedroom held three, however, and a fourth was in the floor. That one was covered up by the trash that had buried Liz. That's where the blood was as well."

"So the shooting took place before she died? And they missed twice standing in the same room?"

He shrugged. "Speculation. There could have been a struggle. We have a lot more investigating to do."

Molly's heart sank. "So I'm out of the house for a while longer."

Greg looked down at the bullets, then spoke without facing her. "We need ... you and me ... to keep our distance as well."

Molly felt an odd sensation wash over her, part amusement, part ... loneliness? "Why?"

"I should not have let you back in the house. We should have continued investigating the rest of the house."

"I'm clouding your judgment?"

Greg finally looked up at her. His eyes lit with a smile. "Something like that. Also, our relationship could taint the evidence."

Molly's eyebrows arched and she pointed at the house. "Sheriff Olson, any lawyer worth his shingle is going to get *anything* found in that house tossed. Let's start with the fact that it's been tented and fumigated, has a history of hoarding, and has had a hundred people traipsing through the rooms in the last week." As a stubborn look crossed his face, she relented. "But I get your meaning. I don't like it, but I understand it."

He tucked the bag in the inside pocket of his coat. "Let's get you back to the hotel."

* * *

Molly watched the Charger pull out, closing the door only after it had vanished from sight. The ride back to the hotel had been uncharacteristically silent, and the odd sense of loneliness she'd felt back at the house settled over her again. "Everyone's leaving," she whispered. Jimmy. Sarah.

Greg.

The last time she'd said the exact same thing, Mickey, leaving for the Marines, had hugged her, one of the few times brother and sister would ever share that moment of affection. The Morrows, he'd once told her, were just not a huggy family.

> *"You're leaving. Everyone's leaving."*
>
> *Mickey released her. "All right now. No self-pity, Squirt. Not allowed in this family, remember. We're the strong ones. We stand on our own and get the job done. Let the rest of them whine. They're good at it. But you, me, and Mama. We get it done."*
>
> *"You could stay. Get it done here."*
>
> *Mickey had grimaced, a look of pain that had puzzled Molly. "What?" she asked.*
>
> *"I'll explain it someday. I can't stay. But you have to. Take care of Mama. She's going to need you."*

Molly had not realized exactly how much their mother would need her over the next two years, or that by the time Molly turned eighteen, their mother would be dead, and Molly would bolt for Oklahoma.

"No self-pity, Squirt," she whispered, looking over the scatter of papers, journals, and butcher-paper-covered walls. "We get it done." She dug back into the journals, emerging just before three from a stupor brought on by unending family stories that left her numb. When the Skype tone sounded for the magazine interview, she was glad for the break.

The journalist, a pleasant-looking man in his twenties, had prepared well. He knew her history and had seen a number of her published photos. Their chat lasted more than an hour, and Molly relished the brief return to her regular world of clouds and wind. She shared some of the more remarkable stories from her years as a storm chaser. After the standard questions (yes, it's expensive; no, you don't make a lot of money; yes, it's extremely rough on family and friends), the reporter asked some pointed questions about both the thrills and the aftermaths, the adrenaline and the letdowns, the dangers and the successes. She uploaded several of her recent photos to him, and he promised to get back with her about updating the contract for their publication.

In discussing the dangers of storm chasing, Molly avoided talking about Sarah, that a piece of wood traveling at seventy miles an hour had put the younger woman into a coma. But the sight of Sarah's pale, bloody frame lingered in Molly's mind, along with Jimmy's extraordinary affection toward their injured friend. She should have seen it then, that with Jimmy and Sarah becoming more than friends, their partnership would change.

"But I didn't want to," she whispered to herself as she put aside the laptop and pulled another journal closer. "I didn't want to see that what we had was coming to an end."

Like Mickey leaving. And Mama's death bringing our time in Carterton to a close.

Maybe it was time to go out on her own. Put Carterton permanently in her rearview. Stop putting others in danger. To take the job in St. Louis, and go back to doing what she did best. Making her own way and getting the job done.

* * *

The text from Linda Allen popped up on her phone as Molly put the finishing touches on the draft of her inventory list for Wednesday. She'd take it to the house as soon as she could to finalize it, hoping she'd be able to do that by Tuesday. But Aunt Liz's journals—and the information she had left with Russell—had been a wealth of organized lists detailing everything that had been dumped on Aunt Liz over the years, as well as meandering rambles about things she'd acquired.

Molly wasn't the only one in the family good at lists.

==

I absolutely hate that I'm acting like an accountant with these lists. They are family. I should be able to trust that when they come back they'll take just what they left. But … then again … I did grow up with them. And Bird. They might just snatch up something they want and pack it "by mistake."

I guess that's pretty cynical of me. Or maybe just realistic. Which is why I'm also going to make lists to go with the will.

Oh, Mollybelle! What have we wrought! Greed is going to kill us all.

==

And it had.

The text tone on Molly's phone sounded its second alert, and she leaned over and picked it up.

We've heard what's going on at the house. Sorry. Come over for dinner? Finn's doing steaks and burgers on the grill, and I'm providing the potato salad and veggies. Campfire with s'mores to follow. His house. Please come. 6pm.

Molly smiled. She liked Linda. And she adored Finn and Sheila. Reminders that not everyone in town snatched and clawed for whatever they could get. Linda had opened her home to her brother after both their spouses had died. Now he provided the main income for the household. Finn and Sheila were unbelievably open and kind to everyone around them.

I'll be there. Thank you.

Linda responded with a smiley face.

Molly spent the next hour or so researching the television station in St. Louis, and making a list of questions she wanted to ask Hunter Bradley. Then she leaned back in her chair, and stretched, working the kinks out of her muscles. It felt good to make plans, to have a touch of certainty in her coming week. She would go to dinner, and she should hear from Bradley tomorrow. Wednesday would be the probate hearing. If the will was approved, she'd start sending out messages to potential heirs to see if they actually wanted the things Liz planned to leave them.

And whatever else happened, she'd cope. And get the job done.

At 5:40, she headed for the Explorer, which coughed but started. Molly made herself a note to talk to a mechanic tomorrow. Now was not the time for the most reliable thing in her life to stop being so. She pulled into a station for gas and checked all the fluids under the hood, but she still arrived at Maple Street just before six.

The neighborhood was hopping, crowded with families of all ages spilling out into the street and across the adjoining yards, playing soccer and tossing footballs. She parked at Liz's house, glancing briefly at the yellow crime scene tape still fluttering in the breeze. A white Chevy Suburban sat in the yard, the blue "Crime Scene Unit" on its side announcing to the world what was going on. The house seemed still, but she knew they had to be working inside.

Molly wandered toward Finn's back yard, dodging balls and heys and hellos from a dozen folks as she went. No one stared at her anymore, as though she were the intrusive stranger. As she rounded the rear corner of his house, explosive laughter burst from a group of kids splashing in an above-ground pool near the back of the property. An array of lawn chairs clustered loosely around the grill, where Finn held court with some of the men. Linda and Sheila directed women here and there as they put out a spread of food on a series of picnic tables. One held nothing but drinks and a cooler of ice. Another held desserts, while two others held buns, sandwich fixings, veggies, salads, and chips.

Molly approached Linda, who greeted her with a quick hug. "So glad you came!"

"Can I help?"

Linda cast a glance around the tables. "Yep. We need utensils." She pointed at Finn's back door. "In the kitchen, you'll find some little boxes of plastic forks and spoons in a bigger box on the table. Just grab the little boxes. In the drawer next to the stove will be big spoons for the veggies."

"You got it." Molly headed inside, amused that Linda knew so much about Finn and Sheila's kitchen. "Kitchen friends," she muttered, a term she'd learned from her mother. "True friends are kitchen friends," her mother had told her. "They live in your kitchen and know as much about it as you do."

Did they know this much about Liz?

When Molly emerged with the utensils, Linda and Sheila helped her distribute them across the spread of food. Then they looked at Finn, and Sheila put two fingers in her mouth and sounded a blasting whistle. Finn turned and held up five fingers.

Linda immediately headed for the pool. "Everybody outta the water! Dry off! Rest! Time to eat!" She began herding children and tossing towels over them as Sheila urged the adults to get a drink and pick a chair. That's when Molly spotted Russell sauntering into the back yard in his polo shirt and khakis. She greeted him with a grin.

"Coming here from the golf course?"

He chuckled. "Yep. Finn called me. Told me you were coming."

Molly's eyes narrowed. "Oh?"

Russell shrugged. "I'd mentioned to him that I wanted to have a chat with you away from … everything else. The office. The house. The sheriff's office."

"How come? Is that why they invited me?"

"Nope. I think it's why they invited me. Finn called after he found out you'd be here." He looked around a moment. "It's not like I'm part of the neighborhood."

"Neither am I."

Russell's brows furrowed. "Oh, but you are. At least …" he gestured around the yard. "… they think you are. Finn and Linda both talk as if you're a permanent resident."

Molly shook her head. "I've already decided to go back to St. Louis. I'll be talking tomorrow to someone about a job."

Russell fell silent long enough for Molly to become slightly uncomfortable. She cleared her throat. "Let's grab drinks and chairs."

He nodded and followed her. They settled, watching as a dozen or more kids grabbed buns and gathered around Finn to collect burgers and hot dogs. Molly opened her soda and leaned forward, watching Russell. "What's up?"

He took a sip of his own drink. "I was golfing with Judge Petrie."

"Who is …"

"The judge who will probate Liz's will on Wednesday."

"And?"

"Scuttlebutt is that Bird is planning to show up with a holographic will to contest the one we have. Kitty is planning to show up with an inventory list of items she knows are in the house. If your inventory doesn't match hers, she's going to claim yours is inaccurate. It won't stop anything, but it could delay the process. Give them time to marshal more resources."

"Holographic?" Molly swallowed. "So Bird claims to have a will in Liz's own handwriting?"

"Yes."

"You think it's legit?"

"Doesn't matter. Handwritten wills aren't legal in the state of Alabama. Even if she wrote it, it's worthless."

"You think he knows that?"

"Maybe. Mostly they are determined to stir the pot."

"As you said, delay the distribution until they can find a loophole."

"Something like that."

"So what happens Wednesday?"

Russell took another sip. "Sometimes these things are held in chambers, but Judge Petrie doesn't want Bird or Kitty anywhere near his chambers. We'll gather in the courtroom, where he'll preside over the reading of the will. The point of the probate is to prove the will is Liz's, not to oversee its execution. That'll be done by you. He'll ask for verification of the will's authenticity, and I'll present the affidavit. He'll ask if you have any objection to being the executrix and for your inventory. Then he'll ask anyone else in the room to present documents to the contrary."

"Which is when Bird and Kitty put their two cents in."

"Yes, and the judge will most likely disallow them. If he doesn't, then he'll ask for more proof on both sides and set another date."

"So this could drag out for weeks."

Russell nodded, then stood, motioning for her to do the same. "I've known probates that took years. But it probably won't. Let's get food before the kids scarf everything up."

"Which is why you played golf with the judge today."

He grinned. "We talked about no specific case. Just generalizations."

Molly laughed. "Even though you both knew what you were talking about."

"Of course!"

They grabbed plates, and Molly went for a burger and potato salad, while Russell chose what looked like a ten-ounce sirloin. Linda finally stopped hovering and joined them, along with some of the other neighbors. From then on, the talk turned to anything but Liz Morrow's hoarding house. Kids, church events, the local doings at the community center. Basketball, upcoming proms and graduations, and the start of the local farmer's market. All of it contemporary small-town life. No one brought up the past or dwelled on what happened twenty years ago. No one asked Molly about her family—and none of *them* showed up to spoil the party.

A blessed evening, and Molly couldn't believe how blissful she felt at the end of it. She hugged Russell and Linda goodbye, and made her way back up to the Explorer. Lights still shone out of the windows of Aunt Liz's house, although she didn't know if it would ever feel like a home again, to her or anyone. She could see shadows of the techs moving back and forth, and wondered how long they'd take *this* time.

Sliding into the Explorer, she pulled her phone and purse out of the glove box. No messages. Not from Greg. Or Jimmy. Anybody. She pushed everything back into the glove box and slammed the door. *Forget about them. You had a nice time. Just cherish it and get on with yourself.*

She turned the key. The Explorer's engine resisted with a grinding noise, but then coughed and cranked. Molly rubbed her hand along the dash. "Wow. You do need a checkup. Tomorrow. I promise."

She put the SUV in reverse and backed out into Maple Street. As she reached the main road and turned, her brakes felt a little soft. "Geez … not them too." Her thoughts strayed back to the last oil change and brake check she'd had on the Explorer, and she frowned, puzzled. Just a couple of months ago. She never neglected her vehicle; it was her lifeblood. Her mechanic back in Missouri had been insistent that everything was fine. Tires still had at least ten thousand miles on them, the brakes probably as much. Molly would not have headed for Alabama if she hadn't thought the Explorer was up to it.

She headed into the downhill curve where her motel was located, the lights and VACANCY sign as welcoming as most of the places she'd spent the last twenty years. And she couldn't wait to wash off the woodsmoke of the campfire and grill. Time for bed. She signaled her turn and pressed the brake.

It slid all the way to the floor. The Explorer picked up speed on the downward grade. Molly pumped the brake. No resistance. She gripped the wheel as the SUV shot by the hotel.

Every muscle tensed. Molly shifted into neutral. The engine roared its protest. The SUV slowed some, but the steep grade tugged hard at it. Molly stamped on the emergency brake. Nothing.

She headed into the tightest part of the curve with only one thought: *Too fast!* She tried to swing right for more space going into the turn. The rear end skidded out onto the shoulder of the road. Molly yanked the wheel into the skid, but her momentum was too great. The right side of the Explorer slewed out over the shoulder and toward the waiting ditch.

Molly felt gravity take over, pulling the Explorer over the edge. She braced herself, waiting for the impact. The SUV slid, tipped onto its side, then pitched hard onto the roof. It slammed to a halt against a tree, the sounds of crunching metal and cracking glass ringing in her ears. She smelled gas, oil, and hot rubber.

I have to get out!

Her entire body quivered, and she fought to orient herself. She hung upside down, the seatbelt still holding her in place. Breathing hurt, but nothing else seemed to be injured. Her legs, arms, ached and trembled, but nothing felt broken.

She reached for the buckle.

No! Don't release it yet. Brace.

Jimmy's words, echoing from a wreck almost ten years ago, when storm winds had tumbled their last SUV. *Don't panic!*

Molly tried again to take a deep breath, but the shoulder harness pressed hard into her chest. "Okay," she said aloud. "Brace."

Molly brought her knees up, pushing her feet against the dash, one arm against the roof, now below her. She released the buckle. She still rolled onto the roof, but not as hard as she could have. She lay still a moment, still assessing.

The stench of gas and oil remained overwhelming. All of the windows had shattered, the doors twisted, but the passenger cage of the SUV had survived. She just needed to get out. The cracked windows still held firm in the frame. She shifted to look at the back. The tailgate had twisted, pulling away from the SUV, tearing the plastic sheet covering the opening for the back glass. *Freedom!*

Pushing debris and clutter aside, she crawled toward the back and clawed at the plastic like a cat tearing its way out of a bag. It shredded, and she yanked it inside the Explorer, thrusting it behind her. Molly scrambled out, scraping her back and one arm on the tailgate, and driving bits of wood and shards of glass into her palms. She dug her fingers into the dirt of the ditch, pushing her way through the dark brush to the shoulder of the road. She collapsed, gasping deep breaths of air, shivering violently.

Sirens. She could hear distant sirens. Someone must have seen it. God bless 'em. Molly choked back a hysterical laugh that came from nowhere. As the sirens closed in, she forced herself to stand, waving as the first headlights came into view. An ambulance slowed, doused its siren, and the doors flew open as the EMTs leaped out.

Molly sat down hard, giving herself over to their care.

17

"Your brake line was cut."

Molly stared at Greg, but his words barely registered. The ER docs had found a number of injuries she'd been unaware of, including a cracked rib, cuts on her right arm and calf that needed stitches, and sprains in her back and shoulder. Tiny cuts and abrasions littered her arms and legs. They had discharged her just before dawn, but she still floated in a painkiller haze.

Now Molly and Russell sat in the front of his Mercedes. They had been about to leave when Greg slipped into the back seat. She looked at Russell. "Are you getting this?" Her speech felt thick. "I can't …"

He nodded. "You just listen. We'll go over it later." In his lawyer tone. This was serious.

Russell twisted to look at Greg. "Are you implying someone tried to kill her?"

"Anytime there are no skid marks before an accident, we look at the brakes and the driver immediately."

"I was with her last night. She wasn't drunk."

"We know. We had her blood alcohol level checked." Greg addressed Molly. "You told the officers at the scene the brakes felt soft when you left the party."

Molly took a moment to process the statement, digging through her memory of the accident and aftermath. "Yes. When I turned from Maple onto the highway."

"We pulled the brake line right after we towed it to the garage. It had a slit in it, about two inches, straight along the line. It had been leaking, and when you touched the brakes during the turn, the pressure probably pushed out the rest of the fluid. The brake fluid container was empty. You parked in Liz's drive last night."

Molly nodded. Something else swam around in her memory. Checking the fluids before the party …

"You parked away from everyone."

"The techs—"

"Were inside. But one of them noticed where you'd parked. There was a substantial amount of brake fluid on the gravel in that spot."

Russell tapped his fingers on the steering wheel. "So this is twice someone has tried to kill her."

"Or just hurt her. Scare her. Something tells me these people aren't big on thinking things all the way through. Where are you staying tonight?"

The question confused Molly long enough for Russell to answer. "I'm taking her to my condo."

"Security?"

"Yes. Residents only admitted to the lobby. No guests without prior permission. Guard twenty-four seven. She'll stay there until after the will is probated on Wednesday."

Greg paused. "If this is even about the will."

All three fell silent, and Molly cleared her scratchy throat. "It's about the money."

Greg shrugged. "Or the jewelry. We got a report from one of the pawnshops in Birmingham. About a week ago, someone tried to pawn a necklace that had been part of a robbery in Gadsden. But the shop owner actually read his flyers from the police and the insurance companies, and called the police. Fake ID on the guy who tried to pawn it, but Birmingham PD crossed the necklace with one of our pieces. They were part of the same robbery."

Molly tried to clear the confusion out of her brain without much luck. "Are you saying Aunt Liz was holding stolen goods?"

"Probably without her knowledge."

"*Definitely* without her knowledge," Russell added.

Greg opened the door and got out, bracing the door open. His words were more clipped, leaving no room for discussion. "Don't come to the house tomorrow. Stay at Russell's and rest. The techs will be done later in the day, and I'm going to set up a perimeter and put a deputy on the premises. You can resume work after the probate hearing." He closed the door and was gone.

Russell watched the sheriff march back to his patrol car, then he turned to Molly. "He's got a bee in his bonnet."

"He hates me." She poked her tongue with one finger, then scowled at her fingertip. Why did her tongue feel numb?

Russell looked Molly over carefully. "No, I don't think so."

"He wants us to keep our distance. Says I'm clouding his judgment." Molly grimaced. She was whining. She hated whining.

Russell chose the better part of discretion and started the car, pulling out of the lot. The streets of Gadsden were mostly empty that time of morning. The sun had edged up over the horizon, casting a gold-and-purple haze over the city. Molly stared out at the buildings, trying not to think about Greg. Maybe he was right. They should stay away from each other, especially with her heading back to St. Louis when this was done.

So why did that thought make her chest ache?

Russell spoke, his voice carefully even. "The docs called in some medicines for you at a twenty-four-hour place. I'll swing through and pick them up, then we're going to get you settled. I'm hoping you can sleep before these meds wear off. When they do, you are going to hurt like the dickens."

"Thank you. What am I going to do for a car?"

"Nothing today. Where's your insurance information?"

"In the glove box. Along with my phone. And my purse."

Russell cast a quick glance her way. "Molly, your purse and phone are in the back seat. The EMTs grabbed them."

"Oh." The scene swirled in her head, now just a blur of flashing lights, encouraging voices, and kind hands. "That's how the hospital had my insurance."

"What about your camera bag and computer?"

"At the hotel." A pulsing throb had begun near the base of her skull.

"I'll get the car insurance from the garage, and I'll follow up with the insurance company. We'll take it from there. One step at a time."

"Thank you. Seriously. I don't know if I could get through this without you."

"You're welcome. We'll overlook that you wouldn't be in this without me."

Molly chuckled, then groaned, pressing a hand to the side of her head. "Don't make me laugh. And don't blame yourself for this. This die was cast before either one of us was born."

* * *

The next twenty-four hours passed in a sleep-riddled haze. Tucked into Russell's guest bedroom, Molly dropped back into a drugged sleep. Russell woke her twice, just checking on her. Pain jerked her awake after eight hours, but more pills took care of that. The smell of coffee awoke her the final time. She found her camera and computer bags tucked in next to a dresser. Her purse and phone lay on top of it. A small duffel bag on a chair near the bed held fresh underwear, jeans, and a clean shirt. She dressed and headed down the stairs, each step made with care and a firm hold on the banister.

Russell sat at a small bistro-style table in the kitchen, drinking coffee and reading something on his tablet. He looked up in surprise and stood. "Well, good morning! How are you feeling?"

Her voice croaked from lack of use. "Like I've been in a car accident. Oh, wait …" She grinned, then grimaced.

He chuckled. "At least your humor survived. Coffee?"

"Please and thank you. Just black." Molly sat at the table. "Thanks for the clothes."

"I thought I was going to have to show Leon pictures of the wreck before he'd let us in. He's gotten quite protective of you." He poured a cup of coffee from a maker on the counter and set it in front of her.

"Us?"

He looked a bit sheepish. "I asked Linda to gather your clothes. One woman to another."

She smiled. "Thanks. And I'm not surprised about Leon. He's sweet. I bring him donuts when he's working late."

Russell sat down. "A little kindness goes a long way."

"What are you reading?"

He pushed the tablet aside. "The morning paper. Easier on the eyes than print." He paused. "I got the car insurance from Greg."

"Thanks. Did you talk to the insurance agent?"

"I did. They're sending an appraiser to the garage on Friday. I asked about a rental car. He said it should be cleared and ready by Friday. You're stuck with me until then."

"I appreciate that."

"And I talked to Greg."

Molly straightened, a little wary. "Oh?"

Russell watched her face. "He confirmed that the house won't be ready for you to resume work until Thursday. He wants everyone to stay away except the techs and his accident investigator."

Molly set down the cup. "But the accident—"

"Molly. It's not open to discussion."

She stopped, fighting an unfamiliar ache in her chest. Greg still didn't want her around. "Fine. I need to go to the hotel anyway. I need to finish prepping for tomorrow."

"I'll drive you. We can bring what you need back here."

She stared into her cup. "So I'm not to stay at the hotel either?"

"It's obviously too dangerous for you to be there alone, especially with you not up to par. And with no car." He took a deep breath. "Greg suggested you start carrying your gun with you."

Molly's eyebrows arched. "I thought he didn't want me to carry it at all."

"He doesn't want you shooting Bird because you've been enraged for twenty years. Defending yourself from people who've already tried to kill you is another story."

"We don't know they did anything. Not for sure. Right? The Explorer was old." Molly felt as if she were fighting a losing battle, but still …

"Brake lines do not deteriorate with long straight splits."

She pushed her coffee cup back. "I honestly don't get it. Taking me out is not going to make this go away. The will, with me or not, will be probated. If I'm not the executrix, someone else will be appointed. Bird and Nina and Kitty and Lyric are never going to get what they want out of this! The law is just not on their side."

"And if it's about something else. The jewelry? Freddy's death?"

Molly had no answer, and Russell sipped his coffee.

"Talk to me, Russell."

"There are two possibilities. One is that this is an effort to get someone else as executrix. Someone on their side. The other is that it's not about the will at all. That it's about getting you and the cops and everyone away from the house long enough to finish what they started."

"It's about the jewels."

"And the murders. And the only connection to Liz and her hoarding is that they chose her house as a hiding place. Greg thinks—" He broke off.

"Greg thinks what?"

He shook his head. "They got another hit on the jewelry yesterday, from a pawn shop in Montgomery. This guy turned away a piece because he suspected it had been stolen. He saw it later on one of the insurance flyers. Both pieces were reported stolen from homes in Gadsden."

"So Greg thinks Aunt Liz and Freddy were just wrong place, wrong time."

Russell stood and picked up both cups, emptied them into the sink, and placed them in the dishwasher. "Maybe. That's one reason he wants you to stay away from everything. He needs time to process the evidence they've gathered and the information collected from the interviews he and his deputies have done. There's suddenly a lot of material."

"And I'm a distraction."

"That, and every time you're around, more stuff happens."

She stiffened, indignant. "I didn't exactly add that blood to Lyric's pillow!"

"No, but if he hadn't been so anxious to let you get back to work on the house, he wouldn't have stopped the techs when they finished upstairs. They would have worked the whole house. As they should have."

Molly stared at him, leaning forward. "Wait. He *stopped* them? He told me they were finished."

Russell smiled knowingly. "Yes. You are a distraction."

She collapsed back against her chair. "This could get him in a lot of trouble, couldn't it?"

"Not till election time. But it could seriously damage the case if it goes to court."

"He sabotaged himself."

"Maybe. Right now, he's just furious with himself, and more than a little concerned he'd take it out on you. So you need to stay away. Let's get through the will process, then make plans. Are you ready to go?"

"As I'll ever be."

They headed for the hotel but were back in Russell's office well before noon. He set her up in a conference room with the files on Liz's estate, the remaining journals, and her laptop. She checked email first, finding a note from Hunter Bradley, the St. Louis station manager, about a time for a conversation about their contract offer. The station had bought a number of her storm photos and videos over the years, so he knew her work. And she knew the offer was a good one, in light of what they normally paid. And it was not one she'd be likely to get anywhere else.

But it felt … wrong.

She couldn't explain it, but there was no time to dwell on it. She responded, explained what was going on, and asked if they could talk on Thursday afternoon. They set the appointment for 4:30 p.m.

An email from Jimmy informed her that Sarah was finally awake but not fully functioning. They were doing more tests. Oh, and a package from a lawyer would arrive soon, with documents separating Jimmy and Sarah from Molly's LLC, which had them listed as full partners.

Oh, joy.

She didn't respond. She couldn't. Molly wanted to take the high road with this, but a sense of betrayal, of abandonment ran deep in her. It made no sense; Jimmy was right all the way around. But he'd made a decision changing her life forever without even mentioning it to her until it was done. That part still hurt. She just needed a little more time.

She hoped.

She closed her email. Time to get down to business. Across the conference table, she spread the last two journals, her notes and inventory lists from the previous journals, and the estate file. She looked over the will and Aunt Liz's specific bequests, then set them aside. She had already accounted for most of these, marked the locations of items in the house, and added them to the inventory. Molly continued to be astonished at the number of friends and relatives Aunt Liz believed to be deserving of help from the estate. They far outweighed the ones she thought should be disinherited, which seemed to be limited to Bird, his descendants, and a few random cousins.

"Elizabeth Morrow, you had a heart of butter," she muttered, as she opened a journal. After several pages of recipes, reports of neighborhood events, and a praise of Finn's work on her water heater, one entry stopped her cold.

==

October 12th
Bird and Leland stopped by today. Poor Leland. He looks so bad. He obviously has the cancer, even though they aren't talking about it. Probably the same cancer his mama had. Hopefully, they'll get better treatment for him than she got. I know Nina told someone at the Piggly-Wiggly that he was getting treatments, but I can't tell they are doing any good.

They came because Bird once again insisted on taking the secretary in the front hall. He keeps saying it came out of the old farmhouse before Mama died, and they should have it back. I suspect he's seen one like it on eBay and knows how much it would bring at auction. I reminded him that his timing was off. That if it had been in the house before Mama died, then it would have been part of the estate that Daddy had sold to Regina—thus, it would have been in the house when he forced Regina to sign it over. Sometimes I have to keep throwing in his face that the reason Daddy didn't leave a will is that he'd deeded everything to Regina before he died, to keep spats like this from happening. Couldn't contest a will if ownership had already been transferred.

Anyway, Mollybelle, you hold the line when this all comes down and don't let Bird bully you. He forced your mother to give up ownership of the farm. Don't let him do the same thing to you.

==

The screech was out of Molly's mouth before she could stop it. "Russell!"

When he burst through the door, she thrust the journal at him. She stood up and tried to pace as he read, but the pain in her side stopped her. She stretched, pressing against the rib.

"Russell, I swear to God I'm going to—"

"Molly. Stop. I warned you. Don't say anything against Bird right now."

She shook her finger at the journal. "But you see—"

He scanned it. "I know." He dropped the journal on the table and crossed his arms, peering over his glasses at her. "But you didn't."

"Of course I didn't know!" She pointed at the journal. "Is she right? Mother already owned the farm?"

"Yes. Your grandfather sold it to your mother before he died. For around $200, if I remember."

Molly couldn't believe it. "She owned it free and clear. She didn't have to give in to Bird. She could have just had him arrested for grand larceny."

He nodded. "And torn the family apart."

"That happened anyway."

"But it wasn't her doing."

Exhaustion swamped Molly. She pulled a chair away from the table and dropped into it. "I honestly didn't know I could despise him more than I did."

Russell sat as well. "Molly, I really thought you knew, or I would have said something. That's one of the reasons Liz wanted to sign her house over to you. So maybe this time you'd stand up to him. But as to the farmhouse, it's done. You can't change it. You have no standing."

Molly threw up her hands. "He can't win every single time!"

Russell responded with the same high emotion. "It's not about winning, Molly! This is not a competition! It's about caring about people and *not* taking advantage of them. *That's* what Liz wanted you to fix. To have some compassion. To hold Bird and his kin at arm's length to do what she couldn't. Not to *defeat* him, but to complete what she wanted to do. To bring healing to the family. Not more anger and separation."

"I'm not Liz!"

Russell's voice dropped back into his professional mode. "That is more than apparent to everyone who's met you. But that's the whole point, isn't it? You can do what she couldn't. But not because you can 'beat' Bird. Because you're not like *him* either."

She stared at him. And the impact of it hit her as it never had before. She scrubbed her face with her hands, then ran them through her hair. "Wow!" she said. "And my guess is you never had to yank her up short like that either."

"Not even close. But what this tells me is that you want to do this even more than you realize. But you need to focus on the real goal here and not on what Bird did to your family more than twenty years ago. It's not about the past. It's about the future."

She stared at him, letting his words sink in. *It's not about winning.* Finally, she reached for her inventory list and passed it to him. "Okay then. How does this look? I think I've covered everything of value I found in the house, even the stuff upstairs that we haven't touched yet. I still can't get into the basement, but that seems to be mostly stuff that needs to be tossed. I've compared it with the journals, and I can't find anything Aunt Liz catalogued that's not on the list. She was pretty thorough."

"That was the teacher in her."

"Will this do for the probate hearing?"

He pulled out his reading glasses and slipped them on. "It should. What else you got?"

She slid more papers toward him. "Her specific bequests, plus some mentioned in her diary. A lot of good, deserving folks, according to her."

He looked over the list. "I'd have to agree." Molly scowled, and Russell peered at her over his glasses. "What is it?"

"I can't help thinking that dumping all this furniture and stuff on other people, deserving or not, is not exactly going to be compassionate or fair."

He took off his glasses. "Why not?"

She pointed at the estate papers and journals. "She wanted to pass on to them the 'family legacy' and things that are worth money to help them. To lift them up. But I can't see that happening if we follow her plan. A highboy isn't cash. They could get taken advantage of. How would they know how to turn an antique highboy into cash? Are they going to prefer a family heirloom to food on the table?"

"Shouldn't that be their choice?"

She tapped one of the journals. "Maybe."

He tucked the glasses away. "Molly, let's focus on the primary goal for a moment."

"Yeah, that's what Greg keeps saying."

"Then he's right. Let's get through tomorrow, settle the estate, then see what's next."

Molly nodded. "Maybe after tomorrow, people will stop trying to kill me."

18

Wednesday arrived with a fierce thunderstorm, which slowly settled into a driving rain. Molly and Russell went to his office to gather their materials and wrap in plastic anything that wouldn't fit in his briefcase before heading to the courthouse. In the passenger seat of his car, Molly watched the clouds, twisting to see in as many directions as she could. Her sky. She missed it.

Russell couldn't hide his amusement. "Looking for something?"

"Patterns." Her voice softened. "I miss work, Russell. I want to get back to my photography."

"I understand. It's why I haven't retired. I love the law."

She spotted a second, then a third break in the clouds. "I think the roughest part of this storm has passed over us."

"At least the one in the sky."

Molly let out a long sigh. "Thank you, by the way. For grounding me yesterday. For making me see I was fighting the battle from two decades ago more than the one in front of me."

"And this one is hard enough."

Russell let her out at the door, then parked. She waited for him just inside, and helped him pull the plastic off and dump the wrappings in a trashcan. After passing through security, they found a long bench near the courtroom and claimed a spot big enough for them and all their baggage. Bird arrived a few minutes later, followed by Kitty, both dressed in their Sunday best and uncharacteristically subdued to the point that Molly had the urge to ask what was wrong with them. She resisted.

Four other relatives arrived, standing in a cluster down the hall, two women, a young man about LJ's age, and a young girl about twelve, who seemed to be along for the ride. She kept her face buried in her phone.

Molly nodded at them. "Who are they?"

Russell peered at them, then looked away. "That would be your cousins, RuthAnn Travers and Tommie Jane Spruill. The boy is Eddie, RuthAnn's son. The girl is Tommie Jane's youngest."

"Why are they here?"

"Probably moral support for Bird. Their father. Also, RuthAnn is one of the nosiest women I've ever encountered. And she'll spread the news. Whatever happens today will make it back to Carterton before we do."

Molly snarled. "The downside of small-town life."

"The good comes with the bad."

As a bailiff opened the doors to the room, they moved slowly toward the entrance. "Boy, we're a lively group," she muttered to Russell, who smothered a grin with one hand.

"And this is why we're meeting in the courtroom instead of the judge's chambers. Petrie wants a bailiff present. And a large, official judge's bench between him and the rest of this crowd."

Molly jerked a look at him in surprise. "Seriously?

"You're not the only one who was around twenty years ago."

Molly and Russell took a place at the defendant's table, while the bailiff ushered the rest into rows behind them. Judge Dean Petrie entered in a flurry of billowing black robe and scurrying, overloaded clerk. Molly and Russell stood, but the judge waved at them to sit. The judge banged his gavel once, and looked at his clerk, who stood and handed him a sheaf of papers. Petrie slipped on a pair of reading glasses, paged through them, then looked out over the room.

"We are here today to start the probate of the last will and testament of Ms. Elizabeth LouAnn Morrow, who was deceased as of March 14th of this year. The word 'probate' means 'to prove,' and the goal is to authenticate the last will and testament as being the only valid declaration of Ms. Morrow's wishes as to the dispersal of her property after her death."

Bird pushed to his feet. "Your honor, I have here—"

"Sit down, Mr. Morrow. You will have your chance to speak later."

"Your honor—"

"Sit or leave, Mr. Morrow. Your choice."

Bird scowled, then eased down, grumbling under his breath.

Judge Petrie did not waver. "We will proceed in an orderly manner, and I will direct these proceedings. Understood? Good." He lifted a section of paper and pulled another set to the top. "Ms. McClelland?"

Molly stood up. "Yes, sir."

He waved for her to sit. "No need to stand every time I address you, Ms. McClelland. You'll throw your joints out."

She sat. "Yes, sir."

"You are listed in the paperwork as Ms. Morrow's executrix."

"Yes, sir."

"I understand you showed some reluctance to act as such when you first heard about this. Is that so?"

"Yes, sir."

"Why is that?"

"Fighting over possessions destroyed my family twenty years ago. I left Carterton and I never wanted to come back. My aunt was my only contact here. With her death, I didn't want anything to do with the family or what she left behind."

Judge Petrie peered at her over his glasses. "Sound reasoning. What changed your mind?"

Molly glanced at Russell. "Mr. Williams, mainly. And letters and journals my aunt left that were addressed to me. She felt that because I didn't want any of her estate, I would be the best one to direct its dispersal. She had specific bequests, and she mostly wanted it to help people who could use a hand up. That was something I could get behind."

"Helping people."

"Yes, sir."

He turned his attention to Russell. "Mr. Williams?"

Russell straightened. "Yes, your honor."

"Good to see you in my courtroom again. Hate the reason why."

"Thank you, your honor."

"You have provided me with quite a bit of documentation. I appreciate that." Judge Petrie paused and turned pages as he read. "A notarized affidavit from Ms. Morrow that this is her true and final will. A notarized statement from her physician that she was in sound mind and body when she signed it. The notarized letter addressed to Ms. McClelland outlining the reasoning for choosing her as executrix and a list of specific bequests." He paused and pulled out a stack held together by a large binder clip. "And more affidavits than I want to read from potential heirs, signing off on Ms. McClelland as executrix. Is that it?"

"That's it, judge. The only heirs who have not waived any objection to Ms. McClelland as executrix are sitting behind us."

"So I see." The judge took several minutes to scan through the pages again, then he grouped them, slipped a rubber band around them, and handed them back to his clerk. "Ms. McClelland, do you have an inventory of the estate, along with a list of recipients?"

"I do, your honor, although they are only *potential* recipients. They have not been contacted, since they were not direct heirs to my aunt."

"Do you have any reason to suspect they would object to receiving a nice *objet d'art* from your beloved aunt?"

"Truthfully, your honor, if someone told me I'd inherited a six-foot by nine-foot wardrobe made from solid cherry that took up half a room, I'd tell them to call Goodwill."

Petrie stared at her, obviously fighting a smile. "Point taken, Ms. McClelland. And there is such a creation in the inventory?"

"Yes, your honor."

"Nice. Please bring the inventory list to the clerk."

Molly did so and returned to her seat. Her hands were clammy and cold, and she twisted them together in her lap. *Why am I so nervous?*

The clerk passed the list to the judge, who went through the list slowly. Finally, he peered over his glasses again. "Would you be willing to swear that this list is complete and accurate as to the contents of the house to be considered part of the estate?"

Molly glanced at Russell, and he nodded. She faced Judge Petrie. "No, sir. I cannot."

He put the list down. "Why not?"

"Sir, the house is currently a crime scene under investigation."

"I am aware."

"Aunt Liz was a hoarder. When I first arrived the house was impassable, except for a few rooms. While I've inventoried the main rooms of the house and most of the attic, I've not been able to get into the basement. While it appears to be primarily garbage that has been thrown down the stairs, I could not swear to the contents beyond that."

The judge looked over the list again, then at Molly for a few moments. "But you would be willing to begin dispersal of the estate based on this list."

"Yes, sir. With an addendum to the inventory filed when I could get into the basement."

He handed the list back to his clerk. "Mr. Morrow, please come to the rail and explain what it is you want to present."

Bird stood and stepped forward. "Your honor, my cousin, Kitty Filbyhouse—" he gestured at Kitty. "Ms. Filbyhouse has a second will from my sister, dated after the one you have there. She also has an inventory list that shows items that are in the house, which are not on Ms. McClelland's list."

The judge stared at Bird a moment. "How do you know what's on Ms. McClelland's list and that there are items on yours not listed by her?"

Molly twisted in her seat to stare at Bird. She definitely wanted to hear that answer.

Bird glanced at Kitty again, and the judge turned his attention to her. "Please stand, Ms. Filbyhouse, and explain this."

Kitty stood slowly. "Sir. She … Ms. McClelland … she just got here. My daughter Lyric has been living with Ms. Morrow for some time. She was her primary caregiver and knew the house inside and out. Ms. McClelland came down here and just locked Lyric out of her home and took—"

"Stay on point, Ms. Filbyhouse."

Kitty swallowed and looked at Bird for support. Bird continued. "Lyric knew what was in the house, including the basement. Ms. McClelland has admitted she doesn't know what's down there, so her list can't be as complete as Lyric's."

Judge Petrie continued to stare at them. Finally, he motioned for his clerk to collect the papers from Bird. The clerk did, handing them off to the judge. He looked at the list first, then the will. He paused, then looked up at Bird. "This will is handwritten."

"Yes, sir. My sister … Ms. Morrow didn't have a computer. But you can see it's a later date, and there are changes to the specific bequests."

Judge Petrie peered at Bird over his glasses, glanced at Kitty, then back at Bird. "Are you aware, Mr. Morrow, that holographic wills aren't accepted in the state of Alabama?"

Bird licked his lips. "Holo …"

"Holographic. It means handwritten. They aren't legal in this state. So this will is worthless."

Kitty couldn't hold back. "But it's what Lizzie wanted!"

Judge Petrie took off his glasses and leaned forward, bracing his elbows on the bench. "Then Ms. Morrow should have contacted her good friend and attorney of record, Mr. Williams, and had him redraw the will. Her letter to Ms. McClelland, which is part of the estate package, is signed and dated *and notarized after* this will, which casts even more doubt on its authenticity. And do not speak out like that again in this courtroom or I will have you removed."

Kitty dropped back into her chair and covered her face with her hands. Bird cleared his throat. "Your honor, what about the list?"

Judge Petrie paused, then looked from Bird to Russell to Molly. "Mr. Williams, do you have any thoughts to share?"

This time Russell stood. "Judge, first, Ms. Morrow did have a computer. She kept in touch with Ms. McClelland via email. She surrendered it to me when Ms. Lyric Filbyhouse moved into her residence."

The judge cleared his throat. "Did she state a reason for this action?"

"She said it was a matter of trust."

Kitty shot to her feet.

Judge Petrie put up a hand. "Don't, Ms. Filbyhouse."

Kitty's mouth opened and closed twice, but no sound came out.

"Go on, Mr. Williams."

"She did have a cell phone. We talked at least twice a week. She never mentioned a new will or a desire to have one."

"Thank you. Sit down, all of you."

Russell, Bird, and Kitty dropped back into their chairs. Russell shot a single glance at Molly and nodded once.

Judge Petrie sniffed and handed all the paperwork to his clerk. "While the second will is not and will never be legitimate in this court, there is a significant discrepancy between the two lists, enough for a dispute to be considered. Ms. McClelland, please refrain from dispersing anything in the estate until the basement is emptied. You will submit a revised inventory at that time, and we'll review the two lists again. This is not because I consider Mr. Morrow's list more authentic but because you admit you have not completed the inventory because of circumstances beyond your control."

He paused and took a deep breath. "The last will and testament as submitted by Mr. Williams, however, is proved authentic and true to Ms. Morrow's final wishes. It is accepted by this court and the state of Alabama. Any further contests to the will must be filed with this court within thirty days from today's date. After that time, the clerk will provide all parties a new date for those contests to be heard."

He paused and pointed his gavel at Bird. "But, Mr. Morrow, I give you fair warning. Do not bring any paperwork this shoddy back into my courtroom. If you want to contest this will, hire a good attorney who can advise you on your standing." He banged the gavel and stood. "We're adjourned, people. Go home." And he was gone with the same flurry of billowing robe and scurrying clerk.

19

"I feel as if I've been put through a wringer."

"You have been." The rain had stopped by the time they left the courthouse, and Russell tucked away his briefcase and their folders in the back seat as Molly got in the front. "Going before a judge is no picnic, even if you've done everything right and it's all on your side."

"It didn't help that Kitty started screaming at me when it was all over with."

Russell chuckled. "I thought the bailiff would have to intervene, the way she kept trying to get to you."

"Hmph. Also didn't help that Bird kept growling and saying they'd have to take this into their own hands."

Russell got in and shut the door. "Yeah, I'm going to let Greg know about that."

Molly didn't want to think about Greg at the moment. She snuggled down in the passenger seat, grateful for the seat heater. "I love this car." Warmth radiated through her sore back and hips. She'd not taken a painkiller that morning, in hopes of staying alert for the hearing. Now everything began to ache, especially her side. She stretched it, trying to relieve some of the pressure.

Russell noticed. "I'll get you back to the condo, so you can rest this afternoon. Because if Greg releases the house this afternoon, I know you'll want to get back to it in the morning."

"I do think a short break from all this would do me good. Maybe watch a movie."

"Mi satellite, su satellite," he responded. "I'll head back to the office with the paperwork. And I do actually have other clients. I need to return some calls." He paused. "How are you doing financially?"

Molly shrugged. "I've had to dip into savings to cover a lot of the expenses, but I'm all right. But it's going to take a lot of storm videos to build it back up."

"Still going to take the job in St. Louis?"

"At this point, I don't have much choice. The contract calls for a signing bonus, which will help a lot, and a minor stipend for April through September. They'll get first option on anything I produce and first rights if they buy it. There are minimums set for purchases, but I doubt they'll ever pay more than that. It's not a great deal, but it's only for a year. It'll give me time to establish my name as the only member of the LLC."

"You don't really sound all that excited."

Molly looked out the window at the passing cars. "It's a default position. I'm not fond of default positions. But it'll give me some stability while still letting me work on my own. I've been a freelancer for more than fifteen years. I suspect I'll have a hard time being tied to one place."

"Do you even have an apartment?"

Molly laughed. "Nope. I have a storage bin in Tulsa, with stuff that I'll probably move to St. Louis. I travel with my computer and camera equipment, and a few clothes. We mostly stayed in motels, sometimes we slept in the SUV." When Russell remained silent, she turned to face him. "Russell, understand. It was not a life I *had* to lead. It was one I *wanted* to lead. I was not only happy, I was *deliriously* happy."

Russell kept his eyes on the road. "But now everything's changed."

"Right."

They rode in silence for a few minutes before Russell spoke again. "When this clears, the estate will pay you back for what you spent on the house. Keep a record and put an invoice in the files."

"You don't have—"

"It's not about generosity. Or me. It's about settling the estate. As her executrix, you'll also have to pay the last medical bills, the funeral bills, her credit cards, the utilities on the house, and the property tax owed when you sell it. You are legitimately one of her creditors, and as executrix you can take out a 10 percent fee. Don't be foolish about this. There's going to be plenty of money in the estate. Even after the bills are paid, even if you don't sell the house, you'll still be able to help a lot of people." He took a deep breath. "And I'm going to only say this once, then I'll drop it. I will not pressure you."

"What?"

"Don't sell the house. Keep it. Rent it, use it as a base, whatever. But don't sell it. After all, the South has a lot of great storms too. And, Molly?"

"Yes."

"Default positions are always the worst options."

* * *

Molly mostly slept. Back at the condo, she took a pill and piled up on the couch with a dozen pillows and the remote control. A half hour into an episode of *Midsomer Murders,* she sank into a heavy, quiet sleep. She only woke when Russell came home bearing a pepperoni pizza and a gallon of sweet tea. Over supper, they talked about basketball, the best pizza in Gadsden, lenticular cloud formations, and whether the Nashville Predators would go to the Stanley Cup playoffs again. Nothing legal, nothing to do with estates or cranky relatives.

But, as Molly took another painkiller before bed, she got the uneasy feeling that this was the calm before the storm.

Which started gathering on the horizon the next morning before she was even out of bed. She woke to a text from Greg, brief and to the point: *The house is clear. All yours.*

Then there was an email from Jimmy, also short to the point of being curt.

> *Sarah's dad has seen a lawyer. Expect papers within the week. Probably just after the ones our lawyer sent. Sorry for the double whammy. I didn't know he was doing this now. I know the LLC will absorb it, if it comes to that, but he's heard (not from me!) that you've inherited a lot of money. Insurance is covering*

Sarah, but he wants copays and damages. I thought you should be warned.

Sorry it's ending this way. Really do hope all is going well in Alabama.

Right. She forwarded the note to Russell with the addendum: *Would it be a conflict of interest for you to be my lawyer in this?*

His response came almost instantaneously, which told her he was up and had his phone handy: *Let me see what I can find out.*

Molly stared at the screen a moment, a little surprised at how good it felt that someone had her back. A relief. A reassurance.

Comforting.

And something she had never felt before.

She got dressed and headed downstairs.

After breakfast, they drove into Carterton, stopping first at the hotel to gather the journals, butcher paper, and all her notes. Future work would be done in Russell's office, with access to a printer and an assistant who would help her with family research. Russell then drove her to the house, where they found a cluster of people in the front yard, waiting patiently. She immediately spotted Linda, Finn, and Sheila, greeting them with a grin and a scold.

"Do you people not have jobs?"

Sheila laughed as Finn feigned shock. "Well, of course we do, Miss Molly! We also have vacation time and friends who need us. Remember, Liz meant a lot to all of us." He dropped his voice to a stage whisper. "Plus, the sheriff says you'll be out and gone back to the far Midwest in a few days. We wanted to take advantage."

Molly bowed. "Thank you, kind sir. It is much appreciated."

Linda giggled. "Stop fawning. What do you want us to do?"

"The basement. It must be emptied, as soon as we can. It's what's holding up finalizing everything."

Russell told her he'd be back by four, then whispered something to Finn she couldn't hear. Molly looked around the yard, taking stock. The pavilions still stood, although limp from the stretched ropes that held them. At least ten other people waited for jobs, so Molly put them to work, assigning tasks with the same efficiency she had in the beginning, just slower.

The third time she pressed her side and bent sideways for relief, Finn went to his house and returned with a big camp chair that had air pockets for cushions. "Sit!" he commanded. "Consider it the director's chair. It's going to take a while to dig out the basement, and you do not need to be going up and down the stairs. Just sit." He handed her a bottle of water.

And for the first time in many years, Molly listened. She sat, watching as bag after box after bin emerged from the basement. With six people traipsing in and out, and another four helping to empty and clean, it went faster than she expected. Most of it, as she anticipated, went straight into the dumpster.

Just before lunch, Nina showed up alone. She pulled the truck up close to the dumpster and motioned vaguely at the "Free" table. "Can I . . . ?" her voice trailed off.

Nina had been noticeably absent at the courtroom; now Bird was nowhere to be found. Apparently, something was keeping them apart, but Molly didn't want to think about that at the moment. "Sure," she said. "As far as I'm concerned, our agreement is still in place. Help yourself."

With a shy grin and a "thank you," Nina began to gather items off the "Free" table, and even stopped to peer at the "Two-dollar" table.

Molly wondered if the rumors about Bird's abuse were true, but her thoughts were interrupted by a bin full of high-heel shoes. As Finn lifted the lid, Molly sighed. Ten years out of date and dotted with mold, none looked as if the four- and five-inch heels would support a child. She looked up at Finn. "Seriously?"

He shrugged. "I know how some women are about shoes."

She pointed at the dumpster.

Just before noon, she called Amanda at Bailey's Bistro and had sandwiches, chips, and drinks made up for lunch. Finn retrieved them, and everyone took a break, ate, and enjoyed the great April weather. Yesterday's rain had cleared the air of pollen and left the yard smelling like honeysuckle.

Back at work, they finished clearing the staircase and the area around the bottom of the steps. Finn kept taking pictures with his phone and bringing them to her, and she would send back directions on what to tackle next. Once the stairs had been cleared of boxes, storage bins, and garbage bags, they found a wall of storage bins and boxes that Molly feared would extend to the back of the basement. It was only two rows, but more than two hundred boxes had been brought outside before her long-forgotten question about the house—what happened to the books?—was finally answered.

Behind the storage bins stretched rows of bookcases and books, a virtual sea of them. Some of the bookcases were magnificent pieces, tall and solid wood with carved ornaments on their doors, but many were just plain, discount-store shelves. But all overloaded with books.

Molly called Linda over. "Can you explain this?"

Linda looked through the pictures, chewing her lower lip. "Oh, Liz …" she finally whispered.

"What?"

"You know Liz loved her books."

Molly nodded. "She was a teacher." She pointed to the left side of the house. "These two rooms were her library. Walls lined with fine bookcases. In the front corner, there was this big wingback chair with an ottoman. She'd read to us kids."

Linda nodded and rubbed one eye. "She loved that chair. When the first family started bringing things to her, she tried to work around it. Then one day I was over here, and the books were gone. The bookcases were gone. And that room was full of someone else's stuff. I never had the heart to ask her what had happened to the books."

"Obviously," Finn interrupted, "somewhere she thought they'd be safe." He handed Molly a book wrapped in muslin. As she peeled the cloth away, she saw the title: *The Hunt for Red October*. She peered up at Finn, puzzled.

"That's a first edition. Fine shape. Signed. Worth about two grand at an auction."

"What?"

He shook his head. "There are dozens like it. Signed first editions." He pointed at the book. "Now flip through it."

She did, slowly, her eyes widening as she kept spotting flashes of green. "Oh, dear Lord," she muttered.

"May He protect us," Finn declared. "Looks like there are more than a thousand books down there, and every one we've opened so far has ten to fifteen twenty-dollar bills in them. Liz trusted banks, but she had a backup plan."

* * *

They spent the afternoon removing the money. Molly halted all other activity, and she even made a careful trip down the stairs. She sat on one of the steps as Finn brought her stacks of books to go through. Everyone working knew all too well why it was vital to gather the cash as soon as they could.

Nina.

As soon as she'd realized what they'd found, Nina climbed in her truck and left, leaving skid marks at the end of the street. With Bird's threat hanging in the back of her mind—*It's time we took matters into our own hands*—Molly dared not leave the cash in the basement. They didn't even count it. They simply piled it into one of the emptied storage bins.

When Russell came to pick her up, he just shook his head. "Liz, you crazy fool," he whispered, but with such affection, Molly remained silent as they loaded the money-filled bins into Russell's trunk. They rode in an equal silence back to her hotel. As he parked, she opened the car door but paused. "I'll stay here tonight. The interview is at 4:30, and I'll have a lot to think about after."

He nodded but didn't respond. She closed the door and went into her room, settling slowly into one of the chairs. She hurt, a bone-deep soreness, but the tightness in her chest was far more than anything the accident brought on. Molly couldn't explain it, and she couldn't imagine what she could do to relieve it. She felt stuck, mired in an emotional mud.

* * *

The interview lasted more than an hour and pushed Molly one step closer to St. Louis. Hunter Bradley was bright, well informed, and curious to the bone, just the kind of station manager Molly enjoyed working with. He asked a dozen questions about her training and experience, but even more about how she saw the job and what she thought about the contract. He was a bit of a weather nerd, and asked if she had ever photographed a Kelvin-Helmholtz wave cloud (of course) or seen the conditions under which Mt. Ranier cast a shadow on the clouds (not yet).

He even made her laugh. When she told him she felt the minimums in the contract were too low, he told her he would check with his "powers-that-be" and get back to her after the weekend. They agreed to talk again on Monday afternoon. It had been a great conversation, but it took the last wind out of her sails. Molly had finally hit a wall.

She set her phone aside, then took two more of her painkillers. Weariness swamped her, as well as the pain. She'd held both at bay just long enough to get through the call, and she wanted nothing more than sleep. She stripped, checked her bandages, then slipped between cool sheets and disappeared for a few more hours into a dream-free sleep.

20

As promised, Molly's rental car arrived at her hotel Friday morning. She rode with the driver back to the agency, but was at the Victorian before nine. With donuts and coffee.

Her crew was ready and waiting.

They cleared the rest of the trash out of the basement but put the books back on the shelves. Molly wasn't sure what she'd do with them, but Linda suggested a couple of the local libraries might be interested. They then turned their attention to the remaining three rooms on the second floor and the attic. Trash bags came out in droves, and the number of things in the pavilions began to dwindle. The dumpster, more than three-fourths full now, had developed the scent of mold and decay, so Molly called the company for a pick-up on Monday. She was now confident they could finish the main clearing of the house by the weekend. She arranged for the cleaners to arrive Tuesday to finish their work.

Finally, she could see a light at the end of the tunnel. As the last areas of trash and debris dwindled, Molly walked around the house, making notes and taking pictures for the revised inventory. Most of what she had missed involved the more ornate bookcases in the basement, but there were two tables on the second floor that had been completely buried and an antique trunk in the attic filled with some fine lace curtains and tablecloths. She had these moved to the first floor, then she called everyone together in the front yard.

Fifteen people. She still couldn't believe it. Fifteen people had given up days of their precious vacation time … and their lives … to help her. Plus the others who had been a part of that first week. She still had trouble accepting it. She knew she didn't deserve it.

"Thank you. I will never be able to repay the kindness—and hard work—you've given me since I got here. I know you loved Aunt Liz, but you owed me nothing. Still, you gave and gave. I will try in some way to pay this back. But for now, just … thank you. I know you must be dog-tired. Maybe, once this is over and we have gotten some rest, we can party and refresh. For now, please go home, hug anyone you love, and get some sleep."

They all hugged her first before wandering slowly back to their homes or cars. Molly slowly sank down on the steps, watching them go. Linda and Sheila were the last, stopping to empty the dirty water out of the buckets they'd been using to clean the items for the pavilions. Sheila waved again as she headed home, but Linda came back and sat on the steps beside Molly.

"What now, girlfriend?" Linda asked.

Molly let out a long sigh. "Right now, I'm going to sit here and catch my breath. Then I'm going to make a couple more rounds through the house, compile more notes for the inventory. Then I'm going to have a sandwich at the Bistro and go crawl into bed. Tomorrow?" She shrugged. "I'm not sure. Probably decide if I'm up for some cleaning. I can't distribute anything until the judge rules on the inventory lists."

Linda looked at her hands, then slid one fingernail beneath another, to push out a bit of trash. "I actually meant, what are you going to do when all this is over with?"

Molly chuckled. "That would be the question of the month."

"So you're still planning on leaving us?"

Molly hesitated. "Linda, I've been through a lot with this. It's taken everything I've got to get through it, emotionally … and financially. I don't know that I have any choice."

Linda gave her a quick hug, then stood, backing away. "Ah, but you do, Molly. You always have more than one choice. You may not *like* any of the choices in front of you, or think that they are good choices, but there will always be more than one." She turned and sauntered back toward her home.

Molly watched her go, finally whispering, "You're right. I don't like any of them."

* * *

The text came in from Linda just after seven. Molly had just finished the last bites of a roast beef and provolone sandwich, while checking social media on her phone and chatting with Amanda. The text scrolled down from the top, making Molly's eyes snap wide. It disappeared before she could tap it, and she frantically clicked over to her messages. Yes, she'd read the words correctly.

I didn't think you were working tonight. Are you moving things out of the house? Do you need help?

Molly stared at her phone, alarm flaring through her. "No!" She shot up from the table, barely taking time to throw a twenty on the table, as she dialed 911. She was already out the door before the dispatcher answered, and she recognized Barbara's sleepy tone.

"Barbara, this is Molly McClelland. Someone's robbing Aunt Liz's house. Please send someone! I'm on my way!"

Barbara was instantly alert. "Dispatching them now, hon. We have someone on patrol. Do not go in the house!"

But Molly had already hung up, rage flaring from her gut all the way to the top of her skull. But she wasn't surprised. Not knowing her family. She was only astonished that it hadn't happened before now.

With the Bistro so close, she arrived at the house before the patrol officer, to find a large blue panel truck backed up to the house. She knew she should wait, but fury drove her out.

You will not do this again. Not this time, mister!

She leaped from the rental, dug her gun case out from under the seat, and marched toward the porch, her Glock clenched in her hand. She pulled back the slide to chamber a round as she headed up the steps and put her finger on the trigger. No hesitation. *Not this time.*

No one was in sight.

Molly stopped to peer into the back of the truck. Several storage bins were stacked against the front wall. Furniture lined the outside walls, and Molly's eyes narrowed as she recognized pieces that had been on Kitty's list at the probate hearing. The ones Molly had missed.

"Kitty," she hissed. "What a surprise." She spun to head into the house.

The first blow came from her right, a blur of motion barely registering in her vision. A vicious spear of fire shot through her head and down her spine, and her world spun as she collapsed. Her fingers tightened instinctively, and the Glock fired, a thunderous echo near her head. A man cursed and something hard hit her arm. The gun skidded away from her hand, slamming into a porch post. Another bolt of pain hit Molly's right side, and she heard the crack of her ribs.

"Where is it!" A woman's voice was followed by a string of profanities, as Molly tried to push up. A third punch slammed into her back, forcing her back down.

"What have you done with it!" A harsh, panicked demand from the woman. "It's gone!"

Words wouldn't form. A fourth blow shoved her face hard into the wooden floor of the porch, splinters slicing into her face. Then Molly's breath caught as something tightened around her neck.

Air stopped. A roaring built in her ears, as the binding on her neck cut into her skin. In the distance, screams. Shouts. Sirens. But a merciful darkness covered her.

* * *

"Molly! My God, *Molly!*"

Molly heard the voice, but the distance was too great, the darkness too consuming, too comforting. She sank back into it.

The voice turned relentless. "No, Molly! Stay awake. Stay with me! Don't leave me."

Not a woman this time. Molly tried to open her eyes, but everything was bright, so bright.

Stay with me, Sarah. Please! Stay with me.

A memory punched through the haze. Jimmy's voice. Sarah hurt. Him cradling her. I should have known then, right? His voice had been that of a lover, not a friend. Sarah, so pale and wan, so lost. *Sarah, my love.*

"Molly!"

Definitely not a woman.

"Jimmy?" Her own voice sounded like a frog's grunt, not even really a word. She coughed, then moaned. Darkness was better.

"Molly, stay with us. Help is here. Please, don't leave me."

That voice again, closer now. *No … not Jimmy.*

Her body moved. A jostle. Her neck confined. A roll. A lift. A landing. The pain hit then, with a fierce roar of agony. Molly screamed. She tried again to open her eyes, but it was too brilliant, too many colors, too excruciating. She clenched them shut.

"We have to get an IV started. Hold her."

A hand clutched hers, caring but firm, strong, holding her arm down. She felt the pressure of the needle, but no pain. Everything else hurt far worse. A slight burning flooded her arm, then blessed darkness came again.

* * *

The beeps came first. Low and muffled, they bounced around the room and inside Molly's head. Then the pain, in her head, her throat, her shoulders, her back, every muscle. She groaned.

"Molly?" Three anxious male voices at once, which made her moan again.

"Give her a minute." A fourth voice, a low, soft alto. A hand gently gripped her arm. "Ms. McClelland? Molly? Can you hear me? You're in the hospital."

"Safe?" The word scraped her throat, and she swallowed.

"Yes, you're safe." The alto tones were calm, soothing. Molly believed her. She tried to open her eyes. Again, too bright. She squeezed them shut.

"Do you know why you're here? Do you remember anything?"

And the images came flooding back. The blow to her head. The gunshot. Then she was down, pummeled by fists and feet. But there were no faces, just limbs and pain. But there were two voices, one cursing, one calling her names, encouraging the others, demanding to know where it was. *Where is it?* Over and over. She remembered the voices.

Tears burned her eyes. "Yes," she whispered.

The alto continued. "We wanted you to wake up, so we reduced your pain medication. I'm going to increase it a bit, to give you some relief. Stay awake for a while if you can. But if you want to sleep, do so. You need to heal and rest will help. Can you open your eyes?"

Molly tried again, but everything was still too blurry and too bright. She squeezed them shut again, then could hear footsteps. The squeak and whiffle of blinds. The light dimmed.

"Try again."

Much better. Molly blinked several times, and the blurriness began to clear. The alto came into focus, with dark brown eyes, auburn hair, and a sweet smile.

"I'm Dr. Kantner."

"How bad?" Molly's voice cracked. Pain radiated around her neck.

The smile dimmed. "You have two additional cracked ribs and a concussion. Lots of internal and external bruising, but no bleeding, fortunately. You're going to be extremely sore for a while."

"Why is my throat so sore?"

Dr. Kantner paused. "Apparently, they tried to choke you. You have lots of bruising and abrasions around your neck. Fortunately, your assailants were frightened off before they could do too much more harm."

"You can thank Finn and Linda for that. They heard the gunshot."

Greg's voice. *Where is he?*

"You can have some ice for your throat but no liquids yet. I want to see how you're doing first. I'll be around later to check on you." Dr. Kantner stepped back. She disappeared to be rapidly replaced by two people beside her bed and one at the foot of it.

Greg, at her elbow, slipped his hand into hers. "Glad you're back." His voice sounded gruff, a little hoarse.

"Me too," she whispered.

Finn's unruly mop of hair shook as he crushed his cap in his hands. "Miss Molly. Man, it's good to see you awake. I was so … I mean, we were so worried."

"I'm too tough to kill."

Silence followed that statement. Then a rich baritone from the end of the bed said simply, "But they did try."

Molly squinted, trying to see who it was. Not one of the neighbors, although his face was familiar. He wore a tunic made from a rough, grayish white fabric, with a brown shift-like apron over it. Around his neck hung a large wooden cross. *A priest? Why would a priest … ?* The fuzz in Molly's head clouded her recognition. She focused harder, taking in the dark eyes, the curly, russet-brown hair dotted with gray. His expression was somber, but his eyes focused on her in the same way her mother's used to …

Her chest tightened. "Mickey?"

Greg and Finn straightened and moved away from the bed. The man at the end gave a single nod. "Brother Michael now. Hello, Squirt."

"You're a priest?" She cleared her throat as some of the pain eased.

"A Trappist monk."

"That's where you've been for twenty years?"

"Not the entire time."

But the pieces began to fall into place, even in Molly's medicine-blurred mind. The reason Liz stopped talking about him. Why he couldn't inherit from her. Why everyone had been sketchy about where Mickey was. Michael. Good Lord in heaven … *Brother* Michael.

"You could have told me."

Mickey tilted his head to peer at her, as he had twenty years ago. "Why?"

Good question. "You left us."

"We both did. And you know why. We had to."

"But you left her."

Her. They both knew who she meant. Their mother.

The room fell silent for a few moments as Molly and Michael observed each other. Every inch of her body ached with throbbing pain, and now her heart did as well. "You owe me some words," she whispered. "Some answers. If only because I'm your sister."

Michael seemed to concede the point and glanced at Greg and Finn. They left, with Greg glancing back just once before the door shut. Michael pulled up a chair and sat next to her bedside. He adjusted his habit, then sat quite still.

"Before you ask anything, let me speak for a moment. Please."

Molly nodded, watching him. This man … this *man* … was a far cry from the angry teenager who had bolted Carterton in a blinding, dangerous rage. Mickey had been angry every day, all day. After the beating by Bird, Leland, and Bobby, Mickey had been in frequent trouble, constantly getting into fights. He'd started drinking.

This man, Brother Michael, had a calmness, a solemnity she would not have thought possible. He straightened his shoulders, and Molly found herself mesmerized by the power of his voice. Deeper than she remembered, almost a bass, and he spoke with a confidence, a resonance, that captivated her.

"I have special permission to come see you because you were in danger. But now that you are awake and healing, I will have to return to the monastery. I want to answer your questions, even though it may be hard for you to hear now, like this. But I cannot stay to see you through all you're dealing with, no matter how much I'd want to. I loved Liz, and Mother, more than you can imagine. When Russell told me about Liz's death, I couldn't move for hours. Like you, I'm still grieving, and the brothers have been good for me during this time. I cannot return to this life, Molly. Being a part of that community is the best decision I ever made."

"I can see that it was good for you."

He paused. "I've changed a lot."

"Me, not so much."

Michael peered at her. "More than you can imagine."

She fought the urge to squirm under his gaze. "Tell me what happened back then. Tell me what happened with Aunt Liz."

He hesitated. "You have to remember that you were five years younger. There were things you didn't know because no one wanted to tell you. I tried to convince Mother you could handle it, but she refused. I had to respect her wishes." He took a deep breath. "Mother was ill—"

"Yeah, she caught something at the hosp—"

"No. She didn't." The words were curt, pained.

Molly waited, and Michael steeled himself and continued. "She had cancer, Molly. Liver cancer. It was aggressive and inoperable. Stage three before they found it, stage four before they tried to treat it. Do you remember her sending you to stay for long periods with Liz?"

An odd numbness spread through Molly, and she suddenly felt very distant from her own body. "I thought she was just tired. Needed a break."

"She *was* tired. Exhausted. But from the treatments, which eventually gave her no hope. So she stopped them. She gave up."

Molly thought over what she'd learned from the journals. "Did you know that Bird never had a right to the farmhouse? That it wasn't even Gram's anymore? That Granddaddy had sold it to Mother before he died? She had the deed in her name."

Michael nodded. "Did you know that his blackmail wasn't just about our possessions? Bird threatened to tell the world that Leland was her son. Worse, he threatened to tell Leland."

Molly closed her eyes. The line from Liz's journal that had made no sense suddenly made all the sense in the world. *Leland obviously has the cancer, even though they aren't talking about it. Probably the same cancer his mama had. Hopefully, they'll get better treatment for him than she got.*

"So all those childhood rumors were true. Leland isn't Bird's son."

"Nor Nina's."

"Why did they take him in?"

"Why do you think?"

She didn't have to think. She knew. "Money."

"Every month. Granddaddy paid every month, and Bird made sure they all never forgot about it. It's why Gram was so quick to give him the farm equipment after Granddaddy died."

Molly's numbness faded into a slow burn of anger. She tried to straighten in the bed, but every inch screeched in pain. She felt as if her entire body winced.

Michael stood up. "Let me help you. What do you want to do?"

"Mostly just sit up a little more. Some ice."

"Hang on." He raised the bed up, then ran his arm under her shoulders. She grabbed his arm, and together they moved her higher and straighter. He handed her a cup from the bedside table, and she spooned a few pieces of ice into her mouth, let them melt. They felt glorious easing down her throat. After a moment, she took a deep breath, wincing. The soreness in her hips, torso, and lower back felt like coals of fire under her skin.

Michael remained silent, sitting again as she waited for the pain to subside. When it did, she looked him up and down. "You're awfully strong for a monk."

He chuckled, and for the first time seemed to relax. "It's not like I sit around reading Scripture all day. The monastery is a working farm. Crops. Cows. Lots of cows. Part of our support comes from selling cheese, chocolate, and artwork the brothers produce."

"So you're Amish in habits?"

"Hardly. And we wear work clothes to farm and make the cheese."

She peered at him closer. "I'd really like to get to know this Michael better. You sound like a remarkable man."

His cheeks reddened. "Thank you. We can make that happen. Letters are permitted. And visits from family. We have a guesthouse."

She nodded. "It's been a long time. We have a lot to learn."

"Indeed."

"Leland has cancer. He looks like Mother did before she died."

"Finn told me."

"Did you know Finn before today?"

Michael nodded and sat down again. "The short version of a long story is that I spent ten years in the Marines, mostly overseas. I asked for it. I wanted to be as far away from Carterton as I could get. Liz stayed in touch. You know I came back twice before Mother died. I came back two other times to see Liz. I met Finn the last time."

"Why did you leave when Mother was so sick?"

Michael looked down at his hands. "I had no choice."

"Explain."

He ran his hands through his hair, and Molly almost laughed. His hair looked so much like her own. And they both had run their hands through their hair when tense since they were kids. He sniffed, then finally looked at her. "After Bird and the boys did what they did, I was angry."

"We all were."

He rolled one shoulder. "Yeah, well, mine took an unfortunate path. Do you remember Bobby?"

"Leland's brother. Joined the military about the same time you did."

He paused. "He didn't have a choice either. I was acting out, fighting, drinking, stirring up trouble. Bobby and I got into a fight that lasted over the course of three days. We basically tried to kill each other. We destroyed a lot of property in the process, including a couple of cars. The cops hauled us up in front of a judge who—like everyone else in Carterton at the time—knew exactly what was going on. He gave us a choice. Jail … or enlist."

"You enlisted."

"Wouldn't you?"

"Why didn't I know any of this?"

"Mother and Aunt Liz made a concerted effort to keep you naïve, innocent of all the tawdry parts of our family. They hoped that if they could protect you, they could get you off to college so you wouldn't be smothered by the family drama."

"I did get away. Probably not the way they planned."

"Which is why Aunt Liz didn't try to stop you. It hurt for you to leave, but she believed you'd have a better life away from here."

"Why did you stop writing her?"

Michael looked off into a distance at something only he could see. "That was her choice. Something … difficult … painful had happened, about six years ago, and she'd written about it. You may have seen it in her journals."

Molly knew what he was talking about. Liz's cousin Gene had gotten ill, and Buddy and Ashley brought his entire house of furniture to Liz's without warning. "The furniture dump. When Gene's family just left everything with her."

He nodded. "I wrote and told her to have the Salvation Army come and take everything out. She called, furious. Read me the riot act about not caring about family and the hard work that had gone into acquiring personal property, that people shouldn't be punished for going through hard times." He paused, looking back up at Molly. "I didn't hear from her for a long time after that. Finally, I wrote to tell her I had joined the monastery, sent her the new address. I never heard back."

"That's when the hoarding started. She became obsessed with what she called 'preserving the family legacy.' Somehow, she connected 'legacy' with 'stuff we've collected.' Russell said it all happened so slowly that it was out of hand before he became aware of it. Then, as she got more frail, it got even worse. People kept bringing stuff. She wouldn't say no and she wouldn't get rid of it." Molly paused. "And I think I started it. Or at least planted the seeds."

"How?"

"She had a lot of our stuff from the little house. Things I left behind when I ran. You said she was hurt when we both left. Did I let her down? Did *we* let her down?"

Michael's eyes widened in surprise. "Did *we—?*" He coughed. "You do remember that three other nieces and nephews live right here in town, and they all have children. Bobby got out, like we did, but Leland, RuthAnn, and Tommie Jane are here. And their children are mostly grown as well. They all had better opportunities than we did to change their lives. They chose not to."

"But we're the ones who—"

"No." Michael's voice was firm. "Molly, you can't take on the burdens of the world. They are not your responsibility." His tone softened, and he leaned closer to her. "When you were still little, maybe eight or nine, you were already a fixer. It was your way of trying to control a life that was already way off track. When Aunt Liz told me you'd started work as a storm chaser, I thought you'd realize how little of life is really under your control. Only God has any sort of control over this existence." He leaned back in the chair. "You could not have saved her. You could not have fixed this."

"But we can now."

He nodded. "Finn told me about the remarkable work you've been doing."

"I don't suppose you'd want anything out of the house. For the monastery."

Michael shook his head, his smile sad. "You and I both escaped the craving for possessions, Squirt. Different paths. But we really *are* the lucky ones, remember?"

She did, and she reached out her hand for his. He took it, squeezing gently. Molly yawned, but tried to shake it off. "I can write when I have more questions?" she asked.

"Anytime. And I don't have to be back to the monastery until Tuesday. I thought we could go back to the house when they release you."

She grinned at the thought. "You're going to cause quite a stir in that getup."

He chuckled. "I'll cause quite a stir just by being Mickey McClelland back from the dead."

Molly blinked as a wave of sadness swept over her. "I was close to thinking you were dead, ya know."

He nodded. "I'm sorry about that. Liz did give me your contact information …" his voice trailed off.

"But you weren't ready." She yawned again.

He shook his head. "Do you remember what you said to me the last time we saw each other?"

Molly felt heat in her cheeks. "I was angry. And I was a kid."

"I believe the exact words were, 'I hope you get shot in some foreign hellhole, never to see the light of day.' They are imprinted on my brain."

"You were leaving us."

"And you were scared."

Molly nodded, then pressed her head back against the pillows. Nodding had not been a great idea. "Terrified. The last thing I wanted was to be left alone with Mother and Bird at each other's throats." She paused. "Forgive me?"

His eyebrows arched. "Oh, I forgave you a long time ago. I know you were furious. I just didn't know if you'd forgiven me. If you'd even want to hear from me."

"Ah." She looked down, plucked idly at the tape on her IV. "We have some healing to do."

"But we'll get there."

Molly yawned yet again. "I think the pain meds are kicking in."

Michael stood, leaned over, and kissed her forehead. "You sleep. Rest. The doc said they might discharge you as early as tomorrow morning. We'll talk then."

Molly nodded, feeling a blissful sleep settling over her. Michael waited until she closed her eyes, then she heard him slip out. As the door closed, she heard Greg ask, "Did you tell her?"

"No," Michael replied. "She needs to rest. Tomorrow is soon enough."

Molly tried to call out, to fight her way back to consciousness, but the meds overwhelmed her. The door closed, and sleep took over.

21

The nightmares arrived later that night, after Dr. Kantner had reduced the pain meds again. The blurred images of arms and legs hitting, and hitting again. The screams that echoed in her mind—*Where is it? What did you do with it?* Then came the fire, a raging inferno that consumed the house, the yard, and flashed up her arms and legs, filling her with an unbearable heat and excruciating pain.

Molly jerked awake, chilled and shivering. A shadow near her bed moved, and she gasped, fear rocking her.

But this time, the shadow grabbed her arm with a whispered, "Sh! It's just me." And Greg stepped into the gray light cast by the moon and streetlights outside. "Sorry. I didn't mean to scare you. Nightmare?"

Shaking violently, Molly nodded.

Greg reached toward the foot of the bed and pulled up a blanket and tucked it around her, helping her to settle back against the pillows. She clutched it, mouthing, *Thank you.* It brought some warmth, but not enough. "Is there another?" she whispered.

He went to the closet and pulled one from the shelf. He shook it out and draped it over here. "These rooms are always frigid. Are you hurting?"

"Not as bad as before. How long have I been asleep?" Her throat remained sore, her voice raspy.

"Want me to get the nurse? I think you're due for some meds."

"What time is it?"

He checked his watch. "Around 3:00 a.m. So you've been out about eighteen hours since we talked."

She wrapped the blankets tighter around her, and the warmth began to ease some of her soreness. "What are you doing here now?"

He sat back in the chair next to the bed, scooting it a bit closer. "We're taking turns. Michael stayed until seven, then I relieved Finn at midnight. Russell will be here around five."

"You don't have to do this. The nurses—"

"The nurses didn't get to see you stretched out on a porch as if you were dead."

Her eyes widened. "That was you? Who kept calling me?" *Please don't leave me.* The panic in his voice lingered in Molly's mind.

He hesitated, then nodded. He looked down at his hands. "Finn was there too. He and Linda heard the shot, saw a lot of it going down, ran the ... the guys fled when Finn and Linda came flying out of their houses with baseball bats. They said the thieves wore masks. Finn got a license plate, but it was stolen."

"Not guys."

He looked up. "What?"

She swallowed hard. "Not *all* guys. One, the voice was too high. A woman kept asking, 'Where is it?'"

"Where's what?"

She shook her head. "No idea." She looked at a small pink pitcher on the bedside table. "Is there ice?"

Greg stood. "It's probably water. I'll get it." He'd snagged the pitcher and headed out the door before she could stop him. In a few moments, he returned, and handed her a Styrofoam cup full of ice and a small spoon. She dug her arms out from under the blanket and took the cup, using the small spoon to scoop a few chips into her mouth. They melted quickly and felt blissful. "I can't believe how good that feels."

Greg winced.

"What?"

He shook his head. "Later. How's the rest of your pain?"

Molly let out a long breath. "I hurt, but it's tolerable. At least for now. Probably the meds. I have a headache. I was still sore from the wreck, so it's a step up."

"We found a fingerprint on the brake line, but it's not in the system."

"So, if you had a finger, you could match it?"

He smiled. "Something like that."

She handed him the cup, and burrowed back under the blankets. "What was Mickey … Brother Michael supposed to tell me that he didn't?"

Greg looked down again. "You heard that?"

She waited, and he finally leaned back in the chair. "They took some of the more valuable pieces out of the house, some of the items designated for specific people. They also broke into your hotel room, probably looking for whatever they were demanding from you. It's completely trashed."

"They didn't find much of anything. Everything of value, even the journals, have been moved to Russell's condo or office."

He didn't respond, and Molly waited for a few moments before she asked, "Are we okay?"

He looked up, an odd brightness in his eyes. "We?"

"You and me."

He stood, leaned over, and kissed her gently on the forehead. "Yeah, we're good," he whispered.

As he straightened, a nurse popped open the door and strode in. "Good," she announced. "You're awake. Time for medicine."

* * *

Molly slept for another five hours. Two nightmares jerked her awake, just before she was consumed by waves of flames, but she drifted off again almost immediately. She finally emerged from a more natural sleep just before nine on Sunday morning, stiff and starved. Her nurse shooed Russell out, who had indeed arrived around five, then she brought Molly some broth, gelatin, and a toothbrush. As Molly opened the small mirror embedded in the bedside tray, she saw why Greg had winced.

The right side of her face was swollen, and her eye a mass of black and red abrasions. A massive bruise extended from her right forehead down to her neck, where it spread across her throat and disappeared into her hairline. The bruise on her throat was hand-shaped, and was a delightful mix of blue, purple, and scarlet. "Oh my word!" she said to the nurse. "Does the rest of me look this bad?"

The nurse, a chipper, efficient woman in her thirties, nodded. "Pretty much. Are you ready for a bath? They tell me you might go home today."

And with that, the lengthy discharge process began. By the time the last paperwork arrived and the IV came out, the cafeteria had sent up more broth and gelatin for lunch, and three men—Greg, Russell, and Michael—waited for her outside the door. As the nurse helped her get dressed in clothes Russell had delivered, she whispered, "We need to get you out of here so they'll stop clogging up the hallway. You're a popular lady."

Molly couldn't answer that. She didn't really know how.

As they all headed downstairs to the lobby, Michael pushed her wheelchair. They got a few odd looks along the way, but Molly couldn't tell if it was because she was a giant, swollen bruise or because the bruise's wheelchair was being pushed by a monk. Russell explained that Linda and Sheila had emptied Molly's hotel room into his guest bedroom, and that Michael was staying with Greg. As they loaded her into Russell's car, she looked around, and said softly, "I want to go to the house. With Michael. Please."

Greg squeezed her shoulder. "I'll see you later." He nodded at Michael, who slipped into the back seat of the Benz.

The silent ride back to Carterton gave Molly a lot of time to think.

* * *

They stood in the yard for a few moments, looking up at the top gables of the house. Molly sighed. "I've spent a lot of time the past few weeks looking at this house. I almost hate to leave it."

Michael shaded his eyes against the sun. "Looking at the house or at the past?"

"You always did love trying to make me think."

His smile was gentle. "You get pushy. People sometimes forget they can push back."

"You know Mother used to call us the irresistible force and the immovable object."

He laughed. "Yep. We could go at each other for hours, snark becoming sarcasm becoming a trial of insults and battle of wits."

"You usually won."

"I'm older. I had read more."

"What do you think would have happened if we'd—"

He held up a hand, shaking his head. "No, Molly. Don't play the 'what-if' game. It goes nowhere, makes you crazy, and discounts what you *have* achieved."

Molly looked at him, feeling a swell of love in her chest. "Always the practical one."

"Someone had to be."

"Are we ever going to talk about who Leland's parents are?"

Michael remained still, his focus on the house. A breeze rustled through the leaves above them. Molly waited.

"You mean the fact that he's our brother?"

She nodded. "Yes."

"Probably not enough for your curiosity. The short version is that Mother and Daddy were in love and thought they'd get married when he got out of the army. Then he went to Vietnam, was declared MIA, which Mother took to mean a death sentence. She found out she was pregnant, and couldn't face it alone. Daddy came back, but by that time, the fix was in and Leland belonged to Bird and Nina."

"You think Daddy ever knew?"

"No. Daddy hated Bird. He'd have fought tooth and nail to get his child back."

"You realize that as Bird's heir, Leland would have gotten the farm, the same as if he'd been Mother and Daddy's heir?"

Michael looked down at her. "You can't always count on a silver lining. If what Greg told me is true, Leland won't be inheriting anything."

"Keep an eye on your liver, will ya?"

Her brother smiled. "We have great health care."

"So when did you become Catholic?"

"In the military. When did you stop going to church?"

"In Oklahoma. Storms are my sanctuaries now."

"Is that where you're closest to God?"

"Sometimes. But they will definitely make you think about Him."

"I'll concede that."

"Do you want to go in?"

"Not particularly. But we need to do this, don't we?"

"I think so. If only for closure."

"Did Russell give you the new key?"

Molly pulled it from her pocket and wagged it at him. "That man is fast on getting the locks changed on this place." She headed for the porch. Walking hurt, but she had to try, to work out some of the stiffness. Michael followed, moving much more slowly, giving her time to reach the steps. He offered his arm, which she took gladly, but still annoyed that she needed help.

It'll pass. You'll heal. Let's just hope the nightmares do too.

Molly slid the key in the shiny new lock and pushed the door open. Michael's steps were measured as he entered the foyer, looking up the stairs, then to the right. Molly waited, remembering all too well how she'd felt first entering the house. He turned and moved into the parlor, looking at the now sparse bits of furniture—a side table, a small desk, a highboy. He paused to run his hand along the edge of the table.

"You've done a lot of work."

She followed him into the room, fighting a wave of sadness. "So much is gone. They took— And there's still a great deal more to do. We haven't brought down everything from the attic, and the cleaning—"

"Molly." He turned to face her.

She stopped, waiting.

"Eventually, you'll have to learn how to accept a compliment."

She smiled, looking down at the recently polished desk. "Bad habit, huh?"

"Always was."

"You're sure you can't stay."

"Just tomorrow. We can talk more then."

"Longer."

"The bus leaves Tuesday morning."

She paused. "I'll take you."

"Thank you." He walked around the room, pausing to open the drawer on a highboy. His brow furrowed as he spotted the paper inside. He pulled it out, scanned it, glanced at Molly, then read aloud. "Highboy, circa 1880, belonged to Loretta and Ronald Jenkins, from

Alpharetta, Georgia. Brought to Carterton after marriage in 1925. Passed to daughter, Rebecca (born 1927), who married Thomas Morrow in 1947." He looked up. "Granddaddy and Gram."

Molly nodded. "Keep reading."

He did. "Loaned to Thomas's nephew, Randall Morrow, in 1966. Returned to Elizabeth Morrow in 1998, upon Randall's death, along with other items in his estate." He looked up at her. "So who does it belong to?"

She shrugged. "You tell me."

Michael put the paper back in the drawer. "According to the law, it would be Aunt Liz. And now you."

"According to Bird, it belonged to Gram, so it should have been his, as her remaining next of kin. The rest of that was just 'loaning'—not gifting." She paused. "I'm surprised they didn't take it as well."

"They probably would have taken more if you hadn't … interrupted. And there are squabbles like this on everything that was here?"

"On almost every piece. Even the dishes."

He paused and looked around the room. "I can see why Aunt Liz and Russell picked you to do this. You're the only one in the family with enough moxie to stare people down."

"Is that another compliment?"

Michael smiled. "Yes."

"Some people have not been so pleased with my moxie." She gestured at her face. "As you can see."

"'Never attribute to malice, that which can be reasonably explained by stupidity.' They apparently have no clue who they're dealing with."

"You still quote Robert Heinlein?"

"Hanlon's razor, actually."

"Ah. Yet another compliment?"

"An observation. If they knew you well, they would know that the more they come at you, the more you will dig in your heels."

She shook her head and crossed her arms, hugging herself. "I don't know, Michael. This took a lot of wind out of my sails. I don't know if I can finish what I started."

"Going to head back to St. Louis early? Leave this as it is?"

She looked out the window, down across the yard toward Finn's. "It might be better for everyone."

"Or maybe just for you. Molly, you've come too far, and done too much, to abandon Aunt Liz now."

"Guilt trips do not become you, brother."

"And giving up has never been your style either. And you have something they don't."

"Righteous indignation?"

He chuckled. "That. And ammunition. And a compassionate heart. The law is on your side, as are Sheriff Olson and Russell. Your neighbors, from what I've been told. And you have all the information you need from Aunt Liz to make the wisest decisions. But they have a greater incentive than you. They are outlaws, guilty of murder, assault, attempted murder, and burglary. If you fail, people will be disappointed, but life will go on. If they fail, they go to prison for the rest of their lives. But I know your heart. That you could use all this to help others drives you, and this is a once in a lifetime chance to help a lot of people. You're not going to give that up easily."

"You may not know me as well as you think."

He crossed to her, pulled her arms away from her body and took her hands. "Twenty-five years ago, when Granddaddy died, you pushed Mother and Gram to sell everything. Get the temptation away from the relatives. You didn't want them to deal with what was to come. Even then you cared more about them and their emotional comfort than you did for possessions. *That* part of your personality has not changed. The reason you so desperately want to walk away is not fear of being beaten up. It's because you seriously don't care what happens to anything in this house. True?"

"True."

"What you do care about are the people who need the help this stuff could bring. True?"

"True."

"So I have a suggestion. It'll make Bird lose his mind, but it might work."

"If it irritates Bird, I'm in."

He squeezed her hands. "Stop trying to divvy up pieces and focus on what will help folks. That would be money. Put it up for auction.

What's left of it. All of it. House and everything. If Bird wants it, he can bid on it. If others want it, they can bid. Then take the money and distribute it to the relatives who need the most help."

"And the people who claim they were just storing stuff here?"

"Buying it at auction is cheaper than a decade of storage fees."

"That's not exactly what Aunt Liz wanted."

"I know. But sometimes you have to look at the intention of the request, not the details. Aunt Liz was overthinking it. She cared about the 'legacy' of these pieces. It is all too clear that no one left alive feels the same. They're only interested in the value these things represent. So turn them into value—money."

Molly squeezed his hands in return. It made sense, almost too much. "You *sure* you won't stay?"

"Now who's indulging in a guilt trip?" He walked over and pulled back the curtains, peering out at the side yard. "When did all those houses go up?"

"Not sure. A few years ago."

"We used to chase lightning bugs and rabbits in that field. We've been gone a long time." He let the curtain fall and turned to her. "I can't come back, Molly. This is no longer home. I'm way past the point of no return. You don't have to either, unless you want to. I made my choice five years ago. You still have time to decide."

"Do you like being a monk?"

"I do. It was not an easy decision, but it was one I was pulled toward until I could no longer resist. Since I answered that call, I've been more content than I ever had been before. There is meaning in my life I wouldn't have understood ten years ago. It's where I am meant to be."

Molly reached out and pulled Michael into a tight hug, which he returned with gusto. As they released each other, Molly took a deep breath. "Russell's waiting. Anywhere you want to stop before you go back to Greg's?"

He paused, then a slow grin spread over his face. "I don't suppose Betty still has that crazy Coke machine."

Molly laughed. "Yep. Right up front. She's going to hug you half to death too."

"I would expect no less."

22

Monday was a day of rest. Greg dropped Michael off at Russell's condo at eight thirty, just as the lawyer headed to his office. Michael had shed his habit for jeans and a t-shirt, which seemed a little more appropriate for the lounging they had planned for the day. Her brother insisted that Molly walk some, to work out sore muscles, but for the most part, they piled up in the living room, and talked about twenty years of who, what, where, when, and how. The past made for a tense morning, but by lunch they had found tenderness and laughter.

Their lives had been troublesome, Michael pointed out, but in the global scheme of things, they had been remarkably lucky. It was a new perspective for Molly, but as the afternoon wore on, it grew on her.

They ordered Chinese takeout for lunch, and by midafternoon, the past had given way to dreams and hopes for the future. Michael fully admitted that his future seemed a lot more solid than Molly's.

"Have you taken your final vows?"

"About a year ago." Michael hesitated, stirring his rice with one chopstick. "I almost tracked you down then."

"Why didn't you?"

"Because, ultimately, it felt wrong to call you to say goodbye, when I hadn't seen you in more than twenty years. Seemed like the 'goodbye' had been over and done with."

Molly thought about where she had been a year ago. "A year ago, I was in Alaska, trying to capture the calving of an uncooperative glacier. Given my frame of mind at the time, I'd say you made the right call on that."

"Still … I didn't expect our reconnection to look anything like this."

"I honestly never expected either of us to show up in Carterton again."

"Have you made up your mind on St. Louis?"

Molly set her food aside and shifted uncomfortably on the sofa. "I honestly don't know. It's a good opportunity. I'm not sure where else I would go."

"And staying here is completely off the table?"

"Can you see me staying in the same town with Bird and Kitty after this is all over and done with? It'd be like eternally existing with two splinters in your butt."

Michael laughed. "But I can see you staying in a town with Finn and Greg and Russell."

Molly released a long, dramatic sigh. "I don't suppose monasteries take girls."

"There are Cistercian nuns, yes, ma'am."

Molly's phone rang, and she realized it was Hunter Bradley. She picked it up. "St. Louis beckons."

He stood. "I'll clean up the kitchen."

Molly answered the call, but the conversation was brief. Her counter offer had been approved, and she'd be getting a new contract via email in a day or two. She could sign it electronically, and they'd be on their way. Easy, over and done. Molly hung up and summarized the chat for Michael.

"Hm," he said, as he settled back in a recliner. "You explained that with all the enthusiasm of a prisoner requesting his last meal."

She shrugged.

"Molly, with the possible exception of the life I've chosen, change is the one common element in everyone's world. Jobs don't last. People move. Parents die. Nothing remains stable forever."

"Your life will. Is that what drew you to it?"

He tilted his head as he looked at her. "Actually, it was the thing I wrestled with the most. And there is some change. We rotate duties, and a farm is never a constant. But change is not as much a part of my world as yours. So I ask you … what if you don't stay here *or* go to St. Louis?"

"I'll get a little money from the estate. I'll go back to shooting storms and freelancing."

"Which is what you were doing when you got here."

"Yes."

"So no worse off."

She wondered where he was going with this. "No. But it's a field in flux."

"So while you freelance, you'll be thinking about a new career."

"Probably."

"What do you want to do?"

"All I've ever wanted to do is be a photographer."

"Which is a hard field unless you have an established niche."

"St. Louis would help me further establish that."

"So would having a home base that costs you almost nothing. There's even room for a studio. So in essence you have two good options, both of which have great potential."

"And the point is …?"

"Which one do you really want to do? In your heart, which one calls to you? Because that's the one that you'll make work."

* * *

The next morning, Molly still did not feel comfortable driving, so Russell played chauffeur for Molly and Michael. Back in his habit, he got the usual stares, but Molly began to feel an odd pride about her brother's choice. He'd answered a drive from deep within his soul. Now if only she could do the same.

Michael hugged her tightly, holding on for several minutes.

"We didn't used to hug," she whispered.

"What fools we were," he whispered back.

She laughed, and he released her, focusing his gaze on her eyes. "Mollybelle, you will know which door to follow when the time comes. Trust your gut. It's the oldest adage in the world, and a horrible cliché, but unbelievably true. You will *know* when it's right. Everything else is just biding your time."

Molly stayed until he stepped onto the bus. He waved one last time, and Molly returned to Russell's car.

And collapsed, weeping into her hands.

* * *

Russell drove her back to the condo, and Molly spent the afternoon making phone calls. An auction company met her in one of Russell's conference rooms the next morning. By that afternoon, the auction signs went up in front of the house, at the end of Maple Street, and at every interstate exit for twenty-five miles around. The auction announcement went in every local paper for two hundred miles.

And life settled into a slow routine. The auction, which would include the entire estate, was scheduled six weeks out, which would give Molly time to finish the inventory and get it back in front of Judge Petrie. Russell arranged for a security firm to watch the house for the next six weeks, and scheduled installation of security cameras. Molly had a much smaller dumpster set to the side of the house. She took down the pavilions, and the block party that had been Liz Morrow's house vanished.

Molly's insurance came through with a small check, and she bought another car, an Explorer, of course, with only 21,000 miles on it. She took a brief trip to St. Louis, met the team, and toured the station. She explained what was happening in Alabama, and asked for an extra month to decide. They agreed, provided she granted them the exclusive rights on the first three videos of merit without compensation. It was a just compromise, and she spent the trip back embedding the "pros" of the job into her brain.

The legal packages arrived from Sarah's dad as well as Jimmy, and Molly turned them over to Russell. Linda, Finn, and Sheila went back to work, and for the first week, the only people at the house were Molly, the guards, and the cleaning firm she'd brought back in. They were efficient and thorough, so Molly focused on the inventory and documenting the "after" of the house with her camera. Between the new storm pictures and the viral video, her social media profile had exploded … along with a half-dozen new requests for pictures through her website. She gave Aunt Liz's house its own Facebook page, and the before and after shots brought in a riot of comments and suggestions for remodeling.

The work kept her mind off everything else. She had not seen Greg since Michael left. Nor Bird, although he'd left an angry voice message on her phone the day the signs went up. She had decided to annotate the inventory with pictures and descriptions, which, once again, put her up close and personal with some remarkable family stories. As she posted some of the stories on the Facebook page, interest in the auction skyrocketed.

Molly added the books to the inventory as well as the cash from the books, which had totaled almost two hundred thousand dollars. With the investments and other found money, Liz Morrow's estate wound up totaling just over seven hundred thousand, not including what the house and furnishings would bring at auction.

As she started divvying it up on paper, Molly could not stop smiling. The money would go a long way to help the people Liz cared about the most. Molly added that list to the inventory as well, so the judge could see her intentions for the disbursement of the estate.

It paid off. When no other contests to the will showed up, they presented the inventory to Judge Petrie in his chambers. He signed off on it and told Russell and Molly to go, be wise, and watch their backs.

Afterward, with nothing to do but wait for the auction, Molly mostly found herself in the basement, going through Liz's books. No surprises, for the most part. Liz had always loved the classics and Southern history. One quiet Saturday, Molly turned out a couple of silverfish that had escaped the fumigation, however, and headed to Carterton Hardware and Feed for some bug poison. Molly hadn't seen Betty since she and Michael had stopped by there for Cokes. Perched on her stool, Betty waved her in. When Molly told her she was looking for silverfish poison, Betty clapped her hands. "Ah! You got to the library!"

Molly stared at her. "You knew?"

"Girl, we both loved books. We'd trade off, and she'd lend me classics." She leaned closer to Molly and her voice dropped. "She didn't used to have that wall of storage bins in front of it. Finn helped her put that up after Lyric started moving in. But there was still one narrow spot she could slip through."

"Why? I can't imagine Lyric being interested in too many books."

"Nah. But rumors have circulated in this town for years that Liz had a lot of cash stashed in the house. Everybody, including Liz, knew that's why Kitty and Lyric were putting the move on her. Probably why they killed her."

Molly shook her head. "Betty, we still don't know—"

Betty shushed her with a wave. "Oh, my girl. Your boyfriend has been putting pressure on all over town, making some of your blood kin nervous as a long-tailed cat in a roomful of rocking chairs. Something is going to crack. And soon."

"He's not—"

Another wave of dismissal. "Molly. I love you. But the only person who doesn't seem to see it is you. No one has seen that man so smitten since his wife died. He tries to hide it, but he is not as stoic as he'd like to believe."

Molly felt the heat sear into her face. "Um … poison?"

Betty laughed. "Aisle 2, down next to the mousetraps. Just make sure you confine it to the silverfish."

When Molly got back to the house, Finn and Sheila were sitting on the front steps. They stood as she got out of the Explorer. Finn snatched his cap off his head, and Sheila greeted her with a quick hug. Finn jumped in with no preamble, his words tumbling, one over the other.

"We want to have a cookout in your honor. No, don't say anything yet. Let me get this out. We know you're leaving, heading back to Missouri. We just want to say goodbye in a Carterton sort of way. Friday night, just come. It'll kick off around dark.

"Okay."

"The whole town is turning out, folks you might not have even met yet, but they all know you. What you've done here is legendary. It's really brought Carterton together. You should see the community social media pages. They are rocking, and not nearly as ugly as they usually are. People just want to say thanks. Wait— You said okay?"

"I love you guys. I'd love to have a send-off."

Finn whooped and slapped his hat against his thigh.

Molly looked at Sheila. "They're going to turn him into a redneck yet."

Sheila grinned. "Maybe."

Finn harrumphed. "And maybe not. Grilling out does not a redneck make." But he grinned again and gave Molly a quick hug. "See you Friday night!"

And, hand in hand, Sheila and Finbar Eccles walked back to their castle.

Molly, on the other hand, began the long, arduous task of trying to rid a basement full of books of all its silverfish.

23

Molly stood in the front parlor, thinking again about the estimate the auction house had given her on the contents … and the house itself. More than she expected, enough to take the estate up over her previous estimate of seven hundred grand. After bills, taxes … and more taxes … still a tidy sum for everyone in Liz's last thoughts. And although Molly knew in her gut this was the best solution, she couldn't shake a lingering sense of loss.

Maybe it was just her grief over Liz finally working its way out into that final acceptance stage. Her aunt was gone. Mickey … Brother Michael … would never be a part of her life again. With the sale of the house, her contact with Carterton would be finally and unequivocally broken. And life would go on, just as it always had.

"Endings," she muttered. "But also beginnings." Her mind and heart had finally accepted the St. Louis move.

The roar of a pickup reminded her that the "party of the year," as Finn had called it, was gearing up two doors down. He had promised that it would be one mighty shindig, with most of Carterton turning out to wish one of their native daughters a final farewell. He'd invited not only locals but some business folk in Gadsden and Attalla he thought would be interested in the auction. "A sneak preview," he called it. She promised that she'd give a tour of the house later in the evening.

But as much as she enjoyed Finn, Sheila, and Linda's companionship, and as much as she looked forward to the send-off, she hated goodbyes. This one would be prolonged, and she dreaded the idea that anyone would turn hangdog looks in her direction and beg her to stay. She hoped … prayed even … that it would just be a celebration of Liz's life, the wake she never got, and a sweet time of hugs and good wishes.

"St. Louis, here I come," she whispered. "Temporary stability, Michael. Until the next change."

Through the window, she could see strings of lights illuminating both the front and back yards, with clusters of folks in both with drinks in hand. Kids darted around the edge of the yard, many with Mason jars, attempting to corral a few lightning bugs. Molly knew they all had phones in their pockets and video games waiting inside, but the whole gathering reminded her of her childhood. A burst of flames from the grill cast wild shadows across the backyard. Even through the closed windows, laughter echoed, and the scent of woodsmoke began to permeate the neighborhood.

Molly looked around the room again. "Goodbye, Liz. I hope you approve. I miss you, and I always will." Switching off the lights, she left, locking the front door and turning.

A shadow on the porch made her back into the door with a startled squeak.

Greg put out his hand, palm out. "Sorry! Sorry. I didn't mean … I thought you might want an escort to the party. Maybe."

Molly pressed a hand to her chest as she caught her breath. "I'm still a little skittish about people surprising me on the porch." Then she smiled, glad they had made their peace while Michael was still here. "I'm sorry, too," she said. "For everything."

He held out his arm. "You were going through a lot."

She slid her hand inside his elbow. "And I put you through a lot."

"All in the past."

"Good. I hope you win the next election."

He laughed softly. "Don't worry about it. The good folks of Carterton and Pine County adore me. Even when I don't catch the bad guys."

"You will."

He shrugged. "I've turned most of the jewelry over to the Gadsden PD. Their case, the crimes happened there, and they'll investigate. I'll help, since it was found here, but I'll be sharing jurisdiction with them. I'm mostly in the info-gathering stage at this point, unless they turn up video or fingerprints."

The noise of the party overtook them, and they separated as Finn threw up his arms, still grasping grilling utensils, and declared, "There she is! Woman of the hour!"

Heat rose in Molly's face as she stepped forward to receive a hug from him. A cheerful buzz surrounded them, as people closed in to wish her well. Molly got the impression that there were more than three times as many people as at the last cookout. After a few minutes, Finn herded them back away from her. "Hear, hear! Let the woman find some food. She looks as if she's going to wither away before the night is out."

She thanked him as folks gave her room, then glanced around for either Greg or Russell. Neither was in sight, although she'd seen Russell at the edge of the crowd earlier. She accepted a plate with a burger on it, made the round of picnic tables for chips and veggies, then settled into a chair next to Linda. "This is quite the crowd. How in the world can they afford to do this?"

Linda laughed. "Believe me, there are plenty of behind-the-scenes donations for tonight." She paused, her face losing its glee. "And a lot of people in this community have adopted you. They admire that you came back to take care of Liz's estate when you didn't have to, and that you've persevered against family objections ... even to the point of violence. They were appalled at what happened. They don't want to see you go, but know why you need to. So we want to send you off in style. And we hope you'll come back someday."

Molly stared at Linda, stunned and humbled. "Thank you. I can never repay what all these people have done to make this work out as well. Y'all have worked hard in the house, and it means more than you know. It reminds me that Carterton isn't all about greedy, manipulative family."

Linda took a bite of her hotdog before responding. "It isn't, but I know how hard it is to see that when you're in the eye of a storm. Plus there was such a history there, how could you not? Bird's a big personality. So is his family. It can be overwhelming." She paused for a sip of soda. "Some of them are here tonight, did you know?"

Molly almost choked. "What?"

Linda nodded toward Finn. "I think he has something up his sleeve. Finn always knows more than he lets on. He invited Tommie Jane, RuthAnn, and their kids. Bird and Nina, but I don't think they'll come. No one's seen much of them since you were attacked. LJ, maybe. Kitty, probably not. Lyric, maybe. I did see RuthAnn and Eddie earlier."

What on earth was he thinking? Molly inhaled deeply to steel herself. "Well, Bird kept saying he'd never go after kin again, so he probably thinks everyone believes he was behind the attack."

Linda sniffed. "He'd be right."

"And Kitty is always going to despise me. I thought Lyric was still in Birmingham with her dad."

Linda shook her head. "Betty said she came in the store yesterday to buy a hammer and screwdriver. Said they were for her dad, but didn't get specific."

"Early Father's Day gifts?"

Linda snorted a laugh.

Molly fell into a comfortable silence, watching the flurry of the party. As she'd seen from the window of the house, it was a community that came together in a relaxed, open way. She couldn't imagine that she'd find anything similar in St. Louis. Even if she found a club, a church, or another small town, she'd still be the outsider.

This party was for her.

Molly chatted with Linda a few minutes longer, then got up to refresh her drink. A half-dozen people stopped her, wishing her well, wishing she would stay, asking questions about the auction. She spotted Lyric at the edge of the crowd. The girl waved hesitantly, but looked away quickly. RuthAnn kept staring at her, and Eddie lurked in the shadows nearby. No Bird or Nina, but as the party grew, LJ appeared on the outskirts of the crowd, a baleful glare on his face.

Molly found Finn and nodded at LJ. "What in the world did you say to get them to show up tonight?"

Finn sniffed and resettled his cap on his head. "That there would be news about the auction and the contents of the house. And Freddy."

Molly gaped at him. "And they came?"

"Curiosity didn't just kill *the cat*, y'know. And there's free food."

"And if you don't deliver?"

He shrugged. "Ya never know what the night might bring."

Molly suddenly had the urge to hide behind the BP station again. Greg was nowhere to be found. Instead, she stayed close to Linda.

Finally, after he shut down the grill and Sheila brought out an array of pies, cakes, and puddings, Finn banged on an oversized pot.

"Okay, everybody! Gather 'round, gather 'round!" He motioned for Molly to join him, which she did, a wary look on her face.

"I'm not going to make a speech, Finn."

"Nah, nah, don't want you to. Just some information."

Slowly, the buzz of conversation died, and Finn had everyone's attention. "Y'all had enough to eat?"

"Where's the desserts?" some guy called.

"Miss Sheila's getting them out now. Hold your horses. I got something to say, and I wanna ask Miss Molly some things."

Molly looked at him, her brow knit in confusion, a tense knot growing in her stomach. But she held her peace.

Finn went on. "We're all here to bid Miss Molly a fond hail and farewell, sending her on her way to new adventures in chasing down tornadoes." He paused and peered at her. "Which makes you braver than I'll ever be."

"Finn hides in the basement," Sheila called out.

"'Cause I like livin'! Ain't nothing wrong with that!" Laughter broke up the mood, then Finn went on. "She has done a fine job of cleaning out Miss Liz's home and getting it ready to sell. Now, all y'all have seen the auction signs. What you might not know is that Molly is not going to keep any of the money from Liz's estate." He paused, and the crowd grew quiet, waiting.

"Molly has made a list of people in the community who Liz wanted to help. You all know Liz had a heart of gold and loved the folks of Carterton. She thought maybe some of the furniture and stuff might be divided up, but mostly what these folks need is money, cold hard cash for food on the table and stuff for their kids. So that's why the auction." He paused again, and Molly recognized that he was going in for the emotional wallop.

"Of course, there would be a whole lot more money in the larder for these folks if someone hadn't broke into Miss Liz's house and stolen a bunch of stuff. You locals may have heard, but some of you others might not. They got some big pieces—" He looked at her. "—a secretary out of the hall—" He motioned for her to go on.

Molly picked up the patter. “A Shaker chest of drawers. A Tudor cup hutch made in Thomasville around 1920. Several others. All of these would have had letters of provenance taped inside a drawer or to the bottom of the piece. Under a table. Most would have had Morrow family connections of some kind.”

Out of the corner of her eye, she saw a woman grab her husband’s arm. She glanced at Finn, but he nodded and mouthed, “Go on.”

“Most of the items were smaller, such as three McCoy pottery vases. Lily vases. I realize those are just gone, but I had hoped to do so much more with what was earned.”

“Wait a minute!” The man with the grabby wife edged his way from the back of the crowd. Molly had never seen him. “How old was that Shaker chest?”

“Late forties, early fifties,” Molly said. “It was made by Cresent Furniture in Tennessee. It was a wedding present to Gene Morrow and his wife from her parents. The provenance was taped in one of the drawers.”

The man’s face turned dark, and he spun, pointing to the back of the crowd. “Eddie Travers! You lying son of a—you told me it had been a gift to your mother!”

All heads turned, and people stepped out of the line of the accusing finger, leaving attention suddenly and boldly on RuthAnn’s son. He bolted, straight into Greg Olson’s grip.

A motion from the other side of the crowd caught Molly’s eye, and she turned to see two deputies clutching LJ between them. He struggled for a moment, then stopped as they handcuffed him.

Eddie didn’t go as quietly. He swung at Greg, and tried to twist free. Greg dodged but didn’t let go. One of the other deputies joined him, and they handcuffed Eddie, pulling him to the center of the crowd. RuthAnn followed, fury clouding her face, but she said nothing. LJ and his deputies soon joined them.

Now at the center of the crowd, LJ stood silently, impassive. Eddie stiffened, defiant. He spit on the ground in front of Molly. “Wasn’t yours to begin with! Like all that money you took. Wasn’t yours!”

Russell suddenly appeared at Molly’s elbow. He put a hand on her arm, but his face was tight with rage. He wedged himself between her and LJ.

RuthAnn thumped her son in the back of the head. “Shut up, boy!”

Greg shot RuthAnn a warning look, as another man pushed forward. “Hey, I recognize him! And that other one.” He pointed at LJ. “They sold me some collectibles, said they found them at a junk store.” His face red, he started toward Eddie, only to be stopped by one of the deputies.

RuthAnn pushed by Greg, looking from him to Molly. “Enough!” She glared at Finn. “Are you satisfied? It’s why you wanted us here. Right?”

Finn rocked back on his heels, a look of pure glee on his face. “More or less, missus. But he’s still got partners to name and talking to do. Right, Sheriff?”

Greg’s face remained impassive. “There’s definitely a lot of unanswered questions.”

“No! They shot Freddy!”

From behind Greg, Lyric lunged out of the crowd, a screwdriver raised over her head. She brought it down toward LJ, who stood blocked by the deputies.

Russell caught her arm. He stopped the downward arc, but her momentum carried them both to the ground. Greg shot forward, grabbing the screwdriver and wrenching it away. Lyric rolled away from Russell, sobbing. Greg helped Russell up, and together they pulled Lyric to her feet.

She gazed up at Greg, tears streaming down her face. “They said he went home, but they shot him.” She jerked her hand toward LJ. “He has a gun. He hides it under one of the hen’s nests in the corn crib.”

“Shut up!” LJ hissed.

Greg took Lyric’s arm and led her to one of the deputies. “Take her to the station. We’ll need her statement.” He looked around at Russell. “You good?”

Russell nodded, brushing dust and leaves off his clothes. “Although I’m way too old to be rolling around in the dirt.”

Greg tilted his head toward Lyric’s disappearing figure. “You call her lawyer?”

“I’ll take care of it.”

He nodded at his remaining deputies, who led Eddie and LJ through a now-jeering mob.

The first man who had come forward moved closer to Molly. "I feel like a fool. I should never have trusted those people. But he had a trailer full of stuff, and he made the rounds to several antique and consignment stores that I know of."

Greg asked, "You said, 'those people.' How many?"

The man didn't have to think. "Three. Those two and an older woman. She seemed to be directing them."

Greg nodded. "Was it that woman? The one with the boy?"

He shook his head. "No. Older. Pale. Really funky hairdo. Like birds had been in her hair."

Finn snorted. "That'd have to be—"

Greg cut him off with a look, then turned back to the man. "Will you make a statement?"

"Right now, if you want me to. They should be horsewhipped, all of them."

Greg motioned for the man to follow him, and they disappeared through the still-murmuring crowd. After a moment, Russell followed them.

Molly turned on Finn, her eyes wide with indignant questions. "You knew?"

Finn ignored her to bang on the pot again. "Excitement's over for now!"

"What about a tour of the house?" called one of the men.

Finn looked at Molly.

She hesitated … but they deserved it. "Meet me there at nine thirty! I'll show you around."

"Excellent!" Finn hit the pot one more time. "But don't forget! Desserts! Pies, cakes, puddings! Right over there! Don't let Miss Sheila have to freeze all that!"

Laughter scattered lightly among the crowd, but his words did the trick, as a lot of them headed that way. Finn set down the pot, took Molly by one arm, and guided her away. They stopped under a sweetgum tree near the edge of the yard. "Yes," he said quietly. "We knew."

"We?"

"Greg and me. I've been listening, and I've been poking about. I knew they couldn't sit on stuff too long. Greg was making it really hot for them, pressing hard in the pawnshops, pulling video from consignments, his deputies hovering around their houses. All he needed was one bit of probable cause and he could get search warrants. He made it so they'd have to move it. I just put ears to the ground."

"And they cracked."

"Like boiled eggs before a tea party." He put a hand on her arm. "They made a huge mistake when they attacked you, Miss Molly. That drove Greg to a place I've never seen him, and this town came unglued. Everyone thought Bird was involved, and the stores refused to sell to them. Nina had to go to Attalla to buy groceries. They couldn't get gas, and every time LJ left his bike somewhere, someone hid it or moved it. The Bistro owner told them that if they didn't do it, they knew who did, and until it was resolved, they weren't welcome."

Molly looked around at the milling townsfolk, a longing burning in her that ran all the way to the bone. Tears clouded her eyes. "What happens now?"

"With them? The law will do its thing." Finn pulled her into a hug. "The rest? I suspect that's up to you."

24

The dominos fell as the party wound down. More shop owners came forward, apologized to Molly, and promised to go to the sheriff's office to make statements after the house tour. Some had video of the purchases. Others could easily identify Nina, LJ, and Eddie. None wanted to be holding stolen goods.

The tour itself turned into more of a joy than a chore. The dealers recognized some of the pieces and plied her with questions. One even cooed over the giant cherry wardrobe, and promised to notify someone he knew would want it. They left, chattering with enthusiasm and promising to spread the word about the auction.

Molly watched them go wistfully, the feeling of loss sinking deeper as she walked back to the party. "Aunt Liz," she whispered. "Every piece will be just as loved with their new families. Cared for by people who really want them. Don't they deserve that? Don't we all?"

Finn had built a campfire for the kids near the edge of the yard, and Molly sat in a lawn chair near it as people trickled away, some walking, others leaving in cars parked up and down Maple. A chill had settled in the air, and a light breeze stirred the flames. She'd offered to help clean up, but Sheila and Linda insisted she just rest, maybe toast a few marshmallows.

Molly skipped that part. Instead she just tried to absorb what had happened tonight. So much had happened since she'd first arrived in Carterton. A lot had changed. And maybe she had as well.

Russell wandered over with another lawn chair and a bottle of RC Cola. Molly looked him up and down as he sat. "I thought you went with Greg."

"I did. As your attorney, although I did call Lyric's as well. Good thing, too. Because of her, Greg has bigger fish to fry than either your attack or stolen goods."

She sat forward. "Oh?"

"Do you know what felony murder is?"

"Yeah. It's when someone is killed during the commission of another crime. Like a shop owner who gets shot during a robbery. Anyone involved with the robbery can be accused of murder."

"Right. Whether or not they pulled the trigger."

Molly couldn't see where he was going. "And?"

"And hiding stolen goods is a crime. Felony murder as a result of it—"

The light dawned. "Freddy!"

Russell nodded. "They had decided to hide the jewels and the cash in Liz's house because it was such a jumbled mess. No one would suspect that something that valuable would be in the house. If any of it were found, there'd be no connection to any of the three. Freddy was just in the wrong place at the wrong time, and wasn't nearly as dim as they thought. He loved Liz. He confronted them, and LJ shot him. When Greg spelled out the legal aspects of felony murder for Eddie and RuthAnn, I thought the poor kid would wet himself. He melted. Young Mr. Travers is on the hook for murder just because he was in the house. Once that domino fell, he let all the secrets spill, including starting the fire and the two attacks on you."

"On the porch."

"And at the hotel. LJ shot Freddy, but he drove the motorcycle that night. Eddie had the shotgun. Nina ran the thefts and fencing, but she didn't know about the first attack or the fire. They started the fire to try to get rid of Freddy's body. They didn't really care about what else was in the house. When Nina found out they'd started it, she just about killed them both for trying to burn all the goodies inside. That's why she was the leader in the second attack. Their main objective was to get what she and Bird wanted out of the house. She was the driving force behind almost everything else."

"God help us."

"Greg is waking up Judge Keeley as we speak, and the deputies are picking up Nina."

"My word. Nina. Poor Stockholm syndrome Nina."

Russell snorted, spilling some of his soda.

Molly grinned. "Sorry." Then another thought crossed her mind. "They killed Aunt Liz, too, didn't they? It wasn't an accident after all."

Russell took a long, deep, calming breath. But he still gripped the soda bottle until Molly thought it would shatter. "Yes. She saw them shoot Freddy. She tried to run, but they caught her and dragged her back in the house."

"The mud on her feet."

He nodded, and they fell silent. Together they watched the fire burn low. Finally, he stood and held out his hand. "Ride with me back to the condo. I don't think either of us should go alone."

She pointed toward the house. "The Explorer …"

"You'll need to save a parking space anyway for the auction tomorrow. People start arriving very early for these things. And the guards are there."

"Bring me over early?"

"Wouldn't miss it for the world."

* * *

The weather could not have been more perfect—high fluffy cumulocirrus clouds in a brilliantly blue sky, temperature expected to top out around seventy-four degrees, a slight breeze. And Russell had been right. The auction was supposed to begin at eleven, and by the time they arrived at eight, Russell had to park down the street.

The preview crowd had been strong, with a great deal of interest in all of the furniture, the collectibles, and even in the house itself. The same storeowners who had been at last night's party were there, spending more time with the documentation Molly had left with each piece. She occasionally heard them repeating information she'd given them to another dealer. One asked her about "true provenance" on a table, not just the family tales, and she suggested he check under the drop leaf. Liz had taped sales receipts, merchandising tags, and anything else she had to the furniture. Some of the pieces still had the original manufacturing tags on them. For the antique dealers, it was a goldmine.

After answering one too many questions, Molly slipped out the back door and out into the yard. Snippets of green were breaking through the burned area of the yard. Before the end of summer, it would be a lawn again. She looked back at the house, abruptly thinking it would look great with a deck. Maybe a gazebo.

Definitely a gazebo. With a swing.

And a dog. Like a collie. Or a Newfoundland. No. Not a Newfie. Too hot. Alabama in August. No. Maybe a Labrador …

At the edge of the pine grove, a flash of orange darted up a tree, finding a resting place on a high limb.

Ah, yes. And a cat. A big, fluffy orange one.

"Molly?" Russell called from the back door.

"Yes, sir?" She headed his way.

"The auctioneer is ready to start. He wants you to confirm with him that you want to liquidate all of Liz's property as well as the house."

Molly stared at him, his words sinking in. "What do you mean, 'as well as the house'?"

Russell returned her stare, his expression puzzled. "Because you contracted with him to liquidate the estate. Only the estate."

"But the house—"

"—is not part of the estate."

Her brain finally kicked out a fact she'd been overlooking. "The quitclaim deed."

Russell paused in astonishment for a moment, then broke into laughter. "Yes, darlin', the quitclaim deed. The house is yours and has been since before you got here. You forgot?"

"I forgot."

"So?"

It felt right. Michael, wise Michael. It was the door that felt perfectly right.

"Just the estate. Just sell the estate."

Epilogue

Stars don't actually fall on Alabama, but snow does. Sometimes. Well after Christmas. By the time the first snow dusted the ground the next February, Molly had had the fireplaces cleaned and repaired, the windows replaced, and enough repair work and painting done that the old Victorian on Maple Street looked like a winter wonderland. She'd hung white lights on the porch for Christmas, and had left them up, so that they twinkled brightly against the night as the guests arrived.

As usual on a wintry Saturday night, the house smelled of hot cider and spiced tea, cinnamon rolls, and coffee. Card tables were set up in the front room for Rook and whist, and she knew her guests would get rowdy before the night was out. They always did. The usual suspects were there—Linda and her brother, Finn and Sheila, Russell, Greg … and Bird.

Her embracing Bird had shocked Carterton. But Bird had aged a lot in the past nine months. He'd also changed. Which was something Molly knew a lot about.

Nina, LJ, and Eddie's arrests had devastated Bird, but he'd remained defensive of them. He put up the bonds for all of them, and he made sure they were at every court appearance. But the dual blows of Leland's death in October, followed by Nina's in November while awaiting trial, had crushed him. Bird retreated to the farmhouse, living in filth and alcohol, until a local preacher had dug him out. When he appeared on Molly's porch, thin and disheveled, he had not even been sure how to ask her forgiveness, but he tried.

Watching him make the attempt, Molly could only think of the changes Michael had gone through. And her brother's last words to her: *Mollybelle, you will know which door to follow when the time comes. Trust your gut. It's the oldest adage in the world, and a horrible cliché, but unbelievably true. You will know when it's right.*

Maybe it was time for all the old rifts to heal.

Most of them, anyway. Kitty still despised her and kept her distance. Occasionally threatened a lawsuit. Molly knew it would never amount to anything, just like the lawsuit Sarah's dad had filed. It had been withdrawn almost as soon as Russell placed the first call. But once Sarah was well enough to address it with her father, it disappeared completely. The partnerships with Sarah and Jimmy, however, had been dissolved. That part of her life forever ended.

The disbursement of the estate could not have gone smoother. In the end, Molly had asked Judge Petrie to oversee it, and he'd agreed. The money from the estate had been enough to help seventy-seven families in Carterton with a check for ten thousand dollars. The books had gone to the town library, which had sold the first editions for enough to expand the building.

And Blossom had come home. Apparently, life as a feral cat did not suit him. Once Molly had him free of fleas, he made no more attempts to leave the house.

"Can I help?" Linda poked her head around the kitchen door.

"Yep!" Molly handed her two plates of cinnamon rolls. "One for each table. Napkins and little plates are in the hutch."

The coffee maker gurgled its success, and Molly checked, yet again, the sugar and creamer levels. Eight cups were lined up on saucers, spoons waiting on a linen cloth. The urns of tea and cider were scalding hot, ready for serving.

The light touch of a warm hand on her back was followed by a soft kiss on her neck. She turned and kissed Greg on the lips, grinning as Finn rapped on the kitchen doorframe.

"Hey! No flirting in the kitchen. It's time to play cards!"

"We're allowed," Greg called back. "We're still newlyweds!"

"Tonight, sir, you are to my right in whist. Get your butt in here."

"Later?" Greg asked Molly.

"Always," she said. "Let the games begin."

The End